From WATERLOO *to* WATER STREET

S. E. Morgan

Matador
9 Priory Business Park,
Wistow Road, Kibworth Beauchamp,
Leicestershire. LE8 0RX
Tel: 0116 279 2299
Email: books@troubador.co.uk
Web: www.troubador.co.uk/matador
Twitter: @matadorbooks

ISBN 978 183859 241 7

British Library Cataloguing in Publication Data.
A catalogue record for this book is available from the British Library.

Typeset in 11pt Adobe Garamond Pro by Troubador Publishing Ltd, Leicester, UK

Matador is an imprint of Troubador Publishing Ltd

To Hywel, my husband.

Acknowledgements

I must thank Richard Hibbs, for being such a kind first reader of my earliest draft. I am sincerely grateful for his tactful advice, constructive criticism and encouragement.

Thanks to Sian Stewart for all her pains in providing detailed comments on the historical, as well as grammatical issues and for giving me enthusiastic support for the project.

I was fortunate to find Rebecca John from Cadogan and Quill as editor. She provided thoughtful feedback with clear and helpful suggestions for improving the novel.

I must acknowledge my great-uncles, Arthur and Alfred Morgan, who, over forty years ago, visited Newchurch to hear of our Waterloo veteran ancestor, and, as critically, took the time to write an account of their visit.

Finally, I should thank Cardiff Writer's Circle members. I count myself lucky to have found such a great group to join as a novice. I have learnt a huge amount listening to their writing, as well as from their detailed comments on my work. Their warmth and moral support has been fantastic.

Chapter One

Saturday 9th April 1843

They were coming for him, sabres raised, he knew it. It was hot, unusually humid for April; thunder was on its way. The old man was restive, jumpy. He paced the farmhouse kitchen, looking around suspiciously. He'd been irritable all morning; he hadn't slept, old dreams had returned to plague him. His wife called out that she was going to the dairy to check the cream wasn't curdled in the heat. Thomas didn't hear, ears drumming. He was swallowed by memories.

Checking the door, he took a ladder-backed chair and leant it tight under the handle. *They won't get in that way,* he thought with grim satisfaction. He limped hurriedly along the passage to the ancient oak door at the front of the house, turned its heavy iron key and bolted it, top and bottom. The door was from Cromwell's time, strong enough to keep the damn French out. He pulled closed the downstairs shutters, setting rusty bars into tight latches with difficulty.

He was sweating from the warmth and exertion, his wound had begun to ache. He felt sick, heart pounding ever faster, his breathing quickened.

Someone was at the kitchen door. They were here, the French, Napoleon's troops. They'd be in, in a second, if he didn't do something. It'd be all over for him. Where was his rifle? Where had Ester hidden it?

Whoever was at the door had realised it was locked. They rattled the latch and started to yell, 'Open the door, open up. Mr Lewis, open up.'

Thomas only heard shouts; he was lost, needed to hide – without his gun, easy prey. He smelt gunpowder, saw blood flowing into sandy soil, heard hooves circle. The taste of saltpetre dried his tongue; he wanted water. Where could he go? There, by the fire in the inglenook, behind the dresser – maybe it would protect him. He cowered, huddled on the floor, hands over his head. The banging at the door merged and echoed with his memories and his nightmares.

Thomas began to cry.

I lay under a pear tree on that first warm day of spring, flexing my shoulders and rolling out my spine with pleasure. It felt good to be lying flat in the sunshine, not crouched over floor joists. Bees emerged from Ester's hives, foraging on the white blossom and the explosion of dandelions, egg-yolk yellow, splashed across the grass.

This last week though, I'd been fitting floors; uncomfortable work, hard on the knees, back and patience. I'd enjoyed most things about the first three years of my carpentry apprenticeship, but not the lancing pains that crouching for hour after hour gave me. Every day I'd longed for the countryside of Newchurch village, to be ploughing or planting, not labouring in a dusty, half-built house on Water Street.

I sighed as Ester's shrill tones and the farm hands' yells travelled across the fields. I guessed it was another of the old man's turns. I'd be called for in a moment, but his bouts happened so often I didn't rush to them as I should. Except for the shouting, it could have been another spring day eight years ago, when I was nearly nine, when my grandfather, known to us all as Gu,[1] and I first became close.

It all involved a pig – well, buying and raising pigs. Gu and I held long discussions all those years before, standing by the old pigsty in the yard. He talked as I listened to his stories of the war, and asked question after question.

Asked what I would like for my birthday in February, I'd told Gu and Ester I wanted a pig to breed. It took them aback; a top to whip, a book, a trip to Carmarthen fair, plausible. A pig, and one to breed at that, was surprising.

For weeks before I'd burned with anger at how poor so many of the villagers were. Often as not, children like my best friend Ellen, who lived next door to Auntie on the Row, didn't have enough to eat.

I'd taken a keen interest when Auntie Gwennie told me about the times before the war with the French. Gwennie

---

[1] Gu pronounced to rhyme with see and key etc. Affectionate term for grandfather in Welsh

Evans, wrinkled as a walnut, was loved in the village and called Auntie by one and all. Auntie had said, "Living was easier when I was a girl. Every one of us in Bank Row had enough to get by on. Yes, we all worked, maybe had two jobs, but most kept a pig in the back yard, reared it to feed us through the winter."

I rushed out my explanation. 'I want to give a piglet to every cottage on Bank Row. I'll ask for a return; my payment will be a hind quarter of the fully grown pig, once it's slaughtered. If they decide to breed from it, not kill it, then they must give me a piglet for the next two years. They'll have meat over the winter, won't go hungry. Ellen's family are always hungry.'

Gu pulled at his beard, doubtful. 'It's thoughtful but you know how pigs smell, Will. We keep our pigs in the back field for a reason; it is well downwind from the farmhouse. Where would you keep it?'

'In the old pigsty behind your barn, of course. I'll clean it out before the pig arrives and then every week, I promise. I won't let it stink.'

Ester spoke up. 'You cannot be serious, William. The sty hasn't been used for maybe fifteen years. It's full of old pig dung, it's deep, deep in dung. A little boy like you can't clean it out.'

She looked severely at Gu.

He scoffed and winked at her. 'Here's the deal, boy. You clean the sty, I'll buy you a pig for your birthday.'

Gu clearly thought there was no chance of that happening, that I would have forgotten the plan by tomorrow. It was that wink that made me determined. How dare he not take me seriously?

Early next morning I was back in Cwm Castell Fawr, called the Big House by the family, wearing my oldest clothes. I went into the sty with an old wooden shovel and two pails. The stench made me retch at first. Ester was right about the size of that heap left by the pigs years before. In places, there was dung three or four feet deep. After a few shovelfuls, I realised it had long since turned to a sweetly scented, well-rotted manure; then the task seemed easier.

I dug in. Slowly, heavy pail after pail went to Ester's muck heap yards away. Ester emerged from the farm kitchen half an hour later, after the farmhands' breakfast. She stared in surprise at what, to me, looked like a mountain of manure beside her vegetable plot.

She smiled. 'Come in for bread and jam. You must be hungry after all that work. Wash your hands first, now.'

She handed me rosemary-scented soap. Gu was sitting by the fire, silent as usual. He wrinkled his nose as I ate, then followed me out to the sty where I began again. He watched me wrestle with the wooden pails. Every minute or so I'd glare at him and he'd return my stare.

He limped off, took up another larger shovel and came into the sty to help. He brought with him a little hand cart that made the task much easier, thank goodness. My jaw dropped. Gu no longer did any labouring himself. He told the farmhands what to do, detailed precisely how he expected it done, and watched them like a hawk. Gu frightened people, an upright soldier pensioner, grey and gaunt with piercing blue eyes. I was wary of him back then, although the puckered scar on his leg, the legacy of a bullet at Waterloo, fascinated me.

I was glad for his help. Panting, I carried on shovelling. Together we piled the manure onto the cart, then pulled it over to the muck heap. We soon had an audience, the whole farm gathered round to watch. Gu swore at them and told the lads to get on with their work or he'd dock their wages.

Saying to the women, 'Go back to your damn butter and cream.'

No wonder they stared. It was the first time Thomas Lewis, veteran and farmer of Cwm Castell Fawr, Newchurch, Carmarthenshire, had lifted a hand to manual labour since he'd walked back, alone, from Waterloo. True, he'd given orders to others. He'd grunted, criticised and cursed the farmhands working his one hundred and thirty acres. He'd grumbled, counted his gold and his pension, and complained of his aches and pains. Not until that day, however, had he lifted a hand himself; not to work the land, nor help in the kitchen garden.

Thomas had gone weekly to market, but never to church, except to see his mother and first wife Susan buried, and to marry her sister, Ester. His only daughter, Elizabeth, my mother, had married and had children. Thomas had not given her away nor seen any of the children named. Thomas had sat, watched the fire, then stumped up to his bed, night after night. Since his return from the army he'd been plagued by nightmares and worse. He would shake, tremble and shout as if the battle was still around him.

I didn't care or notice; it was how my grandfather had always been, as far as I could tell. I was delighted to have him help clean the sty and bounced around, receiving the odd gentle cuff if I got in his way. After an hour it was cleared; a sturdy, white-washed pigsty with a roof of stone tiles. Gu walked round it muttering to himself that it needed some mortar here and there, and bent to pull ivy from the base of the walls. He walked to the well, pulled up the bucket, threw its contents to slop over the cobbles and brushed it clean with a besom.

'Food, Will, my boy,' he said, and off back to Ester and the big kitchen we went.

Fussing happily, she made us wash. 'Properly now, you two.'

Then bowls of steaming stew, thick with potatoes, carrots and lamb, were set before us, followed by curds with sweet preserved plums. They tasted delicious and I told her so.

Gu spoke up. 'Yes, the plums taste of summers gone by, the hint of clove makes them smell all the nicer. Just the thing after a morning's work, eh, Will?'

Ester smiled, delighted at the rare compliment from Gu.

Gu settled by the fire once more. I ignored his back turned to me and went to stand between him and the flames.

'So when can I have my pig, Gu?'

He blinked and came back from his distant preoccupation.

Peering at me, he asked, 'Well, when's your birthday, lad?'

I stamped my foot. 'How can't you know, Gu? It's next Thursday. I'm nine.'

'Nine indeed. We'll have to go to Carmarthen market on Wednesday then, won't we? We'll take the cart with Ester when she takes in her butter and eggs.'

Ester's mouth made a silent 'oh'. The thought of Thomas Lewis doing something as commonplace as taking his grandson to market was astounding.

By Wednesday morning I was hopping with excitement. My mother, Elizabeth, came out from our farm, Cwm Castell Fach, known as the Little House to us all. She walked along the lane to wait beside me.

As the cart pulled up, she asked, 'Are you sure about taking him, Father?'

He grunted, telling her not to be so foolish.

She tried again. 'Would you like John to come in with you then?'

'Damn it, girl, I've been going to market since I was this boy's age, well before you were born. Stop fussing and let us get on.'

I chatted as we went, yelling from the jolting cart to friends and neighbours headed along the same road. We reached the tollgate at Water Street, where Gu paid a shilling for the cart and load with a grumble. The bar creaked open and we were in Carmarthen Town. As the horse pulled us along the crowded road, a cacophony of sounds from cattle, pigs, horses, sheep and poultry got louder, the sharp smell of straw mixed with urine and dung got stronger. We went to the butter market first, leaving Ester there along with the cart and her salt butter, eggs, cheeses and cream.

Most of her produce would be bought by traders from Merthyr and Swansea. Ester could have got nearly as favourable a price from the Newcastle Emlyn carrier buying stock for his cart on his way to Merthyr Tydfil;

she didn't need to go into town but loved her day out at the market each week. She dressed up, wearing a red flannel betgown and cape with a pristine white apron and petticoat beneath. Recently she'd added a tall black hat to the outfit.

'Buyers are often English or Irish immigrants. They believe Welsh country people have always worn these hats. It's not true; my mother only ever wore a cotton bonnet and a proper hat for church. It is a new fashion, but if I get a better price for my eggs, I'll wear any kind of hat you like.'

Ester spent the mornings chatting with her friends from neighbouring villages and selling her produce. In the afternoon, especially when her sister came from Tenby, she'd shop. That morning she looked tense and thoughtful.

'Thomas, you will be careful, no arguments please.'

He pshawed this comment. Then she told him she wanted a pig too and handed him a half guinea.

'Why do you want me to buy you a pig when there is a field full at home?'

'Yes, but those are your pigs, Thomas Lewis. I want one of my own, the same as when I sell the butter and eggs – the money is my own. This is my coin and I want you to buy me a fine young sow.'

'You are my wife, woman, they are yours as much as mine.'

'Now's not the time to talk about this, Thomas. Get me a strong sow like I ask. If I want to make more to set aside, that's my business and you know it. You and the boy get about your day. Will, listen to Gu and learn. Get us two pigs, fit and ready to give us plenty of piglets by and by. You and me, we'll set up well together.' She hugged me. 'Look after Gu.'

'Fuss, fuss, fuss,' Gu mumbled. He grabbed my hand and stalked off, half pulling me along.

I had a grand time in the market. First, we went to the fish sellers on the quay and viewed the catch. Gu, hand on my collar, steered me around two sailors brawling in the gutter and a pile of fish guts, seagulls squabbling viciously over them. Ignoring most of the beggars, Gu went over to talk with two old soldiers, who leant against a wall in tattered and worn uniforms. One was lame with no leg, a wooden stump protruding from his breeches. I stared in fascination at the other man's horribly puckered face, his only eye solid and glistening like the white of a boiled egg. They saluted when Gu dropped a few coins into their tin cups as we walked on.

'It's a hard life for old soldiers who were injured fighting the French. They weren't in my regiment but I give them a few coins when I see them. Could have been me standing there if fate had worked out differently,' he said. 'Now then, I fancy some fish for supper; let's see if there are any fat dabs for Ester to fry.'

After navigating a "gaggle", as Gu complained, of women selling chickens, geese and ducks, we went through the cattle market. Every other farmer stopped him, shook his hand, asked how he was and then talked about the finer points of their animals. Even the thinnest, least muscular of beasts had their finer points, which had to be detailed. After an hour I was impatient and tugged at his hand.

'The best pigs will be gone. Come on, Gu. Come on!'

He smiled, looking as if he might be enjoying himself, and allowed himself to be dragged towards the pig pens. We spent half an hour inspecting the pigs and narrowed it down to two pairs, one pair spotted and one pair pure white. I told him I'd prefer whichever was friendlier and gentler, which Gu told me meant we should get the spotted pair. A call rang out.

'Corporal Lewis, I'll be damned if it isn't.'

Gu paused and stiffened. Looking up, he greeted the tall man in front of him. 'Jones, it's you, is it? Down from Cardigan.'

'Good God, I'm glad to see you, Thomas Lewis,' came the reply. 'Damn shame about our Picton and his top hat, eh? Would be grand to meet for a beer later if you can, talk about old times?'

'Thanks, Joe, but I'm here with the family. Let me introduce you to my grandson, William. He's a fine lad, Elizabeth's second son and nine tomorrow. Already the tallest lad in Sunday school and, so the curate keeps telling us, the brightest. He can read and write wonderfully. They are trying to get me to send him to be tutored with Captain Davies's son. Nonsense, of course, a foolish idea for a lad who's got to earn his way in the world, but we are proud of him. I will pay for a year or two's tutoring, to keep his mother happy.'

Jones and I looked surprised, Jones to hear Thomas Lewis had a grandson who could read and write at nine. I guessed that like Gu, he could only make his mark, the same as most farmers in Carmarthenshire. I hadn't thought Gu ever listened to my mother proudly telling him about my achievements, didn't know I was to be tutored. Gu never did more than stare into the fire; he appeared to ignore my mother telling him about my learning.

The two men talked a while longer. Phrases such as Quatre Bras, green jackets, the Duke, that bastard Price, floated over me. I concentrated on the pigs in the pen. One seemed livelier than the others. Surreptitiously I took out half an apple filched from the store at home. The pig was on to it in an instant, unlike her sisters. My mind was made up, but what if it was too costly? I tugged at Gu's hand again and pulled him down.

'I want this one for my birthday, but if we are to bargain, I think I should pretend to like the other better.'

My grandfather raised an eyebrow and for the second time that day, he cracked a smile.

'Cunning little man.'

He grinned at Jones and negotiations began.

The shouts from the farm were getting louder. I had to stop daydreaming. I hurried. A small group had gathered around the locked farmhouse door. Ester, the farmhands and the dairymaid were there; the dogs barked furiously.

Simon was banging his fist on the door, yelling, 'Let us in, let us in.'

I gave a sigh of exasperation.

'Stop that, Simon. Sam, go and get the hay ladder from the barn. The back window to my room is unlocked.'

I kept that window open for Saturday night trips to the tavern. I used those ladders nearly as often as the stairs if I got home late.

'Now, all of you keep quiet. I'll speak to the old man, then let you in.'

Sam returned with the ladder. Checking its footing was sound, I was up and into the house in moments. I was not surprised to see my poor Gu cowering in the corner of the fire-lit gloom of the kitchen. His body trembled, his arms over his head. In his head, he was back at Waterloo or another long-forgotten battle in Spain. Gu often had turns when he shouted and thrashed in his sleep, and sometimes in the day, he'd retreat into himself and then the horrors would begin for him. His face would change, he'd pale, swallow and start to sweat. It happened more often on sunny days like this one, when for everyone else the world looked bright. This was a bad turn though. I was glad I was there. The family never seemed able to understand how best to help. It confused them to see someone they knew as gruff, hard and cantankerous change and become afraid and vulnerable.

I went over to him, gently saying, 'Gu, it's me, Will, your grandson. Everything is fine. You're back home in Cwm Castell. The war's long over.'

Patting his back, I kept telling him everything was well. Little by little, his body relaxed as he returned from his nightmares back into the kitchen.

He shook his head after a while, saying bitterly, 'I'm a foolish old man, Will, I'm sorry.'

I nearly said no and left it there, but I had an idea.

'Gu, I wonder if talking about the war would help? The rest don't know what to do when your turns come now I'm not here so much. We could try talking about it. You've never spoken to a soul about what happened. You know what they say about sharing troubles. Why don't we go out into the sunshine and talk? You used to tell me about being a soldier and your travels, the happy times, when I was little, that summer years ago as we watched my pigs grow. I enjoyed your tales back then.'

'I'm not sure I can face it, lad. My spells are terrible when they come. It's as if I'm back there in a battle, the noises and memories get louder, sharper and clearer until I can't bear it, I snap. I know it's not fair to Ester or the family. Let me think about it. I dread putting into words how bad it was. A terrible thing, war.

'Go and open the door, let them all back in.'

Chapter Two

Ester and the others streamed into the room. Mother was with them, carrying the baby. Young Sam had been sent down to the Little House to get help.

Simon came up. 'Thank goodness you were here, Will. What would we have done without you?'

'I've told you time and again, shouting and panicking makes him worse. Put yourself in his shoes. He thinks he's in a battle fighting for his life against the French. He's locked the doors to keep them out. You banging and hammering at the door doesn't help. It makes it more real, more like war. Think and remember, will you? Speak calmly and soothingly, don't shout.'

Simon looked at his boots, agreed I had told him that before and said he'd try to recollect next time. I nodded, knowing that the chance of his remembering was slim. Simon didn't listen much, and when he did he forgot most of what he'd been told. He rewarded Gu with fierce loyalty and hard work. My brother Tom complained that

Gu could get someone younger to do twice the work for the money, which was doubtless true; there were many who would take his job in an instant. Times were hard and regular work difficult to find, especially when it came with lodging. Simon would stay; he was part of the family, whatever Tom said. If he didn't work for Gu, we knew it would be the workhouse for him. He'd no family and, like most workers on the land, no savings.

My father John arrived with my brothers, Tom and Shem. They'd heard the commotion and seen Mother dash up the hill.

Tom came up to me. 'You should have called me to help.'

'You weren't needed. I was here. He's used to me,' I replied. Rewarded by the glint of irritation in Tom's eyes.

Gu nodded to them and said gruffly, 'Afternoon, John, sorry you've had your Sunday rest troubled.' Looking at Ester for approval, he asked, 'Maybe now so many of you are here, the little ones can come up too? We can eat Sunday supper together?'

Ester smiled, delighted. She loved to have the family around her. Although we were the grandchildren of her sister Susan, Ester had loved Mother, and now her children, as her own since coming to the farm. Ester had come to Newchurch to look after her younger sister who was in a state of melancholy. She ended up caring for my young mother, along with my battle-scarred, irascible grandfather. Mother was said to look more like her Aunt Ester than her own mother; they were both short, dark and practical women and got on wonderfully. Ester had run the farm quietly and efficiently since then. She was the first to hug us, welcome our friends and defend us, especially my older brother Tom, whenever Gu got irritated with us.

The kindest soul in the parish, she'd give food to any hungry waif or stray who asked when they walked past the gate. There were many such poor souls over the years; the depression after the war, the Poor Laws and then the Irish coming in waves, looking for work, added to the numbers. The Irish walked, hoping for a better life in the mines or factories further east. Gu moaned that it was lucky we were on a side road, not the main road through Carmarthen, or he'd be ruined. We knew he took pride in Ester's kindness and hard work. Mother said barely a woman in the village failed to remark that it was no wonder he'd married his sister-in-law a year after his wife's death, especially with his mother dying a couple of months after Susan. A few added, rather less kindly, that she was a better wife for a farmer than that giddy Susan.

It was rare for the family to gather and include Tom, Gu's heir and eldest grandson. Gu and Tom argued whenever they met. Tom was too much a chip off the Lewis block, too similar in temperament to Gu, unlike Shem and me. Tom wasn't only named for his grandfather; he looked like Gu and, it was said, very much like Tommy – Gu's son. Sometimes the old man flinched to see our Tom at the door, had to turn away because of the likeness. Tom was handsome; lean, dark-haired, with sharp blue eyes like Gu's. The same as Gu, Tom always thought he knew best. The two often disagreed, sometimes within minutes of meeting. Tom was serious, hot-headed and a radical, if shy with women. Although the girls would try to catch his eye, Tom'd never appear to notice. Not like me. I day-dreamed about girls all the time, day and night.

I'd been repairing the arm of a kitchen chair for Ester and decided to sand the replacement arm while Ester laid the meal out. As I sanded, I thought about my older brother.

Tom had stopped coming to the Calvinist Methodist Chapel with Father; he'd joined the Independent Methodists two years ago. But these last few months he seemed to have started back with the Calvinists, which struck me as odd. The Lewises of Cwm Castell had gone to church in Newchurch for generations, so Tom being chapel was another annoyance for Gu. That Gu himself refused to go to church and had no time for religion didn't matter. Tom should go to church.

Tom spoke Welsh, not English, whenever he could. While he dared not tell Gu, he sometimes called himself Twm, not Tom. He'd joined the Ivorites Friendly Society's Carmarthen Lodge. Only Welsh was allowed there, unlike the Oddfellows Society, which I'd visited with Master David once or twice.

Gu was proud of his spoken English, his time in the army and that he was on good terms with the local gentry, including the Rices of Dynevor and Lord Cawdor. He was annoyed Tom would not show he spoke English well, saying, possibly with justification, that when he took over the farm it would damage its reputation. Tom spoke out on the turnpike tolls and against the Poor Law. Everyone complained in private, but Gu thought public criticism of the law was dangerous.

As far as I knew, it was all hot talk and no action for Tom and his friends in the village. There had been no dissent or tollgates broken near Newchurch. Rebecca and her daughters, as we called the protesters who, disguised as women had been destroying the detested tollgates at night across west Wales since the start of the year. Such trouble hadn't come to Newchurch. Farmers and their produce from the north and west of us had further to travel to market. The costs of the tolls for each horse at every gate – fourpence at most gates, and sixpence in Carmarthen, even without their load – was a real burden, as they might have to pass four or more gates. My village was close to Carmarthen, so we paid just one toll, at Water Street. Tom was at home at night, not out breaking gates with Rebecca.

Last autumn, Gu, Tom and I had been sitting in the kitchen when a vicious argument between the two started.

Tom said, 'We must buy new equipment, Gu. Think of the time and money the new thresher saved us; we needed three fewer men at harvest last year. If we get one of those new metal – steel, it's called – ploughshares, the fields will be ready for planting quicker, dug deeper too. The time saved will mean we can plant more fields with crops.'

Gu replied, 'Yes, but many rely on their wages at harvest to get them through the winter; families went without because we didn't employ them last autumn. It's my money you are pushing to spend. Those ploughshares you talk of so lightly are costly. I'm not sure the benefits are there. I'd rather carry on as I always have.'

'Look how well the Swedish turnip worked out. You have to admit I was right about that. You didn't want to pay for new seed then either, but we got double the crops compared with our old turnips, despite the wet spring.'

Gu grunted, irritated that Tom had the audacity to remind him that he had been proven right about the 'Swedes'. I winced as Tom continued, knowing that when Gu was in a mood, it was unwise to push him.

'We should buy clay pipes to drain the Great Oak lower pasture while we are at it. It's so boggy by the stream, nothing grows well, though it gets plenty of sun. I want to plant rye in that field.'

Gu exploded. 'Will you stop your damn meddling and stupid notions. While I'm above ground, it's my farm and I'll decide what's planted. I've sworn there'll be no rye planted on this farm in my lifetime. If you are not careful, you won't inherit the farm once I'm below ground either. I wish to God Will was the older; he doesn't nag at me all the time. He listens.'

This outburst pushed a serious wedge between Gu and Tom and stirred up long-standing ill feeling between my brother and me. I was jealous, not only of Tom's good looks but also that Tom was to inherit Cwm Castell. Usually, land was divided and inherited equally between brothers, but Gu was adamant he'd leave the house and all the land to his eldest surviving grandson: Tom.

Tom, for his part, was piqued that I'd found reading, writing and arithmetic easy; that I'd outpaced him, my elder by two years, so easily. He was envious that I took after Father and was already nearly a foot taller, as well as being stronger and more muscular. That Gu had paid for me to be tutored with the squire's son years before –

another long-standing grudge. Tom had had more than enough of me as a younger brother with my teasing, annoying ways. He made it abundantly clear when we were out in public together that I was younger and much less important than him.

Naturally, I responded by speaking down to him, showing off my learning and using unusual English words and phrases. This regularly ended with him calling me a pompous fool and one of us stalking off.

I finished the sanding. The chair's arm was smooth, ready for me to finish with Ester's lavender-scented beeswax. I looked around and saw Tom gazing at me suspiciously. I was too comfortable in the Big House for his liking. He thought I was plotting to steal his inheritance, that Gu might actually change his will and leave the farm to me.

Smirking, I smeared a dab of polish onto the rag and started rubbing along the grain, back and fore. In reality, years before, Gu had told me firmly, 'I'm sorry, Will, but the farm in its entirety will go to young Tom. Splitting the land is no kindness. I don't agree with the Welsh way; English laws are better for inheritance. This farm with its hundred and thirty acres will give a comfortable living to one family. Your father will rent Cwm Castell Fach for as long as he likes. You will have to make your own way in the world. You needn't worry, I've sovereigns enough to apprentice you to any trade you please and set you up with tools and a workshop. Goodness knows you are bright enough, with energy and ambition. You are shrewd with a shilling too. I don't worry about you making a success of any business. Tom, well, he's a farmer to the bone, it's his passion. We will have to work out how best to look after young Shem though. Tom gets impatient with him, and there's no point in Shem being apprenticed.'

Tom had all the luck, being born eighteen months before me. In my heart, I wasn't sure I wanted to farm, despite my pig breeding years ago. I liked working in Carmarthen, revelled in the inns and taverns, enjoyed bargaining and negotiating. I'd relished learning how to handle wood, making mortice and tenon, lap or scarf joints. The problem was, I wanted the farm too. It was my home. I hated that one day, Cwm Castell and its land would belong to Tom. I made him suffer because I was endlessly resentful. The thought that it would be his, not mine, gnawed at my insides like a hungry rat. I'd never admitted to Tom what Gu had said; part of me still hoped Gu might change that decision and divide the land, or even give the farm to me instead.

Cwm Castell Fawr, the big farmhouse inherited from his father, was my grandfather's pride. It nestled into folds of the rich green fields of Carmarthenshire, in the Hundred of Elvet. It was close to town but far enough away to be peaceful and quiet, deep in a secret valley, tucked below Garn Fawr hill, with ditches and cairns from a time long forgotten; Roman, we were told, maybe older.

The farmhouse was ancient, said to have been built when Queen Bess was on the throne. An uncle of Oliver Cromwell had owned it once too. John Fontaine, a slave master from the West Indies, owned it after that. The land, with two farmhouses and cottages, had been sold as part of Fontaine's estate to my great-great-grandfather years before. Gu added to the land, buying acres nearby whenever he could. The house had been extended in Fontaine's time, over fifty years before. It stood symmetrical and square, like a sampler tapestry house, with a central planked and nailed oak door, five windows above and four below, an older longhouse stitched onto the back of its fine frontage.

It was too big for my elderly grandfather and Ester. I stayed with them on Saturday and Sunday nights now, but most of its rooms were unused. The dark furniture from my great-grandparents' time filled the spaces, but no life or laughter was left within its walls.

I had little choice but to reconcile myself that as the second son I'd have to find my own path. After my talk with Gu and much thought, I'd decided on a carpentry apprenticeship. I'd watched the new National School in Newchurch being built over the summer of 1839, seen how hard and long the craftsmen and workers laboured. I'd weighed up how demanding the work seemed and which masters were most prosperous. I'd admired the skills involved in carpentry, as well as the accuracy the work required. Working with wood and learning a trade seemed a decent prospect to me. I'd been apprenticed to a cousin of my father's, David Morgan, a master carpenter and joiner with a thriving workshop on Lammas Street in Carmarthen.

I was disappointed to have missed going to the new school with a real schoolmaster. In fact, better off farmers' sons and daughters only went to school on and off. The cottagers' children attended less, as by the age of seven they worked, perhaps gathering wood to sell for a ha'penny a bundle in town, picking stones off a field or barking trees for the tannery. The stones were collected to be broken by men from the workhouse to repair the roads. Even a few pennies extra meant a meal or two more on the table. At harvest time the school was almost empty except for the youngest, mothers relieved to have the little ones looked after so they could work all the faster. My father, Da, allowed my sisters to go to the National School, but not Shem; he'd never learn to read.

Shem, my fifteen-year-old brother, loved to sing loudly and tunelessly to the Welsh and English hymns and enjoyed the pictures in the Sunday school books. He missed our sisters in the day, but he was ten years old when the school opened, a strong and willing worker. He did what he was told without question, so his contribution was of real value.

I'd started my apprenticeship aged fourteen, fortunate that home was close. Master David allowed me to walk the three miles back home each Saturday afternoon, to return early on Monday morning. The apprenticeship premium cost Gu a lot of sovereigns from the locked little oak *coffer bach* chest in his bedroom.

I enjoyed showing off my new skills, like with that chair I was repairing for Ester. I mended anything I could find around the farm – doors, window frames – it gave me a chance to practise with my chisels, saws and planes.

I'd overheard Master David tell Father, 'He's got a way with wood, your boy. Economical with it too; he works out where and how to cut it to save the most timber, does it even better than I do after all my years in the trade. I'm delighted with his progress; even if he wasn't kin, I'd still employ him.'

I wasn't sure if any of the less positive reports about visits to the taverns with the older apprentices and our exploits had reached home, but guessed from Tom's comments that he'd heard about them.

I'd slept in the Big House for the last three years; the Little House was full, every bed needed for Tom and the little ones. I liked having a room and a bed with a feather mattress to myself. It suited everyone. Gu and Ester looked forward to me arriving each Saturday night. Ester welcomed me as if I'd returned from a sea voyage, not walked three miles up the road from Carmarthen. She loved seeing my friends and would wait at the door on Saturday evenings for Huw and Ellen to call by and cook us a vast supper. Ester knew it was the best meal Ellen would eat all week, likely her only meal that day.

A ruckus interrupted my thoughts as my little sisters rushed into the farm kitchen, shouting for me to turn their skip rope; Shem had been sent to bring them up to the Big House. Ester served up a Sunday feast: rabbit pie; cold ham with hot creamy herb and leek sauce; early potatoes; carrots from the press; fresh, fine white bread and butter; rice pudding with jam; and then our favourite, spiced cake. The room was soon loud with laughter, squabbles, and cries from the children.

For once Gu and Tom chatted pleasantly about lambing, which had gone well this year, how many hoggets to sell and whether to invest in a new ram in the autumn.

Tom asked, 'What would you say about trying some guano this winter, Gu?'

'Guano? What's that? It is a strange sounding word.'

'It is a soil enricher shipped over from Peru this last couple of years. It is like manure, made from dried bird droppings, but stronger and easier to spread, from what I've read.'

'Peru? That's half the world away. Not sure I'd spend on dung from Peru when we've plenty in Wales. The streets of Carmarthen stink of it; piles of horse and cattle dung as well as human waste on every street corner, and when it rains – well, it's everywhere. What other new ideas have they come up with in those books you read on farming? Any ways to improve my cereal yields, without my spending a fortune?'

After we'd finished tea, Gu looked at my father and asked, 'Brandy, John?'

Gu had several dozen bottles of fine French brandy hidden away below the stairs. To take a glass of fine spirit after supper was a real luxury. Whenever it was mentioned, we grandchildren wondered if there was any truth to village rumours that Gu had smuggled in his younger days. Was that why he had so much brandy in Cwm Castell?

Chapter Three

Gu and I walked out into the sunny evening and strolled down to the pigsty and on up the half mile or so to the Crug. We didn't speak. Passing the sty reminded me of Bluebell. Gu was lost in his own musing and silent, so I drifted back to my nine-year-old self.

I'd loved my Welsh lop ear pig. I'd called her Bluebell. Ester's pig didn't get a name at first. When I asked Ester, she replied, 'Its name is Bacon.'

I'd giggled and that was the name that stuck.

Both young sows were put to the farm's old boar and after twenty weeks produced fine litters; Bluebell had seven and Bacon, six. Those piglets grew fast. My word, did Bluebell and Bacon eat a lot to suckle. The little ones were so sweet. Bluebell had four white piglets and three with spots, including a little runt, always pushed to the back. Four were sows and three hogs. I was kept to feeding them each morning and night, throwing them turnips, milk whey from the dairy, bran husks, rotten potatoes and peelings –

anything edible. They'd squeak and snuffle with excitement, and I'd usually ending up as smelly as their sty. I was made to clear it out once a week on Saturdays. I looked forward to it, although it was hard work, because Gu gave me a penny for the dung each time. I spent half on my favourite sweet: bitter black toffee, so sticky my back teeth would barely open as I chewed. Ester gave the pigs their midday feed and once the piglets reached eight weeks, we started to wean them. Over those weeks, I'd thought long and hard about who should have the pigs to rear, ready for Christmas slaughter.

Auntie Gwennie would be the first to be given one, of course; Ellen's mother too, but I wondered how that would work out. Ellen would do her best, but how would her mother, Isabella Price, known as Bel, feed a pig? I wasn't sure she could. I earmarked the strongest hog for Mother. Sam, the farmhand, said his parents would like to take one and would be sure to give me my quarter at slaughter. After a long, solemn discussion with my father, I decided who would receive the last three piglets.

One Sunday evening in August we set off to Bank Row cottages, five young pigs on ropes in tow. Auntie Gwennie insisted she wanted the runt, saying she and the little one would get on fine. They did, too. Auntie named her Buttercup after hearing her mother was called Bluebell, it being a summer flower. Auntie and Buttercup walked out together every morning and evening, rain or shine, to feed the young pig on the common. Auntie spoilt her with scraps from her table too.

Others on the Row were called on in turn, my father offering them each a weaned pig. He explained my scheme, making it clear we expected a rear quarter of the hogs in return, or for the sows, either the rear quarter or two weaned piglets. My tall, quiet and thoughtful father was respected in the village. A weaned pig was a gift of trust, so each household accepted the offer gratefully. Putting aside eight shillings to buy a pig, nearly a man's wages for a week, had been impossible for most cottagers. But they remembered keeping them as children, and understood the value of having fresh meat, then salted ham and bacon over the hard winter months.

We didn't expect anyone to give us piglets; it cost a lot to keep a pig over the winter and then feed it while it was put to litter. On bigger farms like Cwm Castell, there were easily enough scraps and leavings from the farm and dairy to keep any number of pigs. In the cottages, every morsel was needed to feed a hungry family. From August onwards, though, there would be enough food for a pig from the meagre leftovers, with the additional bounty of Autumn. They'd be fed second drop apples, then windfall apples, mushrooms, acorns, beechnuts, hips and plenty of grass along the hedgerows, enough to fatten a pig. The children would be sent out to collect as many acorns as they could for November. Then, when times got leaner, the pig would be slaughtered and eaten. It was an admirable system but relied on that essential eight shillings outlay that since the wars against Napoleon, few could find.

When we called at Ellen's, Father was shy and clumsy. Bel started to tease and flirt with him. He handled it badly, got embarrassed. Pink-faced, he started to stammer as he tried to explain what was planned.

Ellen rushed up. 'I know all about it, Mr Morgan, thank you very much indeed. We'd love to have one of Will's pigs. I will be looking after it. I'll make sure Will gets his quarter of pork back in the winter.'

Hand on hip, Bel looked at him. 'Time was you and your pals, the Lewis boys, were happy enough to chat with me, John Morgan.'

Discomforted, my father grabbed my hand and hurriedly pulled me away down her path with a brief wave.

I was taken aback. I'd never thought of Bel younger, or of being friends with my father. To me, she was my best friend's mother, ancient. She stood on her step watching us leave in her grubby, old-fashioned dress, cut low, as had been the fashion ten years ago. Bel had Ellen's pretty features; she wasn't really very old at all.

Poor Ellen, a posse of children lived in their tiny cottage. The women whispered that Bel was no better than she should be; she liked ale and men and had no care for respectability. Bel ran a small brewhouse making botanical brews, and stronger beer for anyone passing with a halfpenny spare. It was not the best ale and most in the village avoided her house. That didn't help her reputation either.

Ellen was one of my two close friends in the village, nearly the same age as me. As different in personality from her carefree, dishevelled and cheery mother as it was possible to be, Ellen was a worrier and a worker. It was as if she was the mother, and Bel one more child to be cared for in that tiny cottage. I was sometimes asked in and always warmly welcomed. I knew to say no if offered food. There was little enough of it to go round. Money was earned daily, if at all, odd jobs found here and there. Ellen told me that her mother could be distracted into buying a new ribbon more easily than remembering to buy bread or cheese.

We had reached the top of the Crug hill when Gu spoke.

'There wasn't just one war, you know. People say "the war" now, but it was wars. There were wars across Europe. I'm not promising to be able to tell you about the worst times. Let's see how it goes.' Gu continued, 'I need to do something to help myself, though. It's summer. I'm always worse in the summer.' He grabbed my sleeve urgently. 'Promise me you'll never agree to the recruiter's fine words and join the army, Will. Promise me now.'

I patted his arm. 'I've never wanted to be a soldier, Gu, don't worry, I'd never sign up. Suddenly I felt anxious, wondering *What if talking makes his turns worse?*, but Gu had started his recollections.

'Well then, that war we fought in Spain and Portugal was entirely different from those last few days in Belgium at Waterloo, although we were still fighting the French. I didn't go to America either, but many did; our own first battalion was sent there, but we second battalion of the 44th regiment stayed in Europe. I've tried not to think about that time, although it floods back in my nightmares all too often. It's been nearly twenty-eight years since I came home. I go over and over the terrible memories, but there were better times as well as bad ones. I'll start here in Newchurch, shall I? Explain why I went off to fight.'

He snorted. 'That's another thing, don't you marry too soon, Will. I married too young, you see, besotted by your grandmother. We were eighteen when we met and very different from the start. Susan wanted excitement and town life. She thought marrying a prosperous farmer's son from Carmarthen would give her that. Sadly for us both, Newchurch is not so different from her own Pembrokeshire village of Manorbier. The whirl of dances and parties she'd imagined was exactly that – her imagination. Susan liked to dress up and be admired. Tucked away up this country lane, that couldn't happen. She wasn't much of a cook; my mother was exasperated at how little she knew about running a farm kitchen, kept burning her cakes, she did. Susan wasn't always kind either, my sister Rachel disliked her because of it. Susan expected to be petted and keep her hands soft and clean, not scrub, salt, churn and bake.

'Your grandmother would have been better off marrying a grocer with a boarding house from Tenby, like her sister. In Tenby there are entertainments all summer long, and the gentry flock there. Tenby was bustling and full of building and new business, there were plenty of socials in the Assembly rooms. Newchurch seemed dull to her. To be honest, it did to me too. We argued a lot about what we wanted from life, about money, and after a few years, my enchantment with her was over.

'My father wouldn't let me do as I wanted with the farm; his ways were the right ways and had to be followed.' He sighed. 'I understand how Tom feels, I've been through it, although I won't tell him that. My father insisting, "That is the way things have always been done", it used to infuriate me. I let Tom try new things once in a while, even if I don't agree with him.

'Well, I decided I wanted to see something of the world, not stay in this safe little village. I'd had enough of Susan always wanting new dresses and to be taken into Carmarthen and my father and mother being so disapproving, my poor sister stuck as peacemaker between us; it was miserable. I wasn't paid much more than pocket money. If it wasn't for my trips to Pembrokeshire and around the county, I'd have had no shillings to spend.

'When a recruiter came through Carmarthen on the way back from Ireland in September 1808, to my mothers' dismay, God rest her soul, I took the bounty and joined up, aged twenty-eight. I left my father, mother and Susan with three little ones to run the farm, with only my Rachel and the farmhands to help. I marched off. Looking back, I'm not proud of what I did – it brought me more unhappiness than you can imagine – but at the time it seemed the only way out.'

'I'd wanted to join the Welsh Fusiliers, but as it turned out I joined the 44th East Essex, the regiment that happened to be recruiting in the town square that day. Later we were called the "Little Fighting Fours", a great bunch of lads, the best. We were hard talking, hard fighting, the bravest regiment in the army. I got to see the world, all right, and a whole lot more besides. At first I enjoyed it.'

He paused. 'Enough. I haven't thought of those troubled times in my marriage for years, I'm not sure I want to dwell on them now. Let's to bed. You have an early start in the morning. I think I will walk out tomorrow and see if Tom's right, maybe that lower pasture could do with drainage ditches digging.'

We walked back through the deepening twilight. Bats squeaked and darted around our heads as we crossed the fields. Through the woods, our boots trod silently on springy layers of old leaves. White patches of wood anemones reflected the stars emerging above us. The slow, heavy swoosh of an owl sounded through the dusk.

As he opened the kitchen door, Gu said, 'I realise you wanted to hear about my time fighting, not that old story of why I joined up. I couldn't face the telling tonight. I need more time.'

CHAPTER FOUR

MONDAY 18TH APRIL 1843

Five o'clock the following morning, I was waved off by Ester into the dawn. The robins and blackbirds had started their liquid song, the skylark and thrush would join the chorus soon. I carried a pack of tasty treats: jam tarts and Easter's cheese with a stoneware pot of pickles to keep me going through the week. I had a shilling in my pocket from Gu, too. Gruff and grumpy as he was, he spoilt me. Gu knew there was fun to be had in town, money to be spent in the taverns or treating the girls. He still remembered what it was to be young and happy. I'd set half aside for savings and spend the rest without care or thought over the week. It was a generous allowance for a seventeen-year-old; the other apprentices envied my sixpence. Many families had only pennies or nothing at all to spare after buying the basics. We apprentices might have an evening or two drinking, – there was always a tavern close by where we'd have fun and make mischief – but Master David kept his boys working so hard for long hours, that more often we were glad to eat a decent meal and crawl up to our straw mattresses above the workshop.

I'd manhandle beams with the others, set timber frames to place, lay out floors. We'd make up the window frames and doors. How detailed and ornate the work was depended on who was paying and how much. Times were hard in Carmarthen, but Master David told us that since the new Queen, young Victoria, was crowned things were starting to improve. He approved of the Poor Law; he had resented the costs of supporting so many people under the old system. He believed many who could work chose not to and didn't see why his taxes should pay for them to live at home. That they were the "undeserving poor" was what he, like many, thought.

David held different views to those in the countryside. Tom and his friends talked about the terrible conditions under the new laws and the problems faced by families fallen on hard times. I kept quiet, knowing that Master David, "Dai Chip" as the boys called him – but never to his face, would not appreciate hearing any view not in accordance with his own. Tom would have argued at the drop of a hat, but I knew when to keep people sweet and needed a favourable account from my Master.

In a year's time, I hoped he'd pay me as a journeyman carpenter for the rest of my indenture. I'd learned fast and tried to make myself indispensable. Times were changing, and not before they should. Master David had told us it wasn't compulsory to register with the guild of carpenters anymore, as it had been in his father's time. He knew the value of a skilled workman and wouldn't want to lose my goodwill or have me leave, especially as I was kin and he'd no sons. He'd hate having to pay me a wage, but able work and responsibility has its price.

I was proud of Carmarthen, with its bustling, broad streets built after the war with the French. Our streets were straight, not meandering like Kidwelly or Llandeilo; Gu had said it was because it was a Roman city long ago, and Romans built wherever they liked. Carmarthen had squares and terraces of handsome houses with big windows to let in the sunlight. Old timbered houses had been pulled down to make way for the new buildings. Maybe I would earn enough to have a house like that one day, clean and bright, on Picton Terrace. Lovely houses, those, the work on the curved windows and doors finely done. Every trader and business you could think of was in Carmarthen; no wonder until Merthyr Tydfil grew so big on iron, Carmarthen was the biggest town in Wales.

People were leaving now though, especially those with ambition like my friend Joseph's family. We'd spoken before he left.

'Why are you leaving? Your father's got a decent tenancy, sixty acres of fertile land.'

Joseph replied, 'Yes, but it's not paying, Will. We can't make the rent and feed the family with prices at market so low. We are close to starving. Father and I work to fill the pockets of the landlords and the clergy. My Da says we will follow the money. He wants to see what it's like in the copper works in Swansea. He's heard it's bad for the lungs though, so he's wondering about iron or the coal mines further east. Do you know how much they pay miners? Up to a pound a week. I'd be paid the same, the children can earn too. My father says that without a railway, Carmarthen has no future. Bristol has one and soon it will connect to London. Cattle will be sent to London in one day, instead of the drovers spending weeks walking them to Barnet fields for sale. The world is changing and he doesn't want to be left behind in sleepy Carmarthen.'

'I'll miss you, though.'

'You'll be travelling on the same road soon enough. We'll meet up when you do.'

'No, not while the family is here and there is Shem to think of. He'd not be happy away from home.'

It seemed no time until Saturday afternoon when I could walk back up Water Street towards home. I felt a sense of relief, I acted carefree, but worried about Gu and his turns, Tom's rows, and always what Shem had got up to.

Half a mile before home, there was Shem waiting, sitting on a boulder, kicking his heels, looking dejected. Seeing me, he waved and ran down the hill as if he was eight, not just turned fifteen. We loved Shem dearly and the entire village looked out for him as best they could, but sometimes there was trouble.

Ester talked to me about him the last time he got into a scrape. He'd been knocking on doors and running away, prompted by much younger children of nine and ten.

As she scoured the pine kitchen table clean, Ester said, 'Your Gu and I do worry about Shem and what will become of him when he grows up. Gu has thought of making inheriting the farm dependent on his being cared for, that he has a home for life here. Trouble is, Tom is so impatient with him, that might just make both of them unhappy.

'Shem is a ray of sunshine and we love him, but it's a challenge when a baby arrives that's not the same as the rest. When Shem came, there weren't the usual celebrations. Elizabeth had suffered great sadness just a few years before and by then you were two years old and Tom four; she was worn out. Then Shem was born. I guessed something was wrong straight away. He was small for a Morgan baby, his eyes not set quite right, his cry unusual. Your mother was sad, weeping in pain because he wouldn't suckle and took so long to feed.

'Simon, who is pretty simple himself, said out loud to Elizabeth what a lot of villagers were whispering: that Shem was a fairy baby and should be taken up to the Garn and left, for them to take back their own.

'Your Mother wouldn't consider abandoning him. John said it was for Elizabeth to decide, that time would tell if he'd survive. At first, Shem was weak and sickly, but when he reached two he started to thrive; may be that he was a Morgan with tall, strong ancestors helped, who knows? Now, well as you know, he's the same height as Tom, sturdy and muscular, if tubby with it. We wouldn't be without our boy for a minute, would we?'

I'd nodded vigorously. We called Shem an innocent in the family, rather than an imbecile or natural fool, as others did. Cheerful and obliging, he was easily taken advantage of. He'd help anyone that asked him to do anything at all. He worked hard in the fields or dairy. He was easily led into trouble, however, stealing apples or breaking fences if egged on by the village boys – despite their knowing they'd get a pasting from Tom or, worse, from me.

Shem couldn't concentrate. To get him to finish what he started meant frequent reminders, but he never complained and would work his hands raw. Always smiling and happy, he loved music, singing and picture books. He could not be relied on to sit quietly through a long church or chapel service, but liked Sunday school. There was no teaching him his letters, although he remembered the flowers and animals Ester taught him. If Shem liked you, he showed it; he would rush up to hug anyone, young or old. That was starting to cause problems. Shem arrived, flushed and breathless.

I asked, 'What's with the sad face, brother?'

'Mary-Jane Pritchard shouted at me again, Will.'

Shem loved Mary-Jane, his friend from up the road; they were a similar age and he had known her all his life. Last time I'd seen them together I'd noticed that she was embarrassed by him. While she was still kind, she was resistant to his hugs. A few weeks ago, I'd caught her expression as he'd embraced her; she'd looked disgusted and annoyed. I knew why. Shem gave exuberant and damp kisses to anyone he liked.

'Shem, do you remember when Blackie our dog was a puppy, how he'd play? He'd bark and pretend bite?'

'Yes, he was such fun, his nips didn't hurt anyone.'

'True, but now, while Blackie's the same dog, he's grown over the last two years. You and I know his barking and growls are for show and if he bites it's usually a nip, but a lot of people are scared of him. You must have seen that? It's the same for you now you're older.'

'Do you mean now I've grown big, people will get scared of me?'

'Not exactly scared, as long as they know you – but maybe if they don't, yes, a little afraid. It's the same with kisses. Grown men aren't allowed to kiss and hug girls, except for their mother. Mary-Jane won't want to be your friend unless you act calmly and speak nicely to her. No cuddles or kisses at all, for her or anyone apart from Mother and our sisters. You're no longer a puppy, I'm afraid. Can you try to remember that for me?'

'But I do love her, Will. She's my best friend and very beautiful.'

I had no words. It was going to be difficult as he got older. I felt at a loss as to how to protect him. I remembered Gu wondering what to do for Shem as he grew up. Shem saw our sister skipping up the road and was distracted. He ran off, flat-footed, happy, shouting out to her. I hoped he'd remember what I'd said, but was glad his sadness was soon forgotten.

I walked on up to the Little House. My mother welcomed me with a hug and a quick stroke of my arm. After the week's work and always hungry, I looked forward to my dinner with the family. Already six feet two inches in my stockinged feet and still growing, I took after my father, a giant in the village, where anyone more than five and a half feet was considered tall. I was usually far and away the tallest person in any room, including in Carmarthen.

This brought benefits and problems. People looked up to me due to my height, in every sense. They treated me as if I was older than my years. But there were always shorter or older lads trying to square up to me. I'd manage to stop fights by making jokes or playing the fool, but every so often I'd have no option but to scrap. Father had suffered the same; he'd made sure I could handle most comers, emphasising that the best way to win a fight was to defuse it. Gu, an old soldier, had learned hand-to-hand fighting, so he taught me a trick or two as well. At seventeen I was pretty much left alone, to my relief. I took no pleasure in brawling, unlike some of the little runts from town who seemed to enjoy fighting for its own sake.

My brothers and sisters trooped in; Shem with my three sisters and baby brother. Tom, Shem and Da washed in the cobbled yard outside, joining us as Mother put food on the table. She ladled us each a bowl of tasty stew from the pot – not much meat, marrow-bone stock thickened with barley – as we reached for bread, butter and cheese.

I was itching to be off and meet up with my friends, but put up with the joking and shouting for an hour. Tom and I went out, washed again at the well, then put on cleaner breeches and shirts. We set off chatting into falling light. Tom would meet up with the younger men and boys from his Independent Chapel. As Tom fell more into their company, Gu was anxious and thought Tom was being unduly influenced by them. I suspected Tom might well be leading the others on rather than being led; he was such a firebrand.

One or two of his friends, like John Harris from Talog Mill, were well known to be part of the ongoing disruption across the county. Harris had joined the Rebeccas in breaking down tollgates across Carmarthenshire. The gates were always repaired so I didn't see the point myself; it seemed stupid. We all hated the tolls, but Gu said – and I agreed – that you should work within the law, not outside it. Gu felt he had a place to keep up in our community and that his English-speaking grandchildren should have nothing to do with Rebecca. Let other lads get in trouble, not Tom.

To my surprise, Tom stayed with me on the road as we dropped into the Morrises' to pick up Huw and then went on to Ellen's cottage. Ellen was flustered. She kept going back into the cottage, first forgetting her bonnet, then her gloves. She was hot and blushing by the time she was finally ready.

Tom got embarrassed. He made his goodbyes and mumbled to Ellen, 'See you in chapel tomorrow.'

Huw and I exchanged glances.

Huw grinned. 'So that is why Tom's come back to the Calvinists from the Independents, is it, Ellen?'

He tugged her hair affectionately. I forced a grin but felt confused. My stomach churned. Ellen was my friend, always had been. What did Tom mean by being interested in her? It wasn't that I thought of Ellen as a girl – she wasn't, she was Ellen – but she was mine. I studied her properly. Usually, I wouldn't notice how Ellen looked any more than I would Huw. She looked the way she always did, until that moment. Observing now, I saw her cheeks glowed pink, that she had pretty dimples when she smiled, hair the colour of beech nuts, green eyes, and was small and slim but curving in the right places. Unnoticed by me but not, it seemed, by Tom, Ellen had become lovely. My feelings of rivalry and tension resurfaced. This time I was the one discomforted, Tom oblivious.

Huw, Ellen and I wandered down towards the church. There wasn't much to do in Newchurch except at the May and Michaelmas fairs. On dry Saturday evenings, most of us from the village and surrounding farms would stroll to the church and then on up to the chapel. We might play or watch a game of quoits or kick a ball about against the chapel wall. Those earning wages might call into The Plough or The Rose, or into Bel's front room. A few, like Mary-Jane's brothers, had taken the temperance pledge; many more couldn't afford beer. Next morning most would go to one or other of the chapels or the church and see each other again.

The sunny weather had stayed. It was a lovely walk along the old roads that April evening, high green hedges to each side, dandelions and primroses punctuating the grass along with the celandines, bear leek, and early violets.

I spotted Mary-Jane, Shem's friend, ahead, arm in arm with two girls. I stopped as we passed, motioning to wait and talk. She flushed as she smiled. He was right: Mary-Jane was a darling.

'I've been talking to Shem. I'm guessing it's been difficult with him recently. Is he being too affectionate when he sees you?'

She sighed. 'Yes, it's a problem. Although I tell him not to, he always comes up and hugs me. He is too old to kiss me, but I don't know how to stop him. I've tried telling him, even tried shouting. I know he means nothing by it, but others don't, especially my father. My brothers have told Shem off, but he forgets everything they've said moments later.'

'I've talked to Shem and explained to him that he can't behave the same way now he's fifteen. He seemed to understand, but keep reminding him. Be clear before he hugs you. It's important because it might not just be you he tries to kiss; he may be beaten if he picks the wrong girl or boy. What can I do about your brothers?'

'I'll talk to them again. Explain it is Shem, an innocent, greeting someone he likes enthusiastically. You're right, he has to stop it and not just with me.'

I said goodbye and ran on up the hill to join Ellen and Huw, who had joined more friends.

Huw whispered, 'So it's not only Tom with a love interest, is it?'

I jostled him, saying, 'She's fourteen, Huw, don't be so daft.'

'Lovely little thing though isn't she? Heard my mother say she's going to be the May Queen in a year or so.'

'Well, if you are interested in her, Huw boy, I'd say leave it a while, she's too young. I know her because of Shem. She's nice, and I for one would need answering to if anyone messed her about. To say nothing of her father and brothers.'

I raised my eyebrows at him. I couldn't help but think that Mary-Jane Pritchard's parents would be looking for a farmer's son with a comfortable living to offer for her, like Tom, or Huw come to that. They would not be pleased if she walked out with a carpenter's apprentice. My resentment at being born second bubbled back, spoiling my mood.

The strolling came to an end as darkness fell, so I made my way home to Ester and Gu. As I opened the back door to the kitchen of the Big House, everything was much as I'd left it last week: Gu dozing by the fire in his old chair, Ester mending shirts by the light of a taper, likely as not some of my mother's mending. Mother never stopped but always had too much to do, with father and six children at home and the farm kitchen and dairy to run. Ester bustled me into the cosy room. A plateful of food waited, salted ham with tiny pink radishes, hot and spicy on the tongue, and bread.

'How's the week gone, Will? We've missed you, but things are going well here. In fact, your Gu has been busy, much to the lads' dismay. He's been on to Simon and Sam like a tyrant, out checking the ploughing and planting is done in the right order, inspecting the animals to decide which to send to market, which to breed and which to slaughter. He told me he's going to try to talk to you about the war and get his fears out in the open. I'm glad. He should have talked years ago. I asked him to speak to the vicar after we were first married, but that got me in hot water. He told me he had no plans for sharing his life story with that stuck-up old fool!'

I smiled. Gu suffered fools badly and he was right about the vicar. The new curate was little better. To Mother's horror, I was cynical about religion. I said it was all the same: if the preaching was true and you were reasonably Christian, everyone ended up six feet under in heaven. I couldn't see that church or chapel would make a difference. Gu had agreed. Mother had covered my sister's ears and roundly scolded me.

I slipped up to bed, deciding against a trip to the Plough in Bwlch later. I was tired. I'd save my pennies for another night.

Next morning the weather had turned. It was misty and spotting with rain as Ester and I set off for the church. Mother, Tom, Shem and the children joined us. The little ones would stay on for Sunday school and not attend the whole service. Father would go to the Calvinist Methodist chapel later, or possibly not bother. Recently he'd spent his mornings at home, resting and reading the paper – *The Welshman*, our own Carmarthen-published newspaper, more radical in its editorial views than most.

It cost fourpence ha'penny, a lot when most working men earned around a shilling a day. Father complained bitterly about the penny newspaper "tax on knowledge". There were taxes on everything: bricks, tiles, glass and even windows. My frugal great-grandfather David had two of his nine front windows bricked up years ago to save the shillings in taxes each year. David was still quoted, thirty years after his death, as saying "No room needs two windows, they only make draughts".

Each Friday, Master David bought *The Welshman*. After he'd read it, I'd give him a penny and take it home with me. Father read the editorial and political articles with interest. Sometimes we'd take the paper on to The Plough, where reports were translated into Welsh and read aloud. The same would happen with other weekly newspapers, but the Carmarthen Journal was a Tory paper, so was less popular. Very occasionally someone brought in the London published daily newspaper, The Times, but that would only happen if there had been a big event, like when the young Queen married Prince Albert.

As a child of a mixed marriage,– that is, a marriage between church and chapel – I went to whichever place of worship took my fancy. It was a longer walk to the chapel out on the Bronwydd road, which often weighed in favour of the church, especially when it was wet. I'd decided on chapel this morning and walked on with Tom. Ellen and Bel joined us. Tom stayed with me rather than rushing on to join up with his friends. Bel and her younger brood fell back, Bel chattering like a magpie all the way up the hill. The mist was lifting and the sun filtering through as we went into the chapel. Ellen and Tom talked about a Bwlch farmer who'd been gored by a bull last week, how much it cost to get a doctor and whether one made any difference.

Irritated to see them so comfortable together and cut out of the conversation, I distracted myself by thinking of my thoughtful, kind Father sitting reading the paper, resting his back. He'd been born in the Bank Row and was expected to become a blacksmith, like his father and grandfather before him. Like him, his forebears were brawny men and tall, but they became stooped and old before their time. I had barely any memory of my grandfather Morgan. The Morgans all had bad backs. Da became a little more stooped with each year that passed,

Master David the same. Da had one old aunt who was so crooked, her back was like a dog's rear leg. Like many, Father wanted to better himself. He had gone to chapel Sunday school each week as a youth, determined to learn to read and write well, and had succeeded.

Da had always been friendly with the two Lewis boys, Tommy and George, being between them in age. When Tommy had left, he'd remained friends with the family and often helped out at the farm. It was kind of him as he had to work in the smithy all day. It was little surprise that he caught my mother's eye when she was fifteen.

Gu had finally come home alone, with a shattered leg and spirit. Old Boney had been beaten and the war was over, but his family and farm were in chaos. Fields hadn't been planted, the potato crop had been left over the winter and was starting to sprout. My elderly great-grandfather had died while he was away, leaving my great-grandmother to run the farm alone. She could only manage the dairy. John Morgan did his best with the rest of the animals, but the rest was too much for them.

Susan was said to have never looked Gu in the eye again; she barely spoke to him. Mother told us that Susan had become a harridan, particularly with her, criticising anything and everything she did, and treating her more harshly than she did the dairymaid and farm servants. As thin as a rake, she barely ate, and had no smiles or time for anyone. My great-grandmother was at her wit's end, which was when Ester was sent for. No one had time to notice the growing fondness between young Elizabeth and John Morgan.

By the time Ester arrived and order was restored, things were pretty much agreed between my parents; indeed, it was said the broomstick had been jumped some time earlier. While Gu had been taken aback that his little girl had grown up so fast, he accepted things for what they were. He offered to rent seventy acres along with the Little House and suggested they live there. He taught my sandy-haired, muscular father to farm as he would have his sons, building on the knowledge he had picked up by helping while Gu was away. People said Da had done well for himself and married money. In some ways he had, but he and Mother loved each other with a passion.

The Little House was small and lime-washed in a deep earth red. It perched on a hilltop overlooking the valley. It had lovely views on a clear day but, unprotected, also caught the west wind and rain more often than not. There were two large rooms above and two below in the old style, with one big barn and a stable on one end with a hayloft above.

Father might have had an easier life if he'd remained at the smithy. Times had been difficult for small farmers in Wales since the war. Taxes, in addition to sixteen pounds annual rent for the farm, meant money was tight. As his brood of children grew, Da looked perpetually worried. At times he was sharper than was in his nature as well. He never spent anything he didn't have to; the shilling a week Gu gave me was more than Father would have to spend on himself in a month. Regular trips to The Plough were no longer an option for my father.

Tom and I reached the Calvinist Chapel, taking seats on the hard, high-backed wooden pews for the lengthy, often dull, sermons and lessons; you ached all over after the first hour of the minister's droning. We much preferred standing for the hymns. The congregation enjoyed singing together. Noticing Tom sneaking peeps at Ellen, I could see she was amused and pleased by his attention. Grudgingly I tried to be positive, thinking, *If that's how it is, that's how it is. Get used to it.*

The sun had burnt off the mist by the time the service finished. Tom, Ellen and I went back up the stream and over the top, under the old Crug hill, rather than taking the longer, flatter way by road. It was a beautiful walk. Tom, usually so intense, was laughing and merry for once. It was not unusual for me to take Ellen in for Sunday dinner with Ester, who'd have arrived home in the trap an hour earlier – the church was closer and the sermons shorter, although the pews were no softer. It felt odd to have Tom with us, but Ester was her usual self and plied Ellen with food and packed her up some "little bits for the way home", all of us pretending we didn't know this was to be Bel and the children's best meal of the week.

Tom was dreamy, moonstruck and soft, not his usual sharp self and left, walking Ellen home along the lane. Gu looked disapproving but remained silent. I was disconcerted. In the past, Gu seemed to have had a soft spot for Ellen, going as far once or twice as to slip her sixpence to spend on herself. She didn't, of course; it bought food. When he found out, Gu gave her no more. He wasn't going to fund Bel's foolish ways. While Ellen wasn't a farmer's daughter with any wealth or cows as dowry, she was a sensible, hardworking girl. I couldn't understand why Gu had any objections. It wasn't as if Tom and Ellen were courting. Tom was finally taken with a girl and flirting, was that so bad? She'd been my friend for years and no one had disapproved of me seeing her. Unbidden came the thought, *Ah, but you won't inherit the farm. You don't matter, Will Morgan.*

Irritated by Tom's new fondness for Ellen, I looked at Gu and said, 'Shall we go for our walk, then?' He nodded agreement, so I went to change out of my Sunday best and into everyday clothes. As I came down the stairs, I caught the end of a heated, whispered exchange between Gu and Ester. Exactly what was being discussed, I wasn't sure. It sounded as if Gu was less than happy with Tom's interest in Ellen. They fell silent when I came in. Gu put on his boots and off we set into the dusk, this time walking down the road to the old quarry.

'This evening I'll tell you more about my career in the 44th. I'm not ready to talk about fighting yet, but let's talk about the earlier times. I told you last week that it was 1808, I was bored with life here and thought a soldier's life would suit me fine. I took the new shorter seven-year enlistment. Initially I regretted my rash action. I didn't speak English as easily then; although my mother and Susan were from Pembrokeshire and did, we mostly spoke Welsh in Newchurch. There were only two other lads from Wales in the regiment who I could talk to in Welsh and feel comfortable with. Most of the recruits were Irish; they'd enlisted because it was better than starving at home.

They had their own language. They hated the English for putting down their rebellion so harshly at the turn of the century and assumed I was English too, so were unfriendly at first. I was lonely and isolated.

'The towns we marched through to reach Portsmouth overwhelmed me with their strangeness. Portsmouth was a big city, full of sailors and soldiers. I was swindled out of my shillings as quick as you like. I had a lot to learn. I didn't know it then, but we were headed to the Channel Islands, first to Guernsey and later Alderney. Of all places to be sent when I was looking for excitement, I ended up somewhere smaller and quieter than Carmarthen. Of course, as we were at war with the French, those islands off the coast of France needed to be garrisoned, but my ideas of the racy life of a soldier took a real blow.

'My boots pinched terribly. The army cut the leather and soles identically for both feet, so neither foot fitted. My feet were blistered and rubbed raw, my legs ached. Two weeks in, I was so homesick I considered deserting, but that could have meant being shot. Well, I stuck it out and for over a year did nothing but drill, train and clean my kit. I spent days polishing my boots, buttons and gaiters, hours whitening my belt. The uniform was so hot, stiff and uncomfortable, you wouldn't believe. We were sent on long marches with heavy packs on our backs, and drilled endlessly.

'I was taught to clean, load and fire my musket. I had a head start in that I could already shoot straight. I can still taste the saltpetre from the musket powder. Brown Bess, we called the musket. She was the girl we learned to love and treat kindly. It was drummed into us that as foot soldiers, we either learned to shoot fast and straight, or we would die in our first battle. We tried to get four shots off a minute and close to the target, but that was nearly impossible; getting two out each minute was hard enough. We practised over and over again. I could still load a musket in my sleep. By the end of the year, I'd usually manage three shots a minute. That made me one of the fastest in my company.

'There was a lot to master: how to fight in a square to stop any cavalry attacks from cutting us down; how to fight in line, taking it in turns to fire then kneel and reload, so the man behind you could fire over your head, kneel and reload. Discipline was harsh, floggings doled out daily; they could give you as many lashes as they liked, Will. Men died under the lash. It depended on whether you had a flogger for a captain of your company. The officer's word was law. If an officer took against you, and some seemed to get pleasure from inflicting pain, there was nothing you could do about it.

'The recruits were from very different backgrounds to mine. Some had joined to avoid prison or the workhouse, or, like the Irish, to get regular food in their bellies. There were few volunteers and especially not, I realised, pampered farmers' sons. My early life sounded easy compared to most of those I joined up with. Not many had seen active service; the second battalion had only been raised in 1803. We knew nothing of war, we were raw in every sense. Raw from marching, the beds, our boots, stiff uniforms and the kick of our muskets.

'I was one of the oldest new recruits at twenty-eight, and despite what Susan must have thought, one of those with the calmest heads. It was easy to drink or whore army pay away. Many did both. God knows we already had deductions enough from our pay. I resolved to do neither, keeping back at least half my pay, more if I could. I'm like you with money, Will – careful. I don't mind giving you money because I know you'll save some. I often sold or exchanged part of my rations of spirit or beer for coin. I had no choice but to learn English properly. My life would have been a misery otherwise. Speaking English served me well in the long run. It will you as well, don't you listen to Tom and his nonsense about using Welsh.

'The boys in the company were good lads. Whether cutpurses, paupers, farmers, tailors or cordwainers, we were all the same and in it together. We mucked in, joked, did our best to make the officers look foolish and mostly had a fair old time.We strutted around Guernsey, smart in our red uniforms with yellow facings. The youngest, the drummer boys, were ten years old or less. Only a few veterans who'd served with other regiments or sergeants were older than me. We longed to fight, so little did we know, so foolish we were, so naive. In April 1810, we finally got orders to set sail for Cádiz and to war.'

We were back at the farm now. Gu bent to carry in wood for the kitchen fire. I picked a larger armful.

'There, that is enough talking for now. I'll think about what more to tell you over the week. I can't put off telling you about the fighting much longer.'

Chapter Five

Monday 25th April 1843

We were raising a roof on a new house close to Fountain Hall, near the Water Street tollhouse. It was tricky work in a confined space. I enjoyed being up on the rooftops; unlike many, I'd an excellent head for heights. Mother worried I'd fall and kept asking me to keep my feet on the ground, in every sense. I laughed at her concerns. The green oak had been a pleasure to work with for the main beams, although Master David expected every length and joint to be perfect. The rafters and floorboards were to be Norway pine, shipped into the quay from Riga regularly. Fine weather meant we'd progressed well this last two weeks.

Working on that roof near the tollgate, I pushed and pulled at the beams, straining to get the tenons to fit together, nailing, hammering and joking with my workmates. As I worked I listened. Voice after voice floated up, day after day.

'I've already paid at three gates these last ten miles; half my earnings on these sheep is gone before I get to market.'

'Please, sir, I don't have any pennies to pay until I sell my eggs. Please let me through, I beg you. I'll pay on the way home.'

'You thieving bastard. How can it be that much? It's a load of flannel to ship to London. I haven't spent weeks working at the mill for the damn Turnpike Trustees to take all my profits. The road's in no fit state anyway. I nearly lost a wheel at Rhos.'

Carmarthen was ringed by tollgates as if a fortress; it was the only place to buy and sell stock for a decent price, unless you went the twenty-odd miles on to Swansea, with more tolls to pay.

Local magistrates were on the boards of the turnpike trusts, pocketing profits, handing down swinging fines for those who refused to pay the toll. Trusts were supposed to maintain the turnpike highroads using part of their profits but often didn't. Many roads were so narrow and rough that carts regularly lost wheels. The parishes had to maintain some sections of those highways within their boundaries at their own expense too.

Listening from that roof, I finally understood why tension was rising across the county. Rebecca and her daughters would be taking action and breaking gates in Carmarthen if nothing was done to alleviate the real hardship the tolls were causing. The magistrates showed no sign of being prepared to listen to the people's grievances.

I could hitch a lift on a cart headed for Carmarthen, then jump off before the Water Street toll. Once I'd hopped a few hedges and walls I'd be in town for free. No chance for loads of grain or livestock though; everything had to be paid for at the gate to the toll keeper and written in their book.

We apprentices went out on Tuesday evening, paying threepence each to view a travelling show of curiosities in Priory Field. The main exhibit was the Royal British Whale, its bones one hundred and two feet long, a monster fish. It weighed two hundred tons when found off Plymouth. We were stunned by it.

I whistled. 'Look at that, it's enormous. How can something that size not sink?'

'Just bones left now, dead. I bet it stunk as it rotted.'

'Look at its ribs. You could make a doorway out of them. They are like planks of timber.'

John Jones, one of the oldest of us, said, 'That whale is Will Morgan's cousin, you know, boys. A big lump of a thing with a tiny brain. Tiny you-know-what, too!'

Of course, he and I had a wrestling match after this outrageous slur, much to everyone's amusement. The show had the shrivelled preserved remains of a chief and his wife from Peru. They were wearing strange headgear with long feathers in glorious shades of red, yellow and green.

John whistled. 'What birds could possibly have such lovely plumage, do you think?'

There were other, more familiar, curiosities, including a two-headed lamb entombed in a glass jar of liquid.

Scrunched into its small space, four dark eyes peered out at us, its wet curly fleece looking as soft as any newborn's.

'It's a trick, a fake. A second head is attached under the fur when they preserve it,' I said.

We had a grand time strolling through the field, chatting with the local girls, who pretended to ignore us but then would turn back and giggle. John Jones was the charmer of our group; he could have charmed that whale back to life given enough time, I quipped. We soon had some girls listening to our jokes. A couple agreed to let us walk them home as it got dark.

I admired John. He was three years older than me, ready to become a journeyman and settle down. With darkly handsome looks, he played the field and had strings of women and girls sighing after him.

There were a few he liked in particular, most especially Eliza Jones, a young widow who kept the Waterloo Terrace bakery. We were regular customers, buying bread and buns when we were nearby. John was such a joker; he always made her squeal with laughter. John could never resist flirting with a pretty face, despite her being ten years older than him. Her elderly husband had died some twelve months ago, leaving Eliza the bakehouse and shop. It was hard work but gave a decent income. The baker's first family resented her inheritance bitterly. Eliza had given old baker Jones happiness in his last years and deserved the shop more than his children, not least because takings had improved dramatically when she took over behind the counter. People liked her friendly, talkative manner and she made sure the bakery produce was tasty and sharply priced. Eliza, with her pretty dark ringlets, often seemed lonely, always wanting to delay us apprentices from getting back to work, particularly when John was with us.

I longed to be like John and had modelled myself on his clothes and style. Trouble was, what looked smart on his five feet four frame rarely suited my gangling, still-growing bones. My breeches and shirt sleeves were always too short, my sandy stubble barely visible.

The weather worsened. Days putting up rafters ready for slates had been miserable. The wind blew bitterly cold and we had hail on one particularly unpleasant day. I'd had enough of the roof and longed to be inside the workshop doing some of the smaller, more skilful jobs.

Saturday 22nd April 1843

I walked home weary and cold and, of course, not a single cart passed to beg a ride from. I was relieved to get in the dry. The kitchen was dark, no oil lamps were lit and Mother looked worn. Tom and Da were out with the animals. The change in the weather was a worry. The cold, wet with the biting east wind was bad news for our crops. Next week was May Day, a holiday we'd all looked forward to. Unless the weather improved soon, chances were that pretty bonnets and dresses for the ladies would be left at home for warmer clothing.

As she sat stripping dried rushes, ready for dipping in tallow, Mother updated me on the village gossip.

'I'm sad to tell you that Auntie Gwennie went into the workhouse on Monday.'

'How terrible. Poor Gwennie.'

Mother and I reminisced about those times nine years ago when all I thought about was pigs. Auntie had taken to Buttercup as if it was a pet. Some said they were surprised Buttercup wasn't let into the house, Auntie loved her so. The pig had a long rope lead and every day the two would venture out, either to the common or, more often, the woods, Auntie contentedly watching Buttercup root out treats on sunny days. When it was wet she would tie the rope to a tree to let the pig graze for the day and go back to her little cottage, next door but one to Bel in Bank Row.

Auntie was Ellen's help and support. If Ellen had needed advice or was upset, she'd creep into Auntie's little downstairs room, with herbs and flowers hanging from its rafters, and share a cup of nettle tea. Ellen and I loved to chat with her about the old days before the war with Napoleon, when Gwennie was a girl.

I realised that there was no question of Buttercup ever being slaughtered. It was a loss of profit for me, but I couldn't mind. The little old lady with her big spotted pig walked the roads of the village daily, stopping to chat to anyone, young or old, with the time to spare. Auntie would scratch Buttercup affectionately with her hazel stick, and in summer take her to the pond to cool off in the mud, then throw buckets of water to clean her off. The pig seemed to return her affection; it knew her voice and came when called from the wood or pond. For nearly nine years the two of them had been inseparable and could be relied on to be out and about, characters both.

I asked, 'Tell me again what happened. It can't be true what Ellen told me, that old Buttercup led her to Granny?'

'It is though. If I hadn't seen it myself, I wouldn't have believed it either. One afternoon last December, Buttercup appeared at Bank Row alone, squealing and distressed, rope trailing behind. Ellen guessed something must be up and called people to search for Auntie. She had the foresight to grab Buttercup's lead. Believe it or not, the old pig led her straight back to the wood to where Auntie Gwennie had fallen. Auntie was lying on a path, white with pain; she'd tripped over a root when her foot had caught. I arrived there a few minutes after Ellen. As soon as I saw Gwennie's leg, I could tell something was wrong. It looked shorter than the other leg and was twisted to the side. She couldn't stand or take any weight on it.

'A few of us took it in turns to care for her, popping in twice a day at least, taking meals. For many, finding the spare food was hard. After months with no improvement and her getting weaker all the time, we knew she would have to be looked after elsewhere. You know she's got no close family or savings. I doubt you remember her husband? No. Well, once he died, her only income was from looking after the children of those working in the fields. You know the rest. We women had to tell the Parish Overseer that there was no option but to take indoor relief and go to the workhouse. It was a sad day when she left Bank Row in the Overseer's cart.

'I saw her leave. Gwennie didn't cry, despite the pain, but looked utterly downcast. Two days ago, a distant cousin came from Llandeilo, emptied her little cottage of its few pieces of furniture and took the pig away. It's horrible to think of Buttercup as bacon. She was old, she'll make tough pork, but we've all grown fond of her.'

'But what will happen to Gennnie now?' I asked. 'She told Ellen and me that because she has no family, being taken into the workhouse was her worst fear – that and a pauper's grave.'

'Don't ask, Will, it makes me so angry. You know how it is in that place, folk are treated terribly. Given black bread, watery porridge and soup to eat each day, a tiny portion of meat twice a week and a salt herring on Sundays. Prisoners in Carmarthen Gaol eat better than that. I can't think she'll last long. If only they hadn't brought in the new Poor Law ten years ago. Bel and Ellen would have looked after her if the parish had paid for her food and rent. Instead, the villagers are made to pay taxes to maintain the Union Workhouse, which is mostly full of Carmarthen town folk. It's an outrage that she has to go there. We looked after our own until that cruel law was introduced.'

Father, Tom and Shem came into the kitchen, sitting to remove muddy boots on the bench by the door. Da looked worried, as usual.

'I'll have to go into Carmarthen to sell two of the older milking cows next week. With prices so low and the cost of the tollgates, I doubt that will cover this quarter's rent, let alone the tithes. There will be less milk for the dairy, so there will be less cream and cheese to sell.'

Mother said, 'Don't fret, Gu will wait for his money.'

Father was short. 'That is not the answer, Elizabeth. Delaying will make the money harder to find next time. Gu may wait because I'm family, but it will be grudgingly, and I don't wish to feel indebted to him. I want to be able to stand proud, pay my way. Many with long trips to the market can't make their rent these days. The tolls make everything harder.'

Tom chipped in, 'Farming isn't paying for anyone other than the landlords. All the profits we make go to them, not to those doing the work. They never invest anything back in the land either – spend the money on mansions or in London and Tenby, not here.'

Da replied, 'It wasn't so bad when the church tithes were collected in kind, but finding pounds, shillings and pence is another matter. I'm going to have to sell stock to pay. The barley is fetching half what it did. Last year I got six shillings a bushel, it's selling for three shillings and sixpence now. Your mother's cheese is going for just tuppence a pound instead of fourpence. I have no cash to pay the damn tithe.'

Mother sighed. She'd heard this over and over again. That their complaints were true didn't matter. The real problem was that we felt powerless, and no one in the government listened to our complaints. Mother didn't want to hear it again.

I suggested a trip over to The Plough and Harrow at Bwlch in an attempt to improve Father's spirits. The Plough was further than the Newchurch taverns, but we liked the Bowens, who brewed excellent beer, and Tom and he liked the company. Da nearly refused, then shrugged his shoulders and agreed he could do with a night out. Mother tried to press sixpence into his hand, but he was offended.

'No more Lewis charity for me, thank you.'

Mother shrank at this, blinking a tear away. I was taken aback. My parents had always billed and cooed like a pair of pigeons. This was unlike them. I knew things were tense at home but hadn't appreciated how bad they were until today. I glanced at Tom, who didn't appear to notice anything amiss. I wondered if such bickering had become commonplace.

We three set off into the dusk, a sharp wind blowing us along the road. Shem had asked to come with us but Da said kindly, 'No, not this time. Would you mind taking care of Mother and the little ones for me?'

Shem was pleased and proud at this, and said, 'Of course, I'll look after everyone,' which made us smile.

As we walked along the lanes towards the tavern, Tom and Da began to discuss the Rebecca attacks on tollgates across the county. The countryside was in turmoil.

I asked, 'Da, why are the protesters called Rebecca? Someone said it wasn't after the woman in the Bible, but because the leader first borrowed a dress from a woman called Rebecca, that it was the only one big enough to fit.'

Father discounted that. 'Nonsense, it's no trouble at all to sew on some extra cloth to the hem of an old dress, then all you do is use a belt and leave the skirt undone. A smock suffices at night for a jacket; it's dark, after all. No, they quote from the scriptures to show the right of the cause: "And they blessed Rebekah, and said unto her,

Thou art our sister, be thou the mother of thousands of millions, and let thy seed possess the gate of those which hate them.'"

I brought up the disputes and complaints I'd heard from the roof above the Water Street tollgate.

Tom nodded. 'Twelve gates around one town, it is no wonder people are angry. It's not just that, there's a tollgate nearly every three miles of road in the county.'

'But when the gates are broken, they replace them. It's pointless to take such risks for no real benefit. Where will their farms and families be if they are caught and sent to gaol?'

Tom retorted, 'You've changed, Will. You think like a town person since starting that apprenticeship. You've become stuck up and even more pompous. You are always making excuses for the authorities. You sound like Gu. Don't sit on the fence all the time, for God's sake, you're so careful about everything. Don't you and those living in town understand it is the countryside that feeds you? If farmers can't make a living there'll be no food for Carmarthen, Swansea or Merthyr Tydfil. The government has to see sense, and you – you want to remember where you come from.'

How dare he call me careful and pompous? He was the one with all the luck, with a farm to inherit and now a girl who liked him. My girl, in fact – he'd taken my best friend from me. I seethed and started to reply, but Father spoke sharply.

'That's enough. Aren't there enough arguments at home? I don't need you two fighting too. Ignore Tom,

Will. You have a right to your opinion. Some are wary of the law and taking risks. It's for the individual and their conscience to decide.'

I was stung by Father's comment. He was a man of principle; I knew what he thought my conscience should dictate.

When we got to the tavern we split up with relief, joining the groups of older and younger men, gathered as close to the fire as space would allow. Mrs Bowen carefully filled our tankards with foaming ale from her tall, blue-glazed jug. The talk there was all about the turnpikes and the Poor Law too. There was little doubt the sense of acrimony was increasing across Carmarthenshire. It was no different in Pembrokeshire and Brecknockshire. Loud and boisterous after pints of Bowen ale, we Newchurch boys and men made our way home. Tom disappeared into the Little House with Father, which was for the best as we might have come to blows. I was still furious with him. I carried on up the lane to the Big House where Gu and Ester waited up for me, cosy in their high-backed chairs beside the inglenook. Ester was spinning, the hum of her wheel familiar and calming in the firelight.

I didn't share the tavern discussions with Gu; while he disliked the tolls, he had divided loyalties. Cwm Castell was one of the biggest farms in the valley and he had benefited from the depressed prices of land. He'd bought up extra acres whenever they came up if they joined his land. Gu was one of the few who had any money to spare. He gave a variety of explanations for this surplus; his army pensions and looting on campaign were mentioned. I had heard rumours mention wrecking and smuggling but doubted them, despite the bottles of brandy under his stairs. That Gu had a tough business head and was notoriously careful with money was explanation enough. It wasn't until the next day, after I'd returned from church and eaten my dinner, that Gu leaned back to talk.

'Let's sit in the warm while I carry on my tale, Will. I've told you we set sail for Spain and arrived in early April. We ordinary troops didn't know where we were going but, after what felt an endless sea crossing, it turned out it was Cádiz. That's a pretty, old city on the coast of Spain out at the end of a long spit of land, surrounded by high fortress walls the colour of gold, set in a blue, blue sea. Above its walls float white houses and the spires of churches galore, the sunlight so bright that from far away they look like white paper cutouts. We'd been sent to help the Spanish defend the city against the French. It was the only undefeated city in Spain. Bonaparte had conquered all the rest and put his brother on the Spanish throne. The Spanish Government had just that one little city left.

'The 44th Regiment was sent to a fort called Matagorda, facing Cádiz across the estuary. It was like looking over the River Towy to Llansteffan Castle, if you can imagine it, except it gleamed white in the sun, not grey like our castles. That was a harsh awakening. The French bombed the fort day after day with huge mortar cannon. Stone by stone, that fort was knocked to pieces. The noise was terrible. Occasionally someone would get hit by a flying shard of stone or a cannonball.

'You've no idea of the power of a cannon; the ball screams past, obliterates anything in its path. I saw one man lose his head. One second he was standing a few paces away from me, a moment later a body was crumpled to the ground, blood splattered everywhere – on my boots, my white belt, my lips. His head pulverised, nowhere to be seen, nothing left of it.'

His face mirrored disgust. I knew Gu saw that bloodied body lying on the ground.

'It scares you to hell. You know one day it could be your turn. Gone in an instant.

'There was nothing we men could do to protect the fort or Cádiz, really. We were target practice for the Frenchies. They had three other forts across the estuary, we'd only the one. In the end, our army had to abandon Matagorda. The engineers tried blowing it up so the French couldn't use it when we'd gone, but after we evacuated, the officer who was to light the fuse was shot, so the fort survived. A number of us were killed there for no purpose at all, as far as we could see. The French couldn't get to Cádiz; it was so well defended and supplies could get in along its beach coast, it was all a pointless waste of time. We were sent closer to the city, which was stuffed full of Spanish, Portuguese and British troops, and it got hotter and hotter. All we could do was drill, sweat and wait for our officers to think of a plan.

'I hoped that I'd finally see something of the world; try the taverns of a city, perhaps meet some señoritas, as they call the Spanish girls. Meet them I did, but not there.' He cleared his throat. 'Spanish women, their hair and eyes dark as coal, skin like cream… you'd like them, Will.

‘It turned out for most of the regiments that the soldiers were not allowed in the city. Officers could only visit and had to return to their billets overnight. The city was full to the brim with the Spanish already; their government had retreated to Cádiz. I heard tell they thought we British wanted a second Gibraltar; they didn’t trust our army to go inside the walls in case we kept the city.

‘As rank and file, we were kept away on a marshy island called Isla de León. We were barracked in tents in a huge encampment of over ten thousand men all through that scorching summer. There was one town with a few taverns and whore houses, San Fernando, but it was full of officers and ate your pay. That was if your pay arrived. I boiled my tea rations so I knew the water was safe. It stunk, that marsh – seemed only sensible to boil the water to me. I sold some of my rum rations too; safer not to drink too much spirits when you are in the army. We polished our kit and drilled, day after day. They kept changing our officers but nothing changed for us. They were sweltering, insect-ridden days. It wasn’t pleasant but was safe enough, bar the swamp fevers that carried off nearly twenty of the lads in the regiment. We could see the Frenchies sometimes, doing sorties across the marshes, but Spanish and British ships could get in and out with supplies.

‘It was stalemate, the siege in Cádiz went on for years. It was impregnable, that city, out like a little white pearl on its causeway of land. The French mortars in Fort San Jose could just about reach Cádiz, but they didn’t achieve much. Sometimes smoke went up, a house on fire – and it must have been terrifying if you lived there, but it wasn't enough to damage a big city.

'We saw no more action. After five steaming months, in September 1810, we were marched to join Wellesley. You know him as the Duke of Wellington. We were made to dig and man defensive lines called Torres Vedras near Lisbon in Portugal. Wellington was at the start of his career then; he was yet another officer ordering us around, as far as we were concerned. "Stuck up and cold" was what most said of him at first. It took a while to get from Cádiz to Torres Vedras. It was near enough Christmas by the time we finally marched in. It had gone from being hot as hell to as cold and wet as a Welsh winter.

'The army chased Marshal Massena away the next spring after miserable, bitterly cold months on those plains. The lines were set out along a series of hills across the land as far as you could see. They were deep ditches, well dug and overlapping. We were safe in their protection; the French had no way of moving forward over them and there was no way around. Wellington had scorched the Portuguese countryside for miles, so there was no food for them to forage. The French troops starved, while our army was kept supplied by our navy from Lisbon.

'When the French retreated, our Light Company whipped the French rearguard like a mule's tail. It was a grand victory for the 44th. It was our Light Company that did the real work. They were crack shots and brave, those boys. A few months later I managed to get into the Light Company. Wasn't I pleased with myself? I should have been afraid, not pleased; the Lights were sent first into battle, harrying and skirmishing the enemy. It meant the risks of being killed were higher. If you were a good shot you were given a rifle – slower to load than the musket but much more accurate. I'd been using a gun since I was a boy like you, so I excelled, if I say so myself.

'Our regiment was still in reserve. You'd think we'd be relieved but we got increasingly nervous. There were battles being fought by other regiments around us, we kept seeing wagons of wounded go past. We were allowed to look for booty and coin from the enemy dead. We quickly understood that when we were sent in to fight, it wasn't going to be glorious; it was going to be bloody and hell. Every battle we missed we felt more afraid. A couple of the lads deserted there in Portugal, not speaking the language. We were right to be afraid, Will. Our numbers fit to fight kept falling; if the heat and fevers didn't get the boys, brawls or consumption did. As each month passed there were a few less of us 44th.'

He sighed. I could see he'd talked long enough, so I got up, saying that if he wanted to snooze after dinner, I'd understand.

It had stopped raining so I strolled up to the Pritchards, our closest neighbours, a quarter of a mile along the road towards Carmarthen, to see if anyone was about in their yard. Sure enough, two of the boys were there, kicking around a football made of a pig's bladder. They were pleased to have a third and called their youngest brother out so we could have two teams of two. After a lively game, we stopped, short of breath and panting.

Their mother brought us out cake and tea, adding in a warning tone, 'Mind now, boys, your father will be home any time. You know he won't want to see you playing and having fun on the Lord's day.'

It was true. Old Pritchard was an elder in the Heol Awst Independent Chapel on Lammas Street. He would have been most displeased to find his sons playing games of any kind on a Sunday. His chapel was said to be one of the biggest in Wales. Mr Pritchard was a trustee and had supervised a big expansion some years ago.

He was a queer man, Pritchard; he acted holy, constantly quoted the scriptures and had taken the temperance pledge, so no liquor for him or his boys. Mr Pritchard put his energy into the chapel, not the farm, where he expected his boys to do all the work. They were treated as if they were farm labourers, not sons. Despite two of them being older than Tom, he worked them ruthlessly and gave them practically no pocket money. The family dressed smartly enough for chapel on Sunday mornings and evenings, but for the rest of the week the boys wore clothes scarcely fit for the poorest Irish worker walking the roads.

Mary-Jane and her mother were dressed better in neat, if dowdy, brown gowns for chapel and village socials, but Pritchard's wife looked downtrodden and fearful. Mrs Pritchard was a small, gentle, bird-like woman who tilted her head to one side as she listened, like a thrush. She had been as pretty as her daughter once but now looked cowed and anxious. It was whispered that Pritchard beat his wife and I didn't disbelieve the tale. Years ago, when his horse wouldn't go into its traces, I'd seen him hit it viciously. He had a short fuse. He wasn't liked in the village, partly because he chose to go to the grand chapel in Carmarthen, not our local chapels, but mostly because of his arrogant and condescending attitude; we knew him for a hypocrite. His actions betrayed all he preached about being Christian.

The three's shoulders sagged as their father was mentioned. There was a silence. I took the opportunity to speak about our problem with Shem.

'Boys, I've called hoping you might be able to help me with Shem. I'm away in Carmarthen all week and I wondered if you might keep an eye on him for me, act as I do, as an older brother, guiding him and keeping him out of trouble? He's fifteen now, not a child, but because he's… simple… he doesn't understand that you can't hug and kiss people, men and women, boys and girls, like you did when you were little.'

This took them aback. They'd expected me to deny there was a problem, not ask for their help.

Robert, the eldest, spoke up. 'Yes, we have seen him doing that, with Mary-Jane and others too. You are right – it's anyone, man or woman, boy or girl. If he likes you, he hugs you. We know Shem's got a heart of gold and only wants to make people smile.'

The youngest brother spoke. 'I sometimes envy Shem being an imbecile, you know. He's always happy, he's no troubles or cares. Everyone likes him in the village and he's loved by his family.'

His voice dropped at the end. I could see both of his older brothers regarding him sadly.

Robert ruffled his hair, saying, 'You're loved here too, our boy.'

Robert suggested we ask Mary-Jane to help, as she and Shem had always been friendly. He called for her. She'd been watching us play football from the window and was there in a second. I let the brothers tell her how they wanted to help Shem. She smiled and agreed, not letting on we'd discussed it already. Mr Pritchard rode into the yard, greeting me with a raised eyebrow and nod. Everyone got up, quietly going their own ways. I caught Robert cast a glance of loathing at his father. Mary-Jane looked relieved to see me leave, despite Mr Pritchard greeting me pleasantly enough. I left, reflecting how glad I was to be a Morgan, not a Pritchard. The memory of Mary-Jane's pretty brown eyes as she smiled came to me. I pushed the recollection away. Why would she be interested in me, an apprentice with uncertain prospects and no farm to offer?

Chapter six

Saturday 30th April 1843

I arrived back in Newchurch late, to find my oldest sister waiting at the lane's turning for me. Mother asked if I could go up to Gu's straight away and meet her there. Thinking he was likely having another of his spells, I ran down the lane. When I arrived, Gu was certainly not unwell; he was furious, shouting and swearing. As I went into the kitchen he started over again, waving a letter angrily in his right hand.

'What the hell do they think, sending me this? Damned cheek. If I find out who wrote it there will be trouble.'

He went on and on. I tried to calm things down and asked what had happened. Mother and Ester exchanged looks as Gu started another outburst.

I raised my voice. 'Yes, there's a letter, but what does it say? Who is it from?'

Gu threw it at me, shouting, 'Who knows who sent it? Read it yourself. You can read, not like me, maybe you can work it out,' and brushed past me into the yard.

I scanned the note, which was printed in capitals and unsigned. It said:

THOMAS LEWIS, YOU ARE BENEFITING FROM THE SUFFERING OF OTHERS, BUYING LAND AT LOW PRICES IN THIS TIME OF TROUBLE. YOU WILL SUFFER THE CONSEQUENCES FROM BOTH GOD AND MAN. IF THIS CONTINUES, YOUR BARNS WILL BE BURNT AND YOUR PROPERTY DESTROYED.

I was shocked. I understood why Gu was enraged, it was a direct threat. Gentry around about had received similar letters, but Gu was a farmer, one of the people. The note went to the heart of a grudge in the village. It was common knowledge that Gu had bought two fields, ten acres, adjoining our land when neighbours had sold up and moved to Swansea for what they hoped would be a better life. I was aware of resentful muttering that he had the means to add to his already ample acres. This accusation showed that grumbling in a different light. I went out to stand next to him, trying to think of something helpful to say.

Gu looked grim. 'Go on home with your mother for your dinner, the little ones will be waiting. I want you and Tom up here before church tomorrow. I'm not having it.'

Wondering what he meant, I complied. There was no arguing or reasoning with him when he was this angry, it was a waste of time and effort. Gu in this mood would do what he pleased; neither Ester, Mother nor his grandsons would have the least influence on him.

Next morning, we waited in the yard of the Big House. Tom picked at his nails in anxiety. We were ready for church in our Sunday best, with no idea what Gu had planned. Sam had already harnessed the pony and trap. Gu nodded curtly to us to get in. Ester was still in the kitchen, not dressed for the service; she was staying behind, it appeared. Gu shook the reins sharply and off we went. To our bemusement we trotted past St Michael's church, going on the extra miles to the Calvinist Methodist chapel. To the best of my knowledge, Gu had never attended a Sunday chapel service in his entire life.

As we walked into the dark hall, the congregation fell silent. A village of eight hundred souls, we knew each other and our affiliations to the church and chapels well. My father was already there, looking drawn. He sat across from the pew we'd taken. Ellen looked at us questioningly. I felt a twinge of apprehension. Gu was a silent, malign presence. Preacher Abrahams felt the weight and animosity of this new congregation member; he gabbled the sermon as fast as possible. As the service ended, Gu stood up and cleared his throat. I felt Tom wince.

In Welsh, Gu said, 'I have come to this chapel of nonconformity to discuss in public an anonymous letter I received yesterday. I am aware that there are members of this congregation who have radical ideas and discuss them in taverns and such places. I do not frequent inns these days, but will make my views on the content of this letter clear to all. The letter suggests that I am benefiting from the misfortunes of others by buying land when it is put up for sale. It is true that I have bought land from people who have come to my door, offering it for sale. I use money put aside over many years, saved from my army pension and farming, fair and square.'

I detected behind me a faint scoffing and overheard someone mutter, 'If smuggling is square, that's true.'

Gu continued, 'I want all here to understand the implications if I, and others like me, don't buy land when it's offered, as the anonymous letter so forcibly suggests. It means the only people to buy land will be the local gentry, as is happening in Llandeilo with the damn Rices in Dynever. There will be no market for land and the price given will be as low as the gentry pleases. The profits will go back to England; nothing will remain here in Wales. If any of you decide to move away, you will get bottom rate for any sale, as locals will be afraid to buy. More land for the rich to tenant at barely profitable rents.'

He looked around and glared at the Rees men, and briefly toward my father. Then he marched straight-backed out of the chapel, barely a hint of his limp evident, to an excited buzz of chatter behind. Tom was rooted to the spot. I hesitated and struggled with my feelings, then put an arm over his shoulder as if in a friendly fashion but dug my nails hard into his armpit, kicking his shin.

I hissed under my breath, 'Walk out with him and me, Tom, damn you. You're the heir, it's your land too.'

Tom resisted for a second. I felt his sinews straining. As my words sank in, he started, then joined me behind

Gu and jumped up into the cart. Father stood isolated and alone, an unreadable expression on his face, as his sons left chapel with their grandfather.

Gu dropped us off at the Little House. He carried on up the lane to the Big House alone. We looked at each other.

Tom spoke first. To my relief, he thanked me. 'You were generous doing that for me, Will. You could have left me there and gone back alone with Gu. It might have meant my losing the farm if he felt I wasn't loyal to him or the land. You could have inherited.'

I looked him in the eye. 'Tom, the farm is yours, you are the eldest. Gu won't divide the land.' I forced myself to continue, 'I am happy as a carpenter. I will make money without all the long hours of cold, hard work morning to night with the animals and crops. I like the town. I've never expected the farm. As Father shows, there is little enough money or future as a tenant, if I wanted to try. Gu has said he'll help me set up a workshop with his savings, that's enough. I plan to make a success of it, believe you me.'

Tom looked pleased, so I took another breath and said, 'While we are talking honestly I must speak about Ellen.' He stiffened as I said, 'It is true that Ellen has been my best friend since we were small and I do love her. I was nettled at first when you were clearly interested in her. I've come to realise it's her friendship I value. What I've found hard these last few weeks is that when she comes into the house, all she really wants is to see you, and all she wants to talk about is you. I have been jealous of the loss of her attention.'

Tom interrupted. 'Really? You think she wants to see me? That she likes me?'

I grunted and replied, 'You daft fool, she's never been lost for words, pink and distracted for me! She's a different person when you are around. I like Ellen because she's straight, thoughtful and kind. Just now she's not so thoughtful; like you, she's constantly mooning around. I'd like the real Ellen back, the one I love like a sister.'

Tom was grinning from ear to ear now. 'You think she likes me!' he repeated in wonder.

I rolled my eyes heavenward. 'I know she likes you. The question is what you do about it.'

We turned as Mother called us for dinner.

As we sat, Father said, 'It was a fine speech your Grandfather made. Some of the neighbours may think again about their actions. Truth is, though, with times so hard, what Gu says is a fair price for land is a low price. He is profiting from the misfortunes of others. I accept his point that the alternative – letting the damned English gentry buy up all of Carmarthenshire – is worse, but as they say, two wrongs don't make a right.' He shook his head sadly. 'There has been no profit for the small farmer these last few years. Most don't have the money your grandfather put by when times were better to take the advantages he takes.'

My sister piped up. 'How did he put his money away, Father? Is it easy?'

'That's what the whole village wants to know. I don't know for sure myself and his pension is part of it, but it's one shilling a week, it wouldn't buy any acres. We have made our guesses.'

Mother smiled and turned away.

That night I spoke to the old man again, telling him I was proud of his speech and that Father had said he thought it was admirable and might make people change their minds.

'No man can send me letters like that and not be challenged.'

I agreed with him, but a voice whispered in my head that it was all very well if you had money put by, but however hard you worked, if you were a tenant like my father the chances of owning or buying land were slim.

'Do you want a walk and to tell me more about the wars tonight?'

'No, we've had enough excitement for one day. Let's leave it this week.'

As I drifted off to sleep that night, I thought again of Tom's criticisms of me last week. What hurt the most was that he'd identified those things I recognised and hated most about myself. Did I want to change and be bolder like him and Gu, or should I accept that, like Mother, I was cautious by inclination, always weighing up my options? I was relieved not to have let my resentment spill over into the chapel today. It would have been so easy to have left Tom in the chapel with Father. If I'd not acted, I might have inherited Cwm Castell, but it would have torn my family apart. Tom would never have forgiven me; Ellen might not have either. Would it have been worth it, though? I'd acted on the spur of the moment that morning, but would I have done the same if I'd thought it through?

Monday 1st May 1843

We were lifting a heavy oak roof joist when it happened: a rope slipped, the pully twisted, and it fell. I heard the warning shout and felt a thud as it hit the beams below – and John Jones, who was stood beneath. I could hardly bear to look; his forearm was smashed to a pulp. We rushed down ladders and across to him.

David examined the beam. 'Right, let's get it off him fast. Carefully, mind. Will, lift this end with me. You, lad, put that toolbox under the end once we raise it.'

I strained with all my might, feeling my muscles pressing into my jerkin as David and I lifted the timber a foot off the floor. We slipped John's unconscious body out. The skin was broken, blood and white shining bone shards clearly visible. I gasped at the sight of it. One of the younger apprentices started to retch. Master David took one look and sent for the doctor. John was out cold. He hadn't cried out as the joist hit, it had all happened so fast. Doctor Lawrence looked solemn after examining John.

'The beam has only hit his arm, as far as I can see. He is unconscious from pain and shock. I'm afraid the bone is so badly crushed that the wound can never heal.' He hesitated, then continued, 'There is no choice – I will have to amputate. The skin has been broken; the risk is that it will become infected.'

John came around and cried out in pain. He lay panting and moaning, white, his dark eyes petrified. Briefly, they met mine. I tried to look reassuring but guessed that he saw reflected in them how badly injured he was.

Doctor Lawrence bent over him. 'Young man, could you try to squeeze my hand?'

John's expression glazed with terror. His hand didn't move, not a muscle. He tried to raise himself but failed.

'I can't feel a hand to grip,' he croaked.

'It's there. Try your best, wiggle your fingers,' replied the doctor.

There was nothing, no movement, his right hand had no strength. John couldn't move his fingers, grip or turn his wrist. He was taken away and lost half his right arm that night. It ended his apprenticeship at a stroke; a carpenter needs two hands and two strong arms.

A moment's slip had caused the loss of a man's future. Such accidents were not uncommon for builders. We felt sick at heart for him, and afraid for ourselves. Master David was angry and upset, questioning himself again and again as to how that beam could have fallen. I'd seen it tilt as we hoisted it into place and the heavy unbalanced weight took itself down in a second, but that was no consolation. We waited anxiously to hear how John was. The immediate days after the amputation were the riskiest – would the arm mend? We wouldn't know until next week. David told us of cases he'd known where men had to have higher and higher amputations as fester set in.

Next day, there was another commotion from further up Lammas Street. Rees Tucker, the watchmaker and jeweller, a few doors up from the workshop, was dead. He had taken his own life. He had hung himself using his black silk neckerchief in his coal house. His sister had found him there. Rees was known as a heavy drinker and melancholic. He had often threatened to kill himself, and he'd tried twice before. It was strange, really; his shop was thriving, he rented out several houses in Carmarthen – it couldn't be money worries. He was a quiet and pleasant man, much liked by his neighbours when sober. Master David said that when Rees was in his cups once, he'd told him the drink drove him mad with melancholy. Beer and wine were cheap and there were so many taverns in Carmarthen; they were where a lot of business was done on market days. Rees was not alone with his drinking problems, but it was such a waste.

To my surprise, early on Wednesday morning Ellen appeared at the workshop.

'I want to go and visit Gwennie in the workhouse, but I'm scared to go alone. There are terrible stories. What if they lock me in there? Would you come with me, Will? Wait outside if they let me see her? Tom wanted to come but the weather is dry; he has to finish haymaking, your father can't spare him. Could you ask Master David if there is any way of making them let me in? I've heard that maybe you can bribe the warders?'

'Of course. I'm glad you asked. I'd have liked to see her myself, but they don't let men into the women's wing.'

Master David had agreed I could go to the workhouse at midday with Ellen and work the time back in the evening. He'd shaken his head, saying no one willingly went there. I put small coins in my pocket, then Ellen and I climbed the hill to the workhouse in Penlan. We reached the gate and who should be coming out but Frances Evans, huge with child. We knew Frances well. She'd grown up a few doors from Ellen on Bank Row and worked as a farm servant in Cilgwyn Ucha. A year younger than Tom and a little older than me, she was as friendly and chatty a girl as anyone could imagine, pert, well able to stand up for herself. "Too friendly", was what they said in the village when she became pregnant. I'd heard she'd had to go into the workhouse once she was too big to work.

She stopped, hugged Ellen, and said, 'I know why you're here. I've tried my best for Auntie but she was terribly weak when she arrived. Told me she was ashamed to have ended up here. Said to leave her in peace. I couldn't get her to eat or drink.' Frances' expression changed to concern. 'She even told me to take her share, said it would do my unborn baby more good than it would her. They've taken her into the infirmary.'

Ellen blinked and twisted her cloth pocket. 'What do you think my chances of seeing her are?'

Frances said, 'I'll go to see if the Mistress will consider letting you in to see her, Ellen. Do you have a shilling in change, Will Morgan? I'll need to cross a few hands with coin.'

We knew how it worked. I gave her a silver sixpence and some pennies. A few minutes later Frances returned, shaking her head. Mistress Evans had said no one was allowed in, except to be admitted for relief. The parson had been called to poor Gwennie; she was not expected to last the night. Frances promised to try to make her comfortable if she could. Laughing, she told us they'd have no choice but to take her to the infirmary if she claimed her birthing pains had started. Frances's belly was so large it looked as if the baby might come at any moment. She was a feisty girl, and it was as much of a chance as we had, so I told her to keep the shilling intended for bribing Master Evans and his warders.

She winked. 'I'll do what I can with it.'

There was nothing more to be done. Dejected, we left. I tried to say the same might have happened if Gwennie had stayed on the Row.

Angry, Ellen replied, 'Any human has a right to a better and kinder place to die than that horrible workhouse. I hate that you have to be deserving poor to get into such a place, too. What if the Parish Overseer had decided she was undeserving? She'd have starved. It is wrong, Will, plain wrong. Don't make excuses.'

There was nothing I could say. It was a terrible end for Gwennie: no friends and little food or comfort.

Back at the workshop, I was told John Jones's arm had required the surgeon's attention again. It had been amputated higher, above the elbow. I cringed for the pain of a second sawing and cutting. If the infection spread any further up the arm it would be a mortal; John would not be long for the world. All that trouble for a moment's slip and the misbalance of a roof beam. Sleep came slowly that night.

CHAPTER SEVEN

Next day it rained hard, fat drops falling all day long. I sighed. If it didn't stop, Father's hay – mown yesterday – would moulder. If it failed now there might not be enough to feed the cows through the winter. Maybe Father should have listened to Tom and planted Swedish turnips; they thrived in damp weather, and it was often damp in west Wales.

Frances sent word that Gwennie had died in the early hours. She would be buried on Saturday in the paupers' grave near the workhouse, unless anyone claimed the body – thrown in along with any others who had died that week. Gloomily, I anticipated that without close family, there was no one to take her back to Newchurch and give her what she and all villagers hoped for: a respectable funeral.

With a heavy heart, I slipped through the wet streets to the market to find someone who could pass on the news to Ellen. I found several Newchurch wives selling eggs, butter and chickens. They sighed and clucked like their livestock at the news. Friday and then Saturday morning dragged. Around eleven, I noticed Tom waving to me from outside the yard. He had Gu's cart with a roughly made coffin on the back. The lads and I tutted at the look of it. I could have knocked together something better in half an hour and told him so.

Tom shook his head at me. 'That's as may be, Will, but you were not at home. We did our best, don't criticise.'

He asked David if I could be freed to go up and help him collect the body. The Calvinist chapel members wanted to take Gwennie's body home, felt it was right in Christian charity to bring her back to Newchurch. The funeral announcer, wearing a black beribboned hat, had walked the district with his cloth bag, asking neighbours to spare a penny towards the costs. The men of the congregation were digging a grave, the funeral was set for early evening. Master David agreed to let me off; it was only an hour until we'd be finished. I jumped up beside Tom. This time I had to enter the workhouse gates.

Inside we were confronted with the wide yard, bleak and forbidding, overlooked by tall buildings with barred windows, with a few thin faces staring out. Gwennie's little body was left in the open yard, in a row with four others, each wrapped in a ragged, dirty cloth. We picked her up. She weighed more than I expected. A horrible image of carrying a drowned sheep last winter came back to me. Gwennie weighed much the same as that sheep. We placed her gently into the rough coffin and drove slowly back to Newchurch, up the hill to the chapel.

When we arrived, there were six men, including my father, finishing up the grave. The entire village came out in procession up the hill for the service, whatever chapel they normally attended. It was sombre but uplifting to feel united in our grief for Auntie Gwennie. Most families brought a plate of food or a cake, which were set out on tables to eat after the coffin had been laid to rest. The Minister said a few words, Gwennie's favourite hymns were sung and the coffin was placed in its fresh grave.

Yet again, Sunday was wet and miserable. My mother had to push my father out of the house, he was so low and worrying about his hay being cut but not dried, raked and stacked. She insisted that he went out to chapel; there was nothing to be done at home. I decided to go with him to chapel, after all the congregation's kindness to Auntie.

It was hard looking at the new grave. Rivulets of muddy water ran down the mound of fresh earth as I hurried out of the rain. My throat felt sore with a hard lump of grief. At least Gwennie wasn't lying in a pauper's grave miles from her home, thanks to her neighbours. People complained about the rain, the taxes and the tollgates. Their mood changed from resentment to real and righteous anger. It was as if Auntie Gwennie's death had ignited a fuse. The Poor Law made those with nothing put aside fearful for their future, and that was the majority of the congregation.

Almost everyone who went to chapel, including Father, knew that if they couldn't work for any reason, or when they grew too old to work, their fate and that of their children would be much the same as Auntie Gwennie. They would be sent from the parish, stripped of clothes and dignity, put into louse-ridden rags; half-starved, men would be made to work crushing stone or bones, women set to washing the townsfolk's clothes or sewing. The meagre portions in the workhouse were notorious. If you weren't starved before you got there, you would be in a week, it was said. There were darker rumours of women and girls being made to provide "physical favours" to the Master or warders, or else be beaten and deprived of food. It was whispered that the same was asked of men and boys.

That the parishes were taxed to fund the workhouse and the Poor Law made it worse, although Gu had told me that the complaints were nearly as loud when the parish had to pay to keep people at home, before that law was introduced. He had said that in years gone by, he'd been criticised loudly in church by neighbours for giving his farm workers decent cottages. As they lived within the parish boundaries, it had to pay relief if they couldn't work. In some places, workers travelled miles for work each day because farmers wouldn't house them; they lived in squalid hamlets with no church or roads. Folk on parish relief were ostracised and made to feel ashamed.

Old preacher Abrahams gave a sermon on forgiveness, but the mood in the chapel was more an eye for an eye. Talk afterwards was all about how we could take no more, how the life was being squeezed out of rural Carmarthenshire. There was muttering that the petitions for the People's Charter should have been heeded by the Government. Millions had signed that charter, including my brother and father, although some with landlords from the gentry or with livelihood connected to them were too afraid to sign.

Poor John Frost had been transported after the Newport uprising, more were arrested in England last year when they refused to work and went on strike. I was not surprised at the strength of feeling. Tom had been saying the same for years. A pragmatist, I didn't hold much hope for anything coming of the charter. The deck was stacked against those without money in favour of the wealthy, to my view.

As we walked home the weather changed, the sun came out and the breeze stiffened. My father whooped and thanked the Lord. He rushed, hoping to at least turn the hay, to start it drying. He told Mother to give us anything she had ready, that we'd eat properly later. I was happy to help rake the gently steaming meadow. The early summer sunshine was warm on my back and the mellow scent of the hay, earthy and sour, made me glad to be with my family. An early turn in the afternoon to shake off the rain, with another later, might undo a lot of the last few days' damage. Maybe we would get enough hay in to see the cattle through the winter yet.

Days were long at the end of May. I was aching but content by the time I finally reached the Big House late that evening. Ester had gone to bed but Gu was waiting in the kitchen with a cold feast of pie, bread, pickles, cheese and *bara brith,* currant bread, spread with rich salty butter. As I finished, he produced his brandy bottle, poured himself a large tot and unexpectedly gave me a smaller one. Gingerly I sniffed, then tasted it. The brandy smelt wonderful, smooth and rich, unlike the harsh spirits served in the taverns in Carmarthen, where I'd tried a gin and regretted the pennies.

Gu began, 'I joined in the summer of 1808, as I've told you already. For three years things were safe enough if you were healthy and sensible. I hadn't seen London or Paris, but had marched through Portsmouth and visited the Isle of Wight and then the Channel Islands. We'd visited Lisbon and Cádiz by December 1811. As a trooper, I hadn't spent time in the cities, but I'd seen their villages and towns.

'We soldiers thought the Portuguese were backward and superstitious. Their towns crawled with Catholic priests and nuns, they were everywhere, scurrying around like black beetles. The churches were wonderful, marble interiors full of silver and gold, paintings of saints and statues galore. You may think St Peter's in Carmarthen and the Lammas Street chapel are grand buildings, but let me tell you, they are nothing compared to those churches and cathedrals. Enormous buildings, full of life-sized carved statues gilded with real gold. On festival days – and they were always holding festivals, not just at Easter and Christmas – they'd parade their statues through the streets, along with body parts of dead saints in caskets. Hideous things, mind you – tortured saints or Jesus dying on the cross in agony. Painful to look at. I only liked the Virgin Mary effigies; even then, she was usually shown crying.

'The priests and nuns ran hospitals for the old and the sick but lived in comfort and luxury like the wealthy. It made me uncomfortable. I don't agree with much the church says, but I do agree it's wrong to worship idols, primitive.

'All that money and gold in their churches didn't help ordinary people. They lived in tiny, thick-walled white cottages with dirt for floors and small, shuttered windows to keep the heat out in summer, but which made them dark. Most were more like our barns or pigsties. They lived alongside their animals; chickens and goats went in and out of houses, which were dirty and stank, like their streets.

'Our first action was at the end of March in 1811, after we'd crossed the border out of Portugal into Spain. Wellington needed to secure that Portuguese-Spanish border, you see. We were in a place called Sabugal, by a river. Our patrols told us they could see a troop of French soldiers cooking up their supper on the further bank. We had one of the bravest Lieutenants – Pearce, his name was. He decided we'd give them a scare. As we riflemen loaded up, others took up their muskets, – it takes longer to load a rifle than a musket – and off we set across the bridge.

'The French weren't expecting us so they panicked, had no choice but run for it. A few shots were fired but not one of our boys was harmed. We took a couple of Frenchies prisoner. Best of all, they'd cooked our supper for us. The food was stinking of garlic as usual, but by that time I'd started enjoying its taste. There was plenty of rabbit and sausage in their stew – delicious, it was. They'd left a few skins of wine behind to drink down with it. It was a grand evening. The 44th had drawn its first blood. We thought maybe fighting for King and country wasn't going to be too bad.

'We were completely wrong, of course. Things rapidly turned for the worse. Early May, we were lined up outside a village called something like Fuentes Orono. "Oh No", we men called it. We had our own names for the towns, tried to make sense of those foreign words. Well, "Oh No" was a little town with twisted streets of white houses set on a steep hillside. We were blockading a French garrison in the nearby city of Almeida. The French had to relieve Almeida so their soldiers didn't starve. Our own supply lines weren't working too well either; we'd had no bread for two days and were as hungry as hell. I'd kept a few dry biscuits hidden at the bottom of my pack but scarcely dared eat in case someone saw and tried to steal them. The 44th had its first look at a proper French army then – rank on rank, vast, it covered the plain. I went pale at the sight of it spread out and wondered how we could possibly beat that many men.'

He cleared his throat and began slowly. 'At the start, we British held "Oh No" with our cavalry and light companies but the French attacked and nearly took it from us, their cavalry and brigades filling the town. My light company were part of the first advance; without the full weight of the division behind us, we couldn't do much. After firing in fast order, we withdrew back to our regiment on the left of the line, on a hillside, in reserve. We watched the battle from there. It was a terrible sight and went on for so long. The Highlanders in their tall bonnets fought like heroes that day. That fighting started at three in the afternoon, it wasn't over until it was dark and past midnight. First, our lads in the town had the upper hand and pushed the French down through the streets and out of "Oh No". Our soldiers believed they'd won, got over excited and gave chase to them. Off they ran way into the countryside.

‘The army lost all order. Some started looting as they went. We reserves on the hillside watched, horrified, as the French cavalry regrouped and started chasing after them. Our boys had to run for their lives back to the village. Quite a few didn’t make it. Imagine being charged down by a cart horse with a rider who has a long sword to slice at you like a sausage. It was horrible, arms were hacked off, guts opened, and huge bloody wounds opened in any man the cavalry caught. Man after man fell as we watched from our hillside.’

Gu shivered as if torn by the memory. It was bad enough hearing it described, but Gu still saw that scene in his mind.

He continued, ‘The battle stopped overnight; no one could see to fight in the dark. Fires lit up in the town, so at least the lads there had warmth. We 44th had none. After nearly three days without rations, with the smell of roasting meat wafting towards us, some were nearly tempted to creep over to join them. I say “nearly” because we knew the battle wasn’t finished; we’d seen how brutal combat could be. A truce was agreed by the officers. It gave the armies time to collect their dead and wounded.

‘It was a welcome respite. The French started playing tunes, some danced, others kicked a ball around. Our lads didn’t mess around; they cooked up any food they could find and rested. The following morning, at first light, the fighting started again with the big French grenadiers attacking the town. At first the French looked to be winning; they were forcing our brave boys back and out of the town yet again. We in reserve were told to make ready as the British were beaten down. It was as if we'd never started except for piles of bodies, two and three deep.

'Then the French made their mistake; they were ordered into columns, a plain stupid plan in narrow lanes and streets. It gave our muskets a target to aim at. The French went down like my Tommy's lead soldiers. The British fought in lines two deep, you see. We could keep up a much faster rate of fire, because first, one man fired then knelt and reloaded, while the second-in-line stood up and fired; by then, the first man had reloaded and could fire again. In the French columns, only the men at the front could fire safely; anyone behind risked hitting their own men if they tried. The French were much slower to reload muskets, too. Their columns did far less damage at close range than our lines. That was the end of the French. Our boys pushed back into the village and the 44th wasn't needed after all. The losses were terrible for both sides. Over a thousand of us were wounded, hundreds killed. The French losses looked worse.

'After it was over, we were allowed into the town. We newer recruits were appalled by what we found. Piles of the dead, mounds everywhere, flies already circling them in the heat. A dog was pulling at the insides of one; a little terrier, white and black it was, a man's guts in its teeth. Men were calling for water and crying for their mothers. I see a neatly severed redcoat arm lying in the middle of the dusty road whenever I think of that day.' Gu cleared his throat again and continued, 'The bandsmen carried away any wounded to the church and did their best for them, but their cries were pitiful. After serving three years in the army, it was the first time I'd seen mass death at first hand and I was terrified. I was glad to leave that place and march on, I can tell you'

'Taught me two lessons that saved my life later, that experience, Will. For a start, I learned not to rely on supplies. It stood to reason that supply wagons would be captured or get lost. Quartermasters couldn't always manage to find provisions for so many if things got sticky. I paid one of the Irish wives to make me dry oatcakes and put plenty at the bottom of my pack; light, you see. I bought an old wineskin and put in a couple of the Spanish dried sausages, corked the skin like it was wine and hid that out of reach too. I'll tell you about the times when that sausage saved me, months later. The second lesson was not to run like a rabbit from cavalry chasing you down. Seeing those boys cleaved from behind, I decided I'd lie down, play dead and take my chances, surrender rather than try to run.

'God, it was hot on that fast march away from 'Oh No'. All day, kites and vultures would circle. Before the Peninsular I loved seeing the kites fly over Garn Fawr. Not anymore. The heat was terrible, so bad that men were dying of thirst, our blood boiled dry. Lads would lie by the road or faint away. We'd be told to leave them where they fell. They were nasty, evil things, those kites, darker than our foxy red Welsh ones, no white flashes. They'd wait until we soldiers marched on, then swoop down in a flock. They'd start by pecking at a fallen man's eyes, just like they do with stillborn lambs. The men were still living, but too weak to bat them away. You'd see a dozen or more pulling at a corpse, flesh coming away in shreds.

‘We needed heavy woollen greatcoats when it was cold and wet in the winter, but putting them in our knapsacks meant carrying them. We sweltered, it was like walking through a furnace. I was as dry as a bone, my canteen empty often as not, lips blistered and sore. I learned to suck a smooth white pebble, tried to dream it was a peppermint, to keep my mouth from feeling parched. We were kept marching on and on in the damned heat until noon each day.

‘The 44th hadn't fought so we were sent on at pace to a place called Barba del Puerco, one of four bridges that crossed a river. “Porko” we called it – turned out we were right, it did mean pig – it was called Pig's Beard. By the bridge there was clean, fresh water; at last, we could rest, drink and eat. We had a laugh one night when a man with a lantern came across the bridge.

‘Who the hell's that un-soldier like idiot?’ asked Colonel Egerton.

‘It was Paymaster Williams on his old horse. He'd come looking for the Colonel's signature on his books; he'd issued pay months before without getting the pay books signed. Lieutenant Pearce decided to play a trick on him and set a rifle fuse to go off on his horse's tail. It fired and sparked, the horse kicked, the books were dropped and William's ink spilt everywhere. The Colonel joined in and played up that he wouldn't sign, although I heard later Williams got into trouble for not having kept his books properly. We laughed. It was a relief to be playing silly tricks while we were waiting to fight.

‘A few days later, we were resting on the riverside when new orders arrived. The thousand French troops of

Almeida fortress had managed to creep away at around midnight. Wellington was furious. They'd given him the slip, no one knew how or why, but the rumour was that mad old General Erskine had been drinking and not bothered to read his order to blockade the bridge. Campbell's division gave chase but failed. Turned out we boys in the 44th Regiment were in the right place; the retreating French were making for our bridge. Led by Captain Jessop, we set out in the dark and managed to do what the other divisions couldn't. We caught the French rear at the bridge, made three hundred or so surrender. It made a mockery of the battle at 'Oh No' those days before. All those men died to keep the siege in place, only to have the garrison slip away to join the French army in the night. What a waste; no wonder Wellington was angry.

'We got to know the Duke better at Fuentes Guinaldo – "Guinea", we knew it as. We were there guarding Wellington's headquarters; we were proud to do it. We respected old Nosey, as we called him, by then. I won't say we exactly loved him, he was just another general, but at least he knew his job. He was aloof, didn't smile or joke with us like some of the senior officers, or know us by name, but he was known to be fair, whatever your rank.'

'When the French attacked "Guinea" we were sent to reinforce the Portuguese artillery. Just as well; they were being cut down at their guns. The Duke himself directed us in the battle. As the French cavalry approached the British position, it was clear they were after our cannon, so British guns opened fire against the French columns. The Duke hardly had time to move to the rear before we were charged by a pounding body of their cavalry, which for a moment succeeded in capturing our guns.

'It is terrifying, being attacked by horses, Will. Our cavalry and theirs the same, it's a foot soldier's nightmare. Think of standing next to a cannon, trying to light a fuse, hands shaking in terror. Exposed, standing waiting, not allowed to move from the line, a horse charging straight at you. If that's not enough, the man riding that horse has a wickedly sharp sword, and it's aiming for your head or gut.

'When you're in square with the rest of the company, facing the charge with bayonets and musket, you are probably safe – otherwise, if the cavalry chases after you, you are as good as dead. I was cut down there. I survived because the sabre caught in my backpack and I played dead. The cavalry man rode on without checking. It was over in a trice, a short engagement between the two armies; although, lying on the ground terrified of being trampled, the moments seemed long enough to me.

'When I have my nightmares, that is one of the worst – I live it again. I'm running, running for my life, hooves pounding closer and closer and closer, then I'm struck. Other times I see that arm in its red sleeve lying in the dust on the road again; the horror I felt floods back into my dreams and overwhelms me. I'm running, cowering from the cannon shot and the swords. I want to vomit.'

'The 44th were too clever for the French at "Guinea". Working with the other regiments, we fired our muskets, then followed up with a charge of bayonets. The guns were retaken and the French repulsed. In the thick of the battle you've no idea what's happening; you do what your sergeant tells you. They push you and pull you into place and keep watch. More men of my regiment were injured but the heat killed more than the French. Our numbers kept falling, we were down to less than four hundred men by then, as much from disease as battle. I benefited, was promoted to corporal, not because I was braver than anyone else but because I didn't drink excessively. I was older, level-headed under pressure and used my head.'

He sighed deeply, lost in his past. He'd started to shake and sweat as he told me the tale. Gu had stirred up awful memories. I worried that we were doing more harm than benefit, talking about those times.

'Let's stop, Gu. It sounds terrible, but I liked your story about stealing the French supper and I'm glad to know how you got your promotion.'

Gu picked up, nodding, saying, 'You're right. I'm exhausted with the telling.'

Saturday 13th May 1843

I walked home kicking a cobble with venom that next Saturday afternoon, angry with the world. News had come from the doctor; the wound on John's amputation was inflamed, it looked as if it was infected. We apprentices had started the morning low and miserable. John had been such a joker, he always made us laugh with his antics. To think of him sweating in pain with his right arm half gone made us tremble. Returning to Water Street had been painful. I looked at the spot where John's arm had been crushed and saw a brown stain on the floorboards. We still had to finish that roof, get the battens on ready for the slates.

At the Little House, I learned that Tom had taken my words and for the past week had been walking up to Ellen's most evenings, to my parents' amusement. As I'd guessed, his attention had been welcomed by Ellen. It sounded as if the future was pretty much decided between them. That evening, Tom decided to come up to the Big House with me to discuss marriage with Gu. He wanted to ask whether he and Ellen might be able to live in there with him; after all, there was plenty of room. We walked down the lane and into the kitchen. Gu was, as usual, staring at the fire as Ester bustled around cooking Saturday supper for the farm boys. After some clearing of his throat and shuffling, Tom looked at me for support, then managed to gabble out his request.

'I am minded to ask Ellen Price to marry me. If she says yes, I wondered… that is… could I – I mean we – move into the Big House with you?'

Gu remained silent, his expression grim. Ester looked nervous.

Gu finally replied, 'I want to speak with your Father about this matter. Would you be so good as to ask him to come up to the house? You two had best join the discussion, so you understand why this marriage is impossible.'

Tom and I were bewildered. We'd picked up that Gu was not particularly pleased with the match. I'd assumed that was because Ellen was poor and would bring no land or dowry. Farmers liked to marry their children to other farmers' children, not to outsiders. But until today, we had believed he and Ester were fond of Ellen and would accept Tom's choice.

I ran down the lane to fetch Father. Tom went outside to wait, looking sick. Father looked perplexed, but I caught Mother nodding as if she'd expected it. Da grumbled; he'd just sat down, bone weary after a long day – the weather was finally dry and he'd cut the top field. However, he'd little choice but to join us, knowing how upset Tom would be if Gu refused to consent to the match.

In we trooped. Gu sat at the top of the long kitchen table looking determined. He motioned us to sit and looked directly at my father.

'I have seen young Tom and Ellen forming an attachment and have worried about it these past weeks. Why have you done nothing to discourage them, John?'

My father looked surprised and asked, 'Why should I have discouraged them? It is for Tom to decide who he wants to marry.'

Gu looked indignant at this reply. 'You know all too well why, John Morgan. If you don't speak up and tell the boy it's not possible, I will have to.'

My father looked confused. 'But why is it impossible?'

'Because of your past relations with Bel Price; you fathered a child on her. Don't tell me you didn't,' Gu spat out.

'I did what? Have you lost your mind, old man? What a thing to say in front of my sons. I've no more fathered a child with Isabella Price than King George did,' Father snapped back.

'Bel came to see me after I returned from the war. Said that if I didn't pay her a crown each month, Elizabeth, you and I would regret it. For a crown a month, she'd keep quiet.'

'Why would that mean I'd given her a child? I will add that yes, the whole village knew you gave money to Bel. There were unkind rumours as to why that might be and what exactly your relationship with Isabella Price was.'

My grandfather sat back, flummoxed. 'What rumours about me and that Bel?'

He sounded so outraged at the idea, I pinched myself so as not to laugh. I dared not look at Tom.

Ester spoke up. 'It's true, Thomas, there were rumours. Susan heard them and took them to heart. She told me that when you returned from the war, there was a wall of unhappiness built between you two. Said you were angry with the world and that if things had been bad between you before you left, they were terrible when you came home. That you barely spoke to her. Then Susan heard you were giving money to Bel Price.' Looking embarrassed, Ester continued, 'Susan assumed that because there was no lovemaking, you had decided to seek it elsewhere, and that was why you gave Bel the money.'

Gu looked first dumbfounded, then sorrowful. 'I had no idea Susan thought that, or anyone knew I was giving Bel money. I thought I was protecting Elizabeth from hearing that John had had a fling with Bel, and she'd had a baby as a result. It would have broken Elizabeth's heart. You were not such a bad lad, I know how it can be with young men… so I paid up. How could I have been so stupid? I only gave her half a crown a month, by the way. A crown indeed.'

We laughed. Gu was careful with his money.

My father sighed. 'Well, I suppose although you thought badly of me, it was all done with kind intentions, Thomas.'

Something jangled at the edge of my consciousness, something I couldn't quite grasp.

Tom burst in. 'So Gu, if this is all a misunderstanding, can I ask again? If I marry Ellen can we live here? Also if I work on the farm with you, would you… would you pay me a wage?'

He looked guiltily at Da as he asked. He knew that father could not afford to hire a replacement and the burden at home would be heavier. This day had to come; Tom could not stay at home working for board and pocket money forever.

Gu smiled. 'Let Ester and I think on it overnight, Tom. It will be a big change for us. I admit I'd like to see you start to manage some of the farm tasks now, to make sure you do it properly. I can keep an eye on things to be sure you are doing things the way I like them done.'

Every one of us sighed at that, "The way I like them done". It was not going to be easy. Gu and Tom had argued over farming methods since Tom was old enough to have an opinion.

Father and Tom left for home as Ester, Gu and I got ready for bed.

Gu grumbled, 'I can't believe I paid that woman for so long to protect John for no need,' as he went up to his bedroom.

Ester looked at me thoughtfully. 'My poor sister, she was so unhappy – her husband lost to her, as she thought, to another woman. She assumed Thomas was paying Bel for physical comfort, went to her grave believing that. It may have made her melancholy worse. Secrets, they do no favours to anyone.'

All that night I was searching in my dreams, then lying awake, turning and tossing, thoughts swirling. Before dawn it came to me. I didn't have an answer, but I had more questions and thought my mother might be able to answer them.

Chapter Eight

Sunday 14th May 1843

In the morning we prepared for church, Gu concluding, as always, that he wouldn't attend, but he was unusually mellow and cheerful. Ester put on her Sunday best dress with fine lace at the collar and cuffs. We took the pony and trap at Gu's suggestion; it looked as if it might rain yet again. We called by the Little House. Mother and the two younger children hopped in and off we went in fine style. Tom and Father walked on up to chapel with Shem.

As we walked up the churchyard path, I asked Mother, 'Did Father tell you about what Gu said yesterday?'

'Yes. Why?'

'He said that Bel expected money from him and everyone in the village knew. You must have known and you didn't stop him.'

'No.'

'Well, why not? I don't believe you thought it was anything to do with Father. There must have been something else. When I was first friends with Ellen, I heard whispers about bad blood between the Lewises and the Prices. People were surprised we were allowed to play together.'

Mother sighed and, with a hint of weariness and sarcasm, said, 'Ever the sharp one, William Morgan, eh? All right. After church, you and I will walk back, and let the rest go in the trap.'

I was pleased. I liked having Mother to myself, goodness knows she had little enough time with the farm and us all. I had been wondering all night long whether her brother Tommy had fathered a child.

The service went on and on, ending after the collection plate had been passed around. Little was collected; those with farms bitterly resented the tithe they had to pay to the church, those without certainly had no money to spare for curate and vicar. I saw three people drop in buttons before passing it on. Ester reached over Mother so she didn't have to give and dropped in a sixpence for them both. I doubted that coin would reach the back of the church; times had got so hard, many would have felt their need was greater than the curate's.

We filed out of ugly, squat St Michael's, rebuilt soon after I was born. At least it was comfortable; there was a cast iron wood stove for warmth and the pews were wider and lower backed than the chapel's pews, so you could sit with ease. Cloth kneelers embroidered by the parish ladies saved your aching knees too. The older villagers still complained at the loss of the ancient, whitewashed church that stood before, nestled in its circular graveyard.

The weather had cleared as I took my mother's arm. Mother asked Ester if she'd take care of the youngsters for an hour so we could walk home on the old road past Garn Fawr.

Ester agreed. 'Yes, you could do with a treat. ,You don't see so much of Will now he stays with us and is in Carmarthen all week.'

Mother hummed the last hymn as I chatted about Carmarthen. She liked to know what the ladies there were wearing and I tried my best to sound interested.

'It seems to me that big sleeves are out; I've noticed every girl seems to have a pretty shawl as well?'

'Yes, fashions are simpler than when I was younger. I like them, they are more practical. I fancy making myself a bonnet of linen and lace, like the one Mrs Davies, Trawsmawr, wore at Christmas. Father has a stash of fine lace in the big coffer, I must ask him for a few lengths. Has the cooking at David's yard got any better?'

'No, it's nothing like as nice as yours or Ester's. David's wife stews the flavour out of every meal she makes.'

We'd reached the top of the Garn, with views in every direction of the Carmarthenshire rolling hills and fields. An antiquarian had visited it once. He'd said it was a small Roman fort, one they'd use to camp overnight at on their way west from Brecon. We each sat on a dressed square stone that I'd always liked to think had been put there by a Roman soldier.

Mother sat silent for a moment and then took a big breath, looking down at her hands. 'Will, this isn't a tale

I take any pleasure in telling or remembering. I know you'll not let it rest until you've heard it, so I will share it with you. When it's told, I'm going to ask you to do as I have done and not tell anyone else. You'll understand why when I've finished.

'Although we never dare to mention his name in front of Gu, you already know all about our Tommy leaving. I talk about Tommy often. I loved my blue-eyed brother, you see. Have you ever wondered why I don't talk about George? Well, he and Tommy were chalk and cheese. I shouldn't speak ill of the dead, but there wasn't much good to say about George.

'He was an odd lad from when he was tiny. The other boys his own age didn't take to him. Hard to quite say why. He was nice-looking enough, handsome even, but he was cold and didn't care about anyone else. Sometimes he was cruel to me when I was little, and I suspect he was the same with others. He'd pinch me to watch what I'd do. Tommy found him with one of the cats one day. George had been tightening a harness around its neck and watching it die. Tommy thumped him, then asked him why he did it. George's answer was that he wanted to understand how it felt. We believed him. It wasn't put on; he was a strange one, our George.

'As he grew older, I became scared of him. Sometimes he'd stand too close to me. I saw him doing the same with the dairymaid. It was disconcerting. He didn't understand the rules of how to behave with people or animals. Very different from our Shem, who, although he's an innocent, loves people and animals – and they love him back.

'As I said, George had no real friends, so he'd always tag along with Tommy and your father. When Tommy left, he lost his only companion. He wouldn't admit to being lonely but he had no one then. Your father still came to see me, but we were courting, we certainly didn't want my older brother with us. We'd give George the slip time after time. I think he may have felt rejected then, although I doubt he'd have recognised the feeling. I imagine he spied on us and saw us kissing and cuddling. He had become obsessed with being seen as the man of the family. I wondered if that's what first put the terrible idea into his head.

'George came home one summer Saturday night in a state, shaking and upset. That was unusual for him; normally he didn't show emotion. His face and arms were badly scratched. My mother and my grandmother were out at a church social, John and I were at the house, my grandfather was working in the barn. George saw us and he started to cry; he told us he'd done something bad by Nant Hir stream and asked if we'd save him. We had no idea what he meant. With coaxing, he said the name Bel. We already knew where he meant in the woods.

'John and I set off, not knowing what we'd find. We got to the copse above the brook and could hear sobbing. After searching we found Bel by the stream, lying in the mud and brambles.' My mother's voice dropped to a whisper. 'She was in a terrible state; her face was all right, but her lower body was bloody, her dress torn. Your father didn't know where to put himself. I asked him to go and find my mother and try to look after George. He muttered something about killing George, but I knew he'd not harm him.

'I sat there on the bank with Bel and she told me what had happened through sobs and gasps. George had often followed her on the roads before that evening, ever since Tommy had gone. She'd not worried about it, taking it as a compliment that a farmer's son would bother with her. She had chatted with him as she would anyone else, she was ever-friendly to all, was Bel. That evening he'd told her John and I were having a picnic over by Nant Hir. He suggested he and Bel join us. She'd believed him – she always believed any tale told to her, especially if it was by a boy. Once they got deep in the wood, he'd turned nasty, asking for kisses and then more. She'd told him no, but it had made no difference, he'd got wilder and angrier. When he started hitting her, she'd stopped her resistance.

'It was terrible to see, Will. Poor Bel was humiliated, begged us not to tell anyone. My mother Susan had arrived by now. Of course, protective of her own, she'd agreed not to tell. We took Bel back to the farmhouse, washed her and put her in one of mother's cotton gowns. Mother gave her ten shillings and walked her home. I was ashamed, I had no idea what to do or say. When my mother returned, she was implacable; it must have been Bel's fault, not George's. Bel must have led him on. Mother insisted no harm would come of it.

'Four days later George became ill. At first I thought it was a reaction to his attack on Bel. He'd been subdued and anxious all those following days. It quickly became clear he had diphtheria, starting with a croupy cough and then the horrible membrane closing across his throat. The sound of his gasping for air was terrible to hear. I was sent away to your Aunt Rachel's for fear of catching the illness. In just a few days George was dead.

'Mother was so sad and lost. My father and Tommy had left and might never come home, now George was gone from her too. She didn't know what to do with herself – she didn't eat, didn't wash, it was as if she hated the sight of me. My grandparents were at a loss. They'd lost their son and grandsons too, but watching Susan's pain was hard for them. They sent me to Aunt Rachel's and tried their best to look after her, but week after week of her doing nothing but cry exasperated them. In the end, they sent her back to Pembrokeshire and her family. Ester had to care for her sister there, while I stayed here in Newchurch with my grandparents.

'After a few months, it was clear Bel was with child. Bel knew George had died; she told me it was God's punishment on him. Bel came up to see us one evening before Mother was sent to Pembrokeshire, told us she was expecting George's baby. My mother was insistent the baby could be anyone's. Bel had a reputation for being free with her favours. Your father had to admit the baby might not be George's. I was not so sure. I'd known her for a long time and suspected that it was mostly kisses for the boys. I had to agree that if she'd really been certain it was George's baby, she would have come to us and demanded support. Anyway, when the baby was born, it looked much like any other baby, whoever could know? I sent a letter to my mother but got no reply. She was deep in her grief and had no regard for anything I said or wrote.

'Time went on. My mother was back in Newchurch by then and inconsolable. Gu came home, but Mother wanted nothing to do with either of us. She still didn't sleep or eat, wrung her hands constantly and was terribly agitated, pacing the floor day and night. Then she started to believe my grandmother was poisoning her food and that we were all against her. We thought she had lost her sanity and feared she might harm herself. It was no real surprise when she died; she'd stopped eating and drinking, we couldn't force food on her, she wasted away. Her heart was broken. They were terrible times. If your father hadn't been there for me I don't know how I would have coped.

'John and I married soon after and I was happy. Your oldest brother came quickly after that,' she blushed. 'Jonny was ten months younger than Bel's son Dan. It's a small village; as young mothers we'd often see each other. The two boys liked to play together. I didn't mind. It helped Bel, if she had day work, for someone to take him when Auntie Gwennie couldn't. I liked Dan. As they grew Dan and Jonny were like peas in a pod.' A tear coursed down her cheek. She struggled to continue. I covered her hand with mine.

'I'd heard rumours Bel was getting money from Gu but paid no real attention. I assumed she'd told him about George. I was busy with the farm and had three children by then. I didn't worry about it. I thought Gu must be supporting the child, even if he hadn't acknowledged him.'

Mother continued, 'I knew the boy was George's. It wasn't just how he looked. My mother, Tommy and George had one unusual thing in common: they couldn't see colours properly. To them, reds and greens all looked one muddy orange colour, blues and purples looked similar too. Mother told me it ran in her family and her father and uncle were the same and described it to me. I don't have it, nor does Ester. George said it was one more thing that made him feel different from everyone else. Tommy said he couldn't imagine seeing the world in any other way and it was fine. Imagine not being able to see one green or red as much different from another.'

She paused as we looked out over our lovely rolling hills beyond, with their myriad shades of green fields, trees and flowers. As we sat, a red kite soared over the ridge above and we watched as it sailed over us, tilting and levelling, wingtip feathers like fingers grasping the wind, a creature of wonder.

'Isn't that a coincidence. That's the sort of thing that showed Tommy and George's problem. Once we were watching a kite flying in the sunshine, and as it flashed over us I exclaimed at the glorious red of its belly and arrow tail. The boys scoffed, said I didn't know what I was talking about, it was all much the same colour, except for the white flashes under its wings. We argued and I felt stupid, but when I asked my grandfather, he told me I was right. He'd noticed the boys had a problem with colours when seeing if fruit was ripe. He blamed my mother, her not being able to see if beef was rare or a cake baked. I can hear him saying, "I'm glad you are one of us, not like that Pembrokeshire woman's troublesome tribe."'

My mother went on thoughtfully, 'I've sometimes wondered if Shem might have the same problem but it's so hard to tell with him; he doesn't learn names or understand complicated questions.

'One day the two boys were playing with Tommy's old lead soldiers, some with red hats, some green, blue or orange. They were learning their colours so I asked them to hand them to me. Jonny could do it fine, but little Dan couldn't – he got furious, threw them at Jonny, saying their hats were all the same colour. It was like playing with my brothers all over again.

'In the end, it made no difference. You know what happened, you know about my sadness. Bel's boy Dan died then too.'

I did know about mother's sadness, although no one mentioned it for fear of upsetting her. Years before, the spotted fever had scoured the village. Mother, my brother–Jonny, and two sisters caught it, along with many others. All three of the little ones died, Mother nearly succumbed. I remembered her taking flowers every week to the graveyard. I hated it when she'd sink to her knees and cry. They had haunted my dreams when I was younger, my dead brother and sisters. They cried to me for help, pursued by spirit dogs that waited for the dead at crossroads and the ghost candles that lit the path of coffins. Tales told on dark nights by the fireside lived and frightened me so much that I couldn't sleep on stormy nights.

Mother continued defensively. 'What benefit would there have been in telling anyone? It's a terrible story. Gu would be appalled to hear what his son had done. How would Ellen feel about marrying Tom, the nephew of a man who raped her mother? Bel has never told a soul about it. Only I knew for certain. I still think she was not sure George was Dan's father. Who am I to betray her confidence? It's not as if the Lewises come out of it well, after all.'

I was astonished. I'd guessed there must be a story behind Bel demanding money from Gu, but I had no idea how sad it would be for everyone concerned. I couldn't help but agree with Mother's view; this was a secret that it was in no one's interest to be told. I nodded, patted her hand and told her so.

Mother got up, smoothing her dress out. 'There's lots to be done at home, I must be getting back. I'm glad I've told someone, it's a relief. Thank you for not criticising me, it's been hard keeping this to myself for so long.'

I looked down at her hands, free of the gloves she wore to church, raw, chafed and sore from her weekday chores. I squeezed them, noticing my own large hands, calloused from the chisels and hammers, with plenty of small scars from my early accidents. We linked those hands and walked home along our familiar lanes, full to overflowing with spring flowers. She went into the Little House to all her housework, and I went on up to the Big House and into the old kitchen.

Ester was pleased with the news that Tom might be marrying soon and coming to live at the farm. She chatted on to Gu and me about how Ellen was a nice girl and she knew she'd lend a hand. She wondered out loud if she'd need a dairymaid – the girl she had now was also courting – if Ellen was there. Ester said how lovely it would be to fill up some of the bedrooms, then abruptly stopped.

'Not that you don't fill one at the weekend, Will. We enjoy having you here.' Then she continued somewhat cautiously, 'Are you happy for them, Will? You and Ellen were always so close from when you were little, I'd thought she might have been the girl for you?'

They both watched me closely.

I paused and said doubtfully, 'At first when they started courting, I felt uncomfortable. There was a bit of a divide between Tom and me. She'd been my friend for so long, but truthfully I'm not sure Ellen was ever the girl for me.' Flushing, I continued, 'I've always enjoyed plenty of girls' company in Carmarthen, you see, and I don't give her a thought until I come home. I do love her, but what I miss is that she's my own best friend, along with Huw. She's only interested in what Tom thinks now. He's all she talks about. It's annoying to hear her go on so, although I know that's what people do when they are in love. I am happy for them, Ester. Ellen can be a real sister to me once they marry. I do believe they are well suited. She'll be good for the farm. Gu, you know how seriously she takes everything and how hard she works.'

As I spoke, it came to me that that was the truth. I didn't really want to marry Ellen. We were too alike, good friends, but her smile didn't make my heart race or my mind turn to wickedness, the way certain town girls did.

Ester looked relieved and Gu agreed. 'You're right. I've always been fond of Ellen. She's not silly and squealing like some girls. You're not in love with her, Will. If you were, you'd not be doubtful. You'd be mad with jealousy. When I first met Susan, if another man so much as looked at her, I'd be furious. If she'd taken up with another, I can't think how I'd have reacted. I might have done something stupid. Beaten him, killed him. Love burns.

'Ester, get me a glass of my brandy, bring the lad some beer. We'll sit here by the fire and chat a while. You can do your mending in the parlour, the light's better in there.'

I caught an unusual expression on Ester's face as I turned. Tears filled her eyes, but she looked vexed and affronted.

'I'll bring it through, Gu, save Ester the trouble. I need to go outside and relieve myself.'

I walked with Ester to the parlour.

'Are you all right?'

Her shoulders shook. 'Yes, yes. Get the old bastard his brandy, Will. Leave me in peace.'

'No, I can't do that. Tell me what's wrong.'

She sighed. 'If he can tell you all, why shouldn't I? Your grandfather doesn't know what jealousy is, but I do. I hated Susan. There, does that shock you? I hated my sister, your grandmother. I never liked her, she was a little cat. So pretty, so self-absorbed, but with sharp claws.

'On that night years ago, everything changed for me when Thomas Lewis walked into our kitchen. He was handsome and had a restless energy, blue eyes, dark brown waves in his hair, a crooked, devilish smile. I was lost the second I saw him, but he didn't notice me. His eyes went straight to my pretty, silly sister. Oh, he was polite, but I was invisible.

'Susan was delighted; at last, a way to escape our strict parents. I overheard her talking to our sister Ann about him. "He'll inherit a decent-sized farm when his father dies. He's an only son and lives close to Carmarthen. He'll do. I'll go mad if I stay on this boring farm in this dull village any longer. Who else will I meet? I'll be an old maid like Ester if I wait much longer."

'"He'll do!" I couldn't believe she'd said that when I longed for Thomas to notice me. I'd have done anything for him to like me. Susan was stupid. She'd never listened when my grandmother and mother tried to teach her about running a farm kitchen. All she was interested in was clothes and being admired. She was mean too. We rubbed each other up the wrong way. I was labelled "too good" for doing what my parents asked, cooking and managing the dairy. She swayed Ann against me. Another time when we argued, she said I was so plain I should have been christened Jane and that I'd never marry. That no one would want me.

'Gu's never told me he loves me, you know. Not in all this time; twenty-six years we've been married. I'm a good wife, was a good daughter, but…' She began to cry. I hugged her.

'Ester, it's not true. We all love you, every one of us. Mother adores you, you know that, and Gu – well, he never shows his feelings. I know he loves you. He told me he lost his enchantment with Susan and that's why he joined the army.'

As she rubbed reddened eyes, I had to lean forward to catch her words.

'He did tell her he loved her though. That's what hurts. He told her.'

She pushed me away. 'Go on, go and get him his drink, he'll be shouting if you don't. I've said more than I should.'

I found the brandy bottle and carefully poured amber liquid into a glass rummer and carried it through.

'Good, you are back. You took your time. Where's my drink?'

Until now, it had always been me asking Gu about the past. Tonight he was the one wanting to talk.

Gu started in his low, gruff voice. 'Talking to your father, then hearing Susan had thought I was unfaithful with Isabella Price shocked me last night. I need to set the record straight. I only told you half-truths when we spoke last month. I've been telling myself the same for years and done my best to make myself believe it. I'm going to be honest tonight. It will be a weight off my chest. You already know Susan and I married in haste, it was a whirlwind courtship, we fell in love like a thunderclap. I felt a hypocrite trying to stop Tom marrying. I know what it feels like, you see. You don't, that's clear. Don't worry, the right girl will come along soon enough. You are too young at seventeen. Have fun, don't race into marriage – believe me, it's too big a decision to rush, as you will see.

'I met Susan through her two brothers, who were wild, as was I in those days. They were friends of my cousins from Lamphey, on your grandmother's side. You probably know that in Pembrokeshire, smuggling has been a way of life for hundreds of years. Goods are smuggled to avoid excise taxes. When I was involved, Napoleon was blockading Britain. We have a quiet coast in west Wales, who's to know where boats go to once they have left port for some fishing. It sounds like law breaking here in Carmarthen, but in Pembrokeshire, everyone is involved, including the squires. It was thrilling – avoiding revenue men, trips to collect contraband on dark nights, the secrecy – and of course, smuggling made me a good profit.

'Your great-grandfather disapproved, of course; told me time after time he'd disown me if I was caught, but people were happy to buy. I got to know many of the gentry and publicans in Carmarthen and Llandeilo by selling best quality brandy, port and wine. They sold it on to their friends as it was in such short supply with that French blockade; everyone benefited. I don't see it as wrong; the taxes and tithes we pay the government on everything more than cover the small profits I made. I built up good networks to pass on contraband here in Carmarthen. I'd meet your uncles in a tavern between here and St Clears. We'd swap carts that looked identical, except one was empty and the other full of flat-sided tubs full of strong brandy, so strong I'd have to dilute it with water to stop men going blind. We used flat tubs so they were easier to carry on a man's back, but it did mean they were easy to identify as smuggled, unlike round oak barrels.

'One time the lads asked me to come to their home in Manorbier; their cart was broken and at the wheelwright's. There, sitting in the kitchen, lovely as anything, was your grandmother, Susan. She had brown hair, big grey eyes and the softest, sweetest mouth you've ever seen. It turned out she was sitting next to her older sister Ester. Back then I didn't notice my Ester, beyond a polite nod – my eyes were only for Susan.

'Susan wore an enticing low-cut pink dress – girls wore dresses cut outrageously low when I was young. She was, as the old phrase goes, pretty as a picture. Ester was calm and pleasant but Susan, she was exactly one of those squealing, pouting girls I mentioned just now, she took my breath away. I was besotted in an instant. Susan acted as interested in me as I was in her. I later came to know that their parents, your great-grandparents, kept a tight rein on their daughters. Those girls saw few men outside the family. I wonder now if Susan might have been so impatient to get away that she saw me as a saviour, which added to her enthusiasm. That may be unfair, but whatever, we were in love, practically at first sight. We managed to meet again at the various fairs around the county. Soon I was determined to marry and so was she. Our parents were reluctant, – we were only eighteen, scarcely knew each other – but there was no convincing or stopping us. It's true to say we'd have run off and married if they'd refused. We wed three months later, in July.

'I took my young bride home. Tommy was born ten months later in 1797, George twelve months after that, then your mother. I've already told you that Susan had been disappointed. She'd left one hard-working farm for another. There were no parties and few friends for an eighteen-year-old bride. Three babies in three years didn't help. She spoke English at home in Pembrokeshire, her use of Welsh was poor, so the local women weren't sure of her, thought she was putting on airs, acting like the gentry.

'What I haven't properly admitted is that I felt as tied down as she. I longed to see more of the world. Most nights I left her and went to meet up with friends in The Plough, or on smuggling runs with her brothers. There was money and a few dresses to be sure, but nowhere to wear them apart from church and the occasional village social and fair. Susan didn't fit in at the dances in The Ivy Bush and Assembly Rooms, without friends to go with.

'I'd been to Susan's home often after we first met and got to know Ester better. I liked her calm and sensible older sister. I'd no idea at all that Ester was more than fond of me. I only cared for my pretty Susan. The hardest thing was that year after year, the babies continued to arrive, but either they came too early or, worse, lived a day or two and then died. Susan grew thinner and sadder with each year. By the end she didn't want me to touch her. Ten years after we married, I was afraid to go near her.

'I decided joining the army was my way out of Carmarthen and the unhappiness of our marriage. The recruiters were a regular sight, banging their drum in Guildhall Square. Sometimes they'd march through the villages too. Many men had already enlisted. For most, the bounty of eleven guineas to join, a shilling a day pay and food was attraction enough; drudgery and poor wages the usual alternative.

'Of course, I didn't have to join, but I'd never seen Swansea, let alone London or Portsmouth. In Tenby, there was a lot of talk of far off places as sailors came home from all over the world – South America, the Indies and the like. I felt hemmed in by the farm. I hated the expectation that I would carry on and do what I'd done ever since I was old enough to lend a hand, to work here until the day I died. Susan and I spent ten years quarrelling. I wasn't even sure I still loved her, and doubt she cared much for me. I wanted to join up whatever, so I asked her to become a camp follower. She rightly thought this would be madness; with three little ones, camp life would be impossible for her. I soon learned she was entirely right – it was a terrible life for women – but back then I couldn't have known.

'We had a bitter argument one Sunday night when I got back from The Plough worse for the drink. Next morning, I heard the drum of the recruiters in town. I went off and signed up for the new shorter enlistment of seven years in a trice. The army was desperate for men to build troop numbers to fight the French back then. They knew what I didn't: their battles were going to need cannon fodder. That's what they wanted, food to feed the guns. I took the King's shilling with pleasure, Will, and marched away from Susan, my babies, the farm and my troubles. I was twenty-eight, old enough to know better, but off I went. Much of the failure of my marriage was my own fault, not Susan's. I know your mother doesn't speak highly of your grandmother, but I put Susan in an impossible position. The blame for everything lies at my door.

'I quickly discovered that the bounty of eleven guineas was half spent on the uniform, boots and other necessities; barely five guineas was left to send home to Susan. I paid someone to write a letter a couple of times from Alderney, asked her to sail over to see me. She had the babies and a life here, so she didn't come. We didn't exchange many letters, maybe one or two a month at first, then hardly any. Your Aunt Rachel wrote more often, every few months, with news of the farm and the family. I'd never learned to write, but Susan could. I think she was punishing me for leaving. Rachel told me in one letter that Tommy was entranced by the idea of the army, always playing with his lead soldiers.

'I enjoyed army life. In truth, it wasn't too bad for those first years. I had more fun than at home. That was up until the real fighting in Portugal and Spain began. When I heard Tommy had joined as a drummer boy in spring 1813, I wasn't unhappy. I didn't know what was coming. How could I? The news was that at last, Boney was losing battles in Europe. The next spring, he was to be exiled and imprisoned on Elba. I saw no harm in Tommy enlisting. Unless my father paid for his discharge, and twenty pounds was a fortune to my father, a year's rent on a lot of acres, there was nothing I could do to stop him. Susan was dismayed. I promised her in a letter that I'd do my best to look out for him. Tommy wasn't in my regiment though, he was a drummer in the 95th. I'd be unlikely to see him. I should have known better after the hell that was Badajoz, but I was caught up in army camaraderie by then.'

Chapter Nine

I was fascinated, not to hear again about his unhappy marriage but rather because I'd finally got to the truth about Gu and where his money came from.

I couldn't resist. 'Gu, it sounds as if you may still be involved with running contraband?'

'Well, yes and no, Will. I do have some investments, shall we say. None of the goods come through Cwm Castell now, that would be risky. I've more to lose, I'm not young and impetuous anymore. That said, I'm proud my wife and daughter can wear Brussels lace that is as fine as that the young Queen Victoria might wear. I like my mellow brandy on cold wet nights like this. I've made sure none of it can be traced back to me.'

He looked at me hard. 'I don't regret spending my profits on land, you know. It is my money and if I hadn't bought up those fields, they'd have gone to Captain Davies or his damned magistrate friends instead, and at a lower price. Is it profiting from others' misfortune, or is it giving them a better price than if there were no other bidders, I ask you?'

It was late, the fire had died down. Gu got up, pushed the glowing embers to the back of the grate and threw on a heavy ash log to keep it alight overnight. I would have been happy to carry on talking about Spain and what happened next, but Gu looked tired. I knew I'd have to wait. I nodded reassuringly and off we went to bed.

I was overwhelmed with what I'd learned and the week's events – Bel's sad history, that Gu still had "investments" in smuggling. I itched to know more. I worried about poor John Jones and his arm in Carmarthen, and about Mother and Father and their money worries. Ester's tears had saddened me. Was there any way I could begin to ask Gu to be more affectionate to her? The thought of trying made me quail.

Should I really be envious of Tom? Last week I'd told him I didn't want the farm because of its hardships, but that was not true. I'd lied. Of course I wanted to inherit. I imagined having no option but live with Gu and Ester until they died, Gu constantly interfering, having to agree with him about every decision on the farm, having to ask for a share of the profit and feeling perpetually beholden. It would drain and irritate beyond measure. To expect my own father to pay me rent was an unpleasant thought. What I'd considered as Tom having all the luck might be viewed by some as a lifelong millstone to carry. Gu had chafed at that same burden when he was younger. Was it unlucky to be allowed the freedom to choose how I made my way in the world? Gu said he'd set me up with a workshop when I started; few were that fortunate. Was I the fortunate one, not Tom? I was startled. I'd spent so long resenting Tom's luck in being born first.

Saturday 20th May 1843

Tom had come into Carmarthen on Wednesday with father to sell lamb. He was bouncing with joy and had rushed to the workshop.

'She said yes, Will, she said yes. She wants to marry me.'

'That's wonderful. I couldn't be happier for you both.'

I pumped his hand, then slapped his back.

'Will you be my groomsman? You are my brother and her best friend. I can't think of anyone more suited.'

'Of course. What did her mother say when you asked?'

'I haven't yet. You're right, Ellen's not reached her majority, Bel does have to agree, but why would it be a problem? I've got a farm to offer Ellen, after all. I thought I'd see Bel at the May Hiring Fair on Saturday.'

'How is she with you?'

'Nice enough, now you ask, maybe a bit cool. She hasn't said much when I've called to walk out with Ellen, never asked me in. I think she may be ashamed of their home.'

I smiled encouragingly, but couldn't help thinking Bel was normally warm and welcoming to everyone. She'd always asked me into their home, but there again, I'd never visited courting.

Saturday dawned cloudless, the sky periwinkle blue for once, the sun warm, trees leafed in finest spring green. I looked forward to the fair, the biggest in Newchurch's year although small by comparison with Carmarthen's fairs, but friendly and fun for locals. Farmers from surrounding villages came to hire new servants and farm labourers, flannel traders travelled from woollen mills around the county to sell cloth, horses were traded. Hawkers and stall-keepers set up too – fancy china from Llanelli and Swansea, ribbons, farm tools; you name it, someone sold it.

In the afternoon there'd be games and competitions, a tug of war, races for the children and one for men. The women ran an egg and spoon race with obstacles set out. We followed the old ways and set a harpist to play as we raised a ribboned birch tree for couples to dance around in the evening.

David sent me to the timber merchant in the morning but gave me an hour off, saying I wasn't concentrating. He and his wife planned to drive out to watch me in the men's race and tug of war later. He'd bring any of the apprentices who wanted to come with them on the cart. It was set to be a grand day.

I went into the Little House to change, but Mother told me not to bother.

'You'll only get your new shirt dirty, or worse – I know you plan on joining the games. There's a fat purse for the men's race, ten shillings, I've heard. I'll bring your shirt in my bag for later, you can put it on for the dancing. Come on, hurry up, the children have been waiting all morning, nagging to leave. Ester will be here in a moment. Your father and Tom left to help set up hours ago.'

We stepped outside. To our surprise, Gu and Ester had drawn up the trap, dressed in their best for the fair.

'Come on, get in all of you, or I'll go without,' harrumphed Gu.

Ester's expression and raised eyebrows said it all.

Don't comment, pretend he always comes to the fair, her eyes signaled.

We climbed up and Gu relented. 'I heard you planned on racing, Will. Thought I'd come and watch for an hour or so. Ester's always asking me to join in with the family. I won't stay long, my bad leg means I will need the trap to get home, but well, I thought I'd try. It's been a year or two since I last went to the fair, what with the weather often poor.'

It was an understatement, Gu hadn't been to a May fair for as long as any of us could remember, but we all, even my little sisters, knew better than to comment.

'That's nice, Father. Will'll appreciate your support, I'm sure,' said Mother.

We arrived at the field and I hopped off, making for Huw and my friends by the *cwrw* stand. Villagers had been home-brewing beer, to fund the prizes for weeks; any money over went to charity. It wasn't a great drink but it was cheap and powerful. Every fair in the county had its *cwrw* stand.

Huw handed me a pot. 'Get that down you.'

'I'll wait. You're not drinking, I notice.' I pushed him shoulder to shoulder as he grinned at me.

'No harm in trying to slow my opposition,' he replied. He added, 'Maybe you'd better see to your brother first. He's on his second, looks very downhearted.'

Glancing to where Huw gestured, I saw Tom sat on a log alone, face black as thunder, furious, a quart pot in his hand.

Walking over, I asked, 'What's going on, Tom?'

'Bel said no. I asked her last night. She's said we can't wed this year. She refuses to consent. I tried to argue, Ellen did too, but Bel insisted no banns could be read. Said it was too soon.'

'Oh… Maybe she'll come round.'

'Huh, I don't think so. Anyway, we've argued, Ellen and me. It's off.'

'What?'

'I said we should elope if Bel sticks to her guns, but Ellen wouldn't agree. I told her if she loved me enough she would, but she still refused.'

'You have only been walking out six weeks, maybe rushing…'

'Oh for God's sake, I should have known. Of course you'd be sensible, you're like her. You've no passion. I hate you, you pathetic, big lump.'

'Tom, don't be stupid.'

'Stupid, is it? You know it all, you think I'm stupid, do you?'

He swung a slow punch at me. I caught his arm.

He pulled away, swearing. I heard him mutter, 'Short and weak, why would she want me?' as he staggered off.

I was irritated but knew it was his disappointment and the beer talking. Where was he going? Gu'd better not see him in this state. He headed over to a group of women who were selling pastries, botanical brews; dandelion and burdock and the like. Bel and Ellen were with them. I hurried over in time to catch the group's expressions of surprise. A swaying Tom was arguing with Bel.

'Have you changed your mind?'

'No. I told you yesterday I don't believe Ellen is ready for marriage.'

'But why not? I love her. My grandfather has agreed, we'll have a home.'

'That's as may be, but…'

'I'm not good enough for her, is that what you think? That's a check – I mean cheek. How dare you turn me down? I've better postpects… prospects than you lot on the Row.'

He'd started to slur. Ellen stood frozen, appalled to see Tom arguing with her mother in public. Tears started in her eyes.

Bel's colour raised, she was nettled.

'Don't you speak to me like that. I've every reason to think badly of the Lewises. Their money won't buy my daughter, thank you very much. You're drunk. Go home and sober up.' Her eyes focused on me. 'Will, take him away before I say something I regret.'

She turned. Tom made to grab her. I pulled him, struggling, away. Fortunately, by now Father was beside me and helped. Everyone nearby had stopped to watch their argument.

Da said, 'Tom, come with me. Will, don't worry, I'll manage your brother. You get ready for the races.'

He marched Tom away towards the family. Ellen sobbed silently. Bel looked embarrassed. She attempted to put her arms around her daughter, who pushed her away.

'How could you, Mother, in front of everyone?'

She half ran towards the field gate.

Bel gestured to me helplessly. 'Go after her, tell her I'm sorry. If he loves her, he'll wait.'

The women around Bel nodded agreement. I knew they'd be delighted. What a story: Bel Price turning down Thomas Lewis's grandson's offer, when he was due to inherit all those acres. One or two had daughters of an age with Ellen; they'd not be disappointed if Tom took against Ellen after this.

I ran after Ellen and caught her up.

'Wait, Ellen. Don't leave, don't go. Tom's not used to strong beer, he's drunk. Because he's in love with you, he has behaved terribly. Your mother was right to tell him off.'

'But in front of the whole village.'

'I know, but it's because he loves you that he did it. Don't go, my race starts in a few minutes, come and watch. If you go, I won't be able to run, I'll worry about you. Hold your head up and ignore the gossips; you'll have to face them soon enough. I think I'm in with a chance of winning the race this year.'

Sad green eyes gazed at me. She knew I wouldn't leave her and would miss the race.

She sighed. 'I suppose it's true. I'll have to face them, so will he, the idiot. I'll have to apologise to Mother too.'

As she called Tom an idiot, her voice softened with affection.

'Come on then, let's see you run. You'd better win after all this. I need something to make me smile.'

CHAPTER TEN

We went over to a marked track where around twenty men and boys were making ready, the final children's race just finishing.

I took off my shoes. We ran barefoot to give everyone an equal chance. I peered round to weigh up the competition. Huw was there, Sam Bowen from The Plough, the younger Rees brother and Robert Pritchard. Excellent, his sister Mary-Ann would be watching. I wanted to impress her – only because she was Shem's friend, of course. There was a redheaded man, maybe thirty, nearly as tall as me, slim and muscular, wearing ragged clothes. I wondered who he could be. He looked the only serious competition; I'd keep my eye on him. The race was to the summer birch pole and back, near enough half a mile. A crowd was gathering to watch. I saw Gu out of the corner of my eye but didn't look for the rest of the family; I wanted to keep focused.

The race martial sounded the starter pistol and we were off. I'd decided to keep some energy back for the end of the race, not push too hard at first, but my legs were long. Without real effort, I had drawn away from Huw and the rest by the birch turn. As I'd guessed, only one man had kept up: the tall stranger.

By the last quarter we were back to the crowd. He quickened his pace, arms pumping, and drew ahead by half a pace. My breath came raw and ragged; I'd have to push now, flat out. I ran with all my strength. The thought of David and the lads, Mary-Jane and Gu watching made me desperate to win. My strides were longer and as we reached the rope, I just pipped him. We sank to our knees, gasping on the grass as the crowd cheered, glad to see the local win.

When we'd stopped panting, he shook his head as if to clear it, then put out a hand for me to shake.

In soft Irish tones, he said, 'Well done… would you know if there is a second prize by any chance?'

'Yes, it's a ten shillings purse for first place, five for second and a shilling for third.'

A wave of relief passed over his face. His eyes flickered to a woman with a child at her skirt and a baby wrapped in a worn shawl at her breast.

'You're travelling the roads from Ireland?'

'Yes, from Cork. Hoped to find work on the way, buy food. We spent our last on the passage, but it's the same at every gate: no Irish, and no work.' He looked down. 'None of us have eaten since yesterday. Five shillings will be a God send.'

'If you'd been fed, you'd have beaten me,' I replied, shamed.

'I might, I might not. Who knows? You're young. I'd have beaten you ten years ago.' His face lit with a warm smile and he laughed.

I liked him instantly. Despite losing, he was stoic.

'Come and meet my family, bring your children. If I know Ester, there'll be a fine picnic in her basket.'

I was congratulated by all, including Huw, who'd come fourth, and looked forward to the prize giving and dancing later. By the time I was free, Ester was doling out food to the travellers, after my earlier whispered explanation. Watching my thin opponent eating a slice of tipsy cake with an ecstatic expression, I understood myself blessed. Ester offered the family shelter in our barn overnight. I knew she'd send them on their way with a pack of food and was glad for them.

Mother beckoned me over. She had to shout to be heard above a ballad singer who was entertaining the crowd, bawling out a song about the shipwreck of the *Pickering Dodge* at Cefn Sidan four years ago. Shem's eyes were enormous as he listened; he loved to hear new songs. He'd buy the printed sheet with the words and lurid pictures for a penny and would happily sing that tune over and over for weeks to come.

Mother said, 'Your father has taken Tom home to sleep it off. What was he thinking? Gu's wondering what's going on. I'm afraid to tell him Bel's refused to agree to the betrothal. I've tried to speak to Bel but she wouldn't look me in the eye, said she wasn't prepared to discuss it. Let's try to enjoy what's left of the afternoon. Take Shem and the children, try to win them a coconut, will you? Buy them some fancy biscuits and tea with this.' She handed me a shilling. 'No beer for Shem, please. I've had enough problems with Tom. Shem can't handle beer at all. Ester and Gu are going home soon. I'll take the young ones back with them, can't face any more sympathetic looks from my neighbours, but you stay. Enjoy your triumph. Don't you get into trouble, now.'

I reached home late that evening after a grand time. Predictably, when I reached the Big House Gu was angry; he'd heard his fine grandson had been refused permission to marry by Isabella Price.

He ranted and raved, 'Ellen will never cross my threshold again. When I think of the money and food I've given that family. You gave them a piglet one year, squandered of course. Sold for fripperies, not slaughtered to feed her children. Bel Price should be damn grateful to the Lewises, not insulting us.'

I snorted when he mentioned the piglet. A sad but telling tale of how things had been in the Price family. Ellen was delighted with her pig, rightly thinking it would give the family food the winter long. Like Auntie Gwennie, she doted on it, walking it to the common each day, her little sisters in tow. The pig grew fast, then one evening in September, she and I returned after playing up at the farm to find its pen empty. Ellen rushed to her mother to ask if she'd seen it. Bel had smiled cheerily and told her she'd sold it to a passing trader on his way to market that morning.

'I got ten shillings and sixpence and have already bought a round of cheese and a rabbit for supper. I mean to buy a new dress tomorrow, I really need one. I'll get you a ribbon too. Won't that be a fine thing?'

Ellen, at nine years, couldn't hold back her tears. She'd loved that pig, but more than that, young as she was, she knew the difference that sides of pork and bacon would mean to the family later in the year. Bel didn't care for the future, a creature of immediate pleasures. "Nothing set by for a cold winter night", Ester would have warned.

Ellen had looked worried. 'But we owe Will for a quarter of the pig, Mother. You know what he and Mr Morgan said when we were given it.'

Bel had frowned. 'I'm not giving Will half a crown when that pig was such a tiny thing when it arrived, now, am I? That's nonsense. I need that money far more than Will, with all those acres in the family. Will, I'll have to owe you the money until I have two shillings and sixpence spare.'

She smiled at me, both of us certain that day would never arrive. Initially, I was resigned, thinking at least Ellen's family had got a cheese and rabbit out of her work. Then an idea came – how to protect Ellen's efforts.

I said firmly, 'No, I deserve my quarter – you know what Father said when we gave it to you. You owe me that money fair and square. Tell you what, if you give me a half-crown, I'll keep it. You can either have another piglet next year, so more profit, or, if you really need the money at Christmas, I'll give it back, on loan of course.'

All three of us knew the money would be handy later in the year. Bel could see the sense in my proposal.

Grudgingly she handed the coins over, but said, 'There's no ribbon for Ellen from the market, mind.'

Ellen and I nodded, knowing that was all we'd get, but at least some of the profit would go towards food over the winter.

Later I whispered to Ellen, 'I'll hand the money over in sixpences, so you'll have five decent meals out of your pig.'

Ellen and I were cut from the same cloth, careful and sensible, always weighing up our decisions. I didn't tell Gu or Father, but soon everyone in Newchurch knew that Ellen's pig had gone and guessed why. No one was surprised when, the following Saturday, Bel wore a gaudy, green gown to serve her beer. The dress was not new but she was delighted with it. Even I, a nine-year-old, could see she looked fetching. It was probably the most money she ever spent on a dress in her life.

Looking back, I reflected on how hard life was for her, with no frills and fancies. I was irritated by her dismissal of Tom and Ellen's marriage, but I couldn't begrudge her that pretty green dress those years ago. The dress was far more flattering than the daily wear of the village women. Bel hadn't bought a woollen betgown and jacket that would have lasted years, but had chosen a frivolous tea gown. Ester and my mother, like most women in the countryside, wore traditional striped flannel for every day. Only wealthier farmers' wives had day dresses with lace for Sundays and holidays. Mrs Davies, Miss Bowen-Morgan and the ladies of the shire were the only ones to wear day gowns habitually. That Bel chose to spend what little money she had on such a dress had made the women annoyed and, I guessed, envious.

Poor Tom and Ellen; Bel was determined, and she had always been single-minded. I couldn't see her being persuaded to let them marry, not now Tom had been so insulting at the fair.

Chapter Eleven

Monday 22nd May 1843

The weather was still pleasant as I left for the week. Tom and Father were up and working; once the dew dried they'd be haymaking all day, so getting an early start on the daily chores would help. Back at the workshop, there was better news about John Jones; there was no further sign of infection, the doctor hoped his wound might heal.

Master David said firmly, 'Right, let's get more work out of you this week, Will. Less time spent on Newchurch matters, more on carpentry, if you please.'

I nodded. He relied on me to keep an eye on the other apprentices and set them right if mistakes were made or they needed guidance. I was strong and clever, and as David's second cousin, my advice and directions were rarely questioned by those who had started years earlier than me. We needed to get the house finished and move on. Master

David had other work he wanted attended to; he was the carpenter for Carmarthen Gaol and they had jobs waiting. I was determined to go with him, fascinated to see inside the prison. All of us would know one or two of the inmates; it didn't take much to be sent to gaol. Times were hard and any theft or misdemeanour heavily punished.

The building had progressed and our work on the Fountain Well House was ending. We'd put up the rafters and roofers were using north Wales slate to make the house watertight. The floorboards and skirting were nearly finished. By Friday evening, we were pleased, there was not so much left to do. After a tidying on Saturday morning and our Sunday rest day, we could move on.

When we arrived at Fountains Well the next day, the street was abuzz, full of people standing and staring. We instantly saw why; the Water Street tollgate was broken, the tollhouse roof completely demolished, slates and stone were strewn across the road. Bystanders told us that in the early hours of the morning, hundreds of men, most dressed in women's clothing with faces blackened, had marched on the gate and destroyed it. Traders travelling to market were delighted to pass through without paying. I watched as one whooped then kicked the splintered wood and rubble aside. The tollgate keeper stood to one side, wringing his hands. He looked bemused and afraid. Rebecca and her daughters had struck, and in Carmarthen itself! We boys were excited to see the wreckage, and to Master David's disgust, hardly any work was completed that morning; all we could do was talk about the gate and fool around.

I pushed past the broken, tangled wooden gate pike later that afternoon on my way home. The news had long reached Newchurch. I was stopped at almost every cottage and farm along the three miles. People either asked about the night before or speculated as to who might have joined Rebecca and taken the hated gate down. Several names suggested were men I knew well from chapel. It felt stirring and part of me longed to have joined in this battle, but another part wanted to avoid trouble with the authorities, keep out of the farmers' and carters' dispute. This was an argument Tom and I had time and again. He told me I had to stand up for what I believed in and the equal rights of every man, not one law for the rich but another for working people. I was cautious, I could always see both sides of any argument.

I went straight into the kitchen. As I'd expected, Tom was there. Mother looked tense as Tom described how Father had been up very early getting the cows in and had heard the news hours ago. When Tom had woken, he'd been aggrieved not to have been asked to join the good work and was cross when I told him the size of the crowd of "sisters".

Mother tutted, 'You can do without the trouble, Tom. The magistrates will send out constables to arrest those suspected of destroying the property of others soon enough. I don't want a knock on my door, or to have to worry about my family.'

Tom was all for going down to Carmarthen to see the gate. Father returned from the yard, looking bone weary; in fine weather, he worked all hours.

He listened to what I had to say, nodding at the state of the gate.

'No doubt it will be repaired by Monday, in time to charge working folks to use the road'.

Mother said, 'Now, I'm having no talk of Rebecca over tea.'

We settled down as she called in the younger ones. There was a fine spread on the table. The kitchen garden had started to produce broad beans, radishes and lettuce. Mother had made a delicious trifle from cake and early raspberries, with creamy yellow custard, and used last year's elderflower wine to soak the sponges.

When Tom left the room, Mother whispered, 'At least the toll's destruction has distracted him from Ellen. He's barely spoken all week; he was distraught after the fair, talked again of running away with her, having the banns read somewhere they aren't known, like Merthyr or Pontypridd, getting a job in the iron works. I've reminded him that Ellen has already refused to go against her mother, it is not in the girl's nature. His best course is to wait a while. I don't want him down some mine, getting killed in an accident, lungs filled with filth. I'm worried. See if you can speak sense to him, will you?'

After I'd teased my little sisters and tickled my baby brother, I suggested to Tom we walk up the Crug. It was a calming stroll, the cow parsley at its frothy spring best, with pink campions, early foxgloves and bluebells adding colour to a green tapestry. Tom spoke about the gate and who would have been there, naming a number of the younger farmers from around about. As expected, his talk soon turned to Ellen.

'I'm in despair, Will, I want to marry her, I can think of nothing but Ellen. Her mother's snatched my joy away. I've been so happy these last few weeks, like I'd come out of a shell and into the sunlight. I thought Ellen felt the same, thought she loved me with the same passion. How could she not try to reason with Bel? Night and day, my stomach and thoughts churn round and round. I wonder if she really loves me as much as I thought.'

'Tom, you know she loves you, you...'

'How dare Bel refuse permission? I can't believe her impudence. We have one of the biggest farms in Newchurch. Everyone's said what a match it is for Ellen; their family is poor. I've so much to offer Ellen. I love her and I thought she loved me. Then again, I think to myself, no, Ellen is a girl who always does what her mother says. The law stopping people marrying without consent until their majority is absurd. How many women do you know that are with child at sixteen, let alone twenty-one?'

He ranted on until I was weary of him repeating himself.

Eventually, I managed to get a word in. 'Tom, knowing Ellen as I do, there is no question that she loves you if she has said so. Ellen is not a girl to take any advantage. You know that. She has kept house, cooked and cared for her mother and the children for years, as if Bel was a child and she the mother. Maybe that's why Bel doesn't want to let her go. You have to support Ellen and be patient.' We returned to the Little House with Tom somewhat mollified.

I carried on down the lane to the Big House, Gu and Ester, where I managed a second supper with no problem at all. Ester said she loved to see me eat so much. Over six feet tall at seventeen, with the constant exertion of carpentry and farming, I was perpetually ready for food. How it would have been for me if I'd been in the circumstances of those in the workhouse, I couldn't imagine. I told the old folks I was going to the tavern. I wanted to hear all about the taking down of those gates on Water Street.

Gu said, 'Aye, and you can tell me all about it in the morning. I'm not going to ask after that letter I had those weeks ago. I feel completely let down by my neighbours.'

Off into the evening I went, calling in for Tom. Father said he'd rather stay home with Mother. We arrived to a full house, the tavern's doors open, huddles of men spilling out, all in animated discussions about the tollgate and how a few more turnpike trusts needed to be taught a lesson. Tom was welcomed by his friends. They shouted out for him to join them.

Evans the cobbler yelled, 'Where were you last night, boys? Too fast asleep to join the good work. We look to the Morgans for muscle.'

I felt as if Evans looked pointedly at me as he shouted. There was a lot of back-slapping and congratulating going on. I knew the three Rees brothers were likely to have been involved, but it sounded like half the men there had gone out the night before. I was relieved; there was safety as well as comfort in numbers. Tom still looked disgruntled and annoyed. Seeing Huw across the room, I made my way over to him and his father. We pulled away from the older men. I bought us both a frothing pint pot of ale from Bowen's wife and we went outside.

'Did you go?'

'Yes, practically every one of the younger farmers in the villages around joined. Quite a number of farm labourers and carters did too. Tailor Jonah Davies and your blacksmith Morgan cousins came.'

Maybe the look from Evans hadn't been so pointed after all, I thought.

Huw's eyes shone. 'Will, it was so exciting, there was such spirit amongst us. Around midnight we put on old flannel dresses, found wigs or white caps if we could. Some cut their horses' tails for hair. We blackened our faces with soot and travelled silently down the valley. You could only hear the tramp of feet and horses' hooves. There must have been a couple of hundred of us from Elvet in the march.

'When we arrived the horns sounded and we gave a great shout. The toll-keeper came out very polite, saying he'd expected us. He asked us not to damage his furniture as his wife and family were in bed. Rebecca and her sister Charlotte were leading, high up on their big horses.'

Huw hesitated, as if waiting for me to speak, but then continued, 'Rebecca and Charlotte were pleased that the keeper was so cordial. They ordered no harm come to the inside of the tollhouse, but that we, their daughters, should start work. Guns were fired down Water Street, so no witnesses would dare come out from their houses. We tore down the gate bar and chopped it to pieces, we took off the tollhouse roof slates and timbers with pickaxes and saws. Then we knocked down the oak posts of the gate. One daughter accidentally put her foot through the ceiling.

Charlotte, in her white turban and gown, told her off, said, 'I expected to see no more damage done', and made the man apologise. With so many labouring it took no time at all; there was nothing left of the damned gate. After half an hour we could melt away into the darkness, the work complete. Some were having such fun they fooled around, started squealing like pigs as we left. I'd do it all again tomorrow. Next time you've got to come with us.'

I felt torn. It did sound exciting. Life in Newchurch was dull. Our cause was right; the tolls had more than doubled over the last few years, but roads were no better – worse, if anything. The turnpike trusts auctioned off tollgates to the highest bidder, who had to make a return on their investment. Carters had to pay as much as five shillings a load to get lime to us to keep our land fed and fertile. Times for farmers were worse and worse in recent years, good harvest or bad.

People could take no more. However hard you worked, keeping a roof over your head and food on the table was all most could manage. Plenty couldn't do that. Farmers couldn't afford to pay the wages for labourers, who were demanding higher pay. Many were selling up or surrendering their leases like Joseph's family, then moving to Swansea and Merthyr.

I longed to be part of the protests, but as an apprentice living in the town, I felt an outsider now. It was not my battle. I had no real stake in it beyond the claims of family. I'd never have either Gu or Father's farms for my own. The tolls were an annoyance to us in town, but not the burden they were for Father and the village.

The sour taste of resentment at being a second son rose in me again. I pushed it away. I'd make damn sure my life would be better. With my trade I aimed to prosper, to be richer than Tom.

'What will happen next?' I asked.

'Our success will lead to more gates being destroyed around the Hundred. The Government in London had better start listening or Wales will be going the way of France.'

His words took me aback; the French revolution had shaken the whole country and led to war. While most agreed with the Declaration of the Rights of Man, we still had respect for the King, and these last six years the new young Queen, Victoria. Parliament would send in militias if things carried on like this in west Wales. I thought of what had happened in Newport in Monmouthshire not so many years before, when troops fired on the Chartists: over twenty men had died.

I squeezed Huw's arm. 'Yes, but the authorities won't take this lying down. Be careful, and don't you mention France to anyone, ever. That's treason.'

The evening wore on in high spirits and it was late when Tom and I walked home. He was bitterly resentful of not being asked to join Rebecca.

'It isn't that you are distrusted, everyone knows how you support the people's charters. It's that no one wants to put you in a difficult position with Gu. Cwm Castell is one of the biggest farms hereabout; Gu has been buying up land offered for sale. He's richer than most, better able to weather the times, to turn them to his advantage. He's an ex-soldier and pensioner, remember. If he was younger, he'd have been called on to support law and order, take up arms in the militia. Same as Captain Davies, the village thinks of Gu as part of the establishment, not one of those suppressed.

'You can't have it both ways. You are his heir, that means folk see you in that light. Right now you are poor with no money, but in years to come, as long as Gu doesn't cut you from the will, you will be wealthy. Gu is famously cantankerous; people know he is perfectly capable of disinheriting you if crossed.'

Tom sighed and looked miserable. 'Everything is going wrong. I hate my life.'

He sloped into the farm while I carried on down the hill to the Big House. I was pleased to see Ester had left me out a slice of her currant cake on the kitchen table; I was hungry again.

The next morning dawned dry and bright. Father sent my oldest sister up to the Big House before six to tell us that chapel or no, he meant to cut the lower pastures while the weather held. She had been told to tell me to come and lend a hand. Ester looked shocked. Working on the Sabbath was not done.

Gu said firmly, 'The saying "make hay while the sun shines" is right. John doesn't want to lose cows over the winter for the sake of a sermon in chapel, now, does he? You don't want to see the grandchildren go hungry either.'

'It's the Lord's day, Thomas, it's not right. Poor Will has been working all week, he needs a day of rest, surely? As if we'd let the family starve.'

'The boys are young and healthy enough to work the odd Sunday morning. Will and Tom don't know what hardship is, and I don't want them to. John is right to do this after such a wet May. You women and the preachers may not understand, but the Lord, if he has any sense, will.'

Ester, mortified, stalked out of the room. I agreed with Gu. I'd be needed, I was deft with the scythe. Between Father, Tom and me, we'd likely mow the pastures in a few hours and still make chapel. Shem wasn't trusted with a scythe but could help with the raking and stacking. Who was to know, would the Lord really begrudge us mowing? I doubted it. Hopefully, neither the vicar nor Minister Abrahams would get to hear about us working. That big field was tucked away, out of view.

I walked quickly up to the house and joined Father in the pasture. Tom was slower and looked dour, but worked hard enough, scything the long grass with a bitter energy. I kept three paces behind him to the right so there could be no accidents. After three and a half hours of solid shoulder-aching labour, the field was mown to father's satisfaction. It was harder work than it would have been earlier in the year. The grass was high and tougher to cut now.

Father nodded. 'Excellent. With luck and decent weather I'll get a second cut in early September. Off you go to chapel now, boys, don't say a word. If it stays sunny, I might turn the hay tonight. Thanks, Will. I appreciate the extra pair of hands.'

I decided to go to church with Ester and Mother rather than chapel. It would make Ester feel better about my working on the day of rest, and I wanted to hear what churchgoers thought of the tollgate destruction. Mother had a freshly laundered shirt of Father's ready for me. I'd outgrown my shirts. I'd one new one being made in Carmarthen but resented paying out my savings for something as dull as a Sunday shirt, especially as I knew in a few months it might be too small again.

The congregation was agog and buzzing with the news. People were circumspect in airing their opinions, and if they supported the taking down of the tollgate, they avoided saying so publicly. The Davieses and Miss Bowen-Morgan were there. We were in no doubt what the views of the local gentry would be. They would see it as an affront to their superior status and a risk to law and order.

In fact, they appeared anxious. Mrs David Davies looked worried. Despite his bluster, I caught a hint of fear in her magistrate husband's eyes. No wonder, Magistrate Timothy Powell's plantation nearby had been set on fire at the end of April, four acres burnt. The magistrates in Carmarthenshire had good reason to fear for their property and safety these days, especially those that were trustees of and investors in the turnpike trusts. Feeling was strong against them; after all, the magistrates were the ones imposing fines on those refusing to pay at the tollgates, but it was their own profits they were protecting.

After the service I sauntered up for a word with those in the front pews, as if talking to the gentry was something I did every week. Edwin Davies, Captain Davies's son, was about my age and when we were younger, before he was sent away to school, we'd been friends. The curate had tutored us and we'd liked each other. We'd nod and have a quick word when we met, but somehow as we'd got older, the connections had withered, neither of us knowing quite what to say, but we still felt friends.

'What's the word in the village and in Carmarthen, Will?' asked Edwin.

His father, along with other men in the front pews, leant forward to hear my response.

They needed to hear the truth. 'Many, probably the majority of, farmers in all of Carmarthenshire and Pembrokeshire, support Rebecca. The trusts have allowed gates to be sublet and gates have been set up on side roads that are not on the highway or maintained by the trusts. There is a lot of profiteering and cheating, and of course, the tolls keep rising, although market prices for crops are lower, not higher.'

When I told Edwin how many gates there were, and how much it cost for a load of lime, coal or other wares to get from Carmarthen to many of the outlying farms, he whistled.

'Profits are down for us in Trawsmawr too,' he said.

I replied, 'Farmers are going bankrupt, it's getting harder for them to pay their rents and taxes. Unless something is done about the tolls soon, it's going to hit the landlords' as much as the farmers' pockets.'

His father joined us. 'What about people in Carmarthen, do they support the destruction?'

'Up to a point, although they benefit from the low prices in the market so, unless they have reason to travel, they are less likely to feel strongly about it. That said, the townspeople hate the Poor Law as much as the villagers.'

Captain Davies asked, 'Do you think there will be more trouble here? There has been destruction of gates and property across west Wales since the New Year.'

I replied carefully, distancing us in the village from my reply. 'Honestly, I have no idea; no one knows what will happen next. We are pretty close to Carmarthen, you see, so it's less of a problem in Newchurch. We've only one gate – Water Street – where we have to pay to get produce in or out of town.'

Captain Davies knew I was talking nonsense. Feelings were as high, if not higher, here. It was whispered that local men led the Rebeccas. Of course, no one dared say who those men were for fear of reprisals.

Mr Enoch came over after they left. 'Well handled, William Morgan. You're clever with your use of the English. None of us could have said what you did so clearly and tactfully. We noticed you told them it has nothing to do with Newchurch folk – very clever, considering.'

I grinned and thanked him, relieved he and the others had heard the conversation. I didn't want the same reputation as Gu. It was only later in the day that I wondered why he added the word "considering". Considering what?

Mr Enoch was right, one of the problems in Carmarthenshire was that the majority of farmers spoke Welsh and their ability to use English was limited. Many spoke no English at all. This made it difficult for them to reach any understanding with their landlords, who largely spoke English, and the same with the turnpike trustees. The chasms ran deep between the farmers and the gentry, who may have lived in Wales for centuries and might have Welsh surnames but married amongst themselves. Most had little direct contact with or knowledge of those who farmed their lands as tenants.

Back at the Little House I was not surprised to see Da out turning the hay. Mother was with the girls in the garden in the early afternoon sunshine, podding broad beans ready for drying, although we'd eat some fresh with our tea when the men got back from the fields. I sat helping and teasing the little ones. It felt very good to be home and laughing. When Tom, Shem and Father returned, we had the Sunday tea Mother loved to make, although I couldn't help notice there was no cold meat and wondered if she was scrimping and putting it aside to sell, with money being so tight. Our tea, even without ham, would have been a feast in many cottages around us. I said my goodbyes an hour or so later, after playing a few games of dominoes with my sister, whose counting was coming on nicely.

Gu and Ester were waiting with, of course, a meal set out on the kitchen table. I'd held back at home, knowing it would be there. I tucked in a second time: a cold leg of chicken, thick ham slices with mustard sauce, plum cake and jam tarts filled me up to bursting. Mother was a talented cook, but Ester's cooking was wonderful. She weighed everything by eye and made the lightest, tastiest pastry in Carmarthenshire. I told Gu about the Water Street gate's destruction.

He was sharpening his axe on the whetstone and paused, then scowled. 'No good would come of it, Will.'

‘The authorities will have to listen. The feeling is so strong across the countryside, there will be no stopping Rebecca now.’

‘I hope so, but doubt they’ll listen. The damn generals certainly never did. They are all the same, the gentry – think they know best because they’ve read a book or two. Most of them have never done a day’s work or fought a man hand to hand. Experience and intelligence count for nothing, only coin.’

He put down the axe. ‘Come on, Will, it’s a lovely evening. I have a mind to walk to Garn Fawr and back. It was my Tommy’s favourite place for a walk when he was little. I’d make him a wooden sword from hazel and he’d play at being one of Owain Glyndwr’s men, killing the English. He’d make his little brother George play the English soldiers, of course.’

He smiled at the recollection as we set off up the hill. I was surprised to hear him speak Tommy’s name. None of us ever mentioned Tommy in front of him. Maybe Gu talking was helping.

‘That man you beat in the races last week, I liked him. Gave him a few days’ work digging ditches, so he had some money in his pocket to see him to where he needs to go with the children. I let his children earn a bit gathering stones from the back field too. He told me his father was a soldier in the 42nd and died at Waterloo. He never knew his father.’ Gu shook his head sadly. ‘I’m pleased to have helped his son. His family wanted to move on, try for higher wages in the mines, or I’d have offered him employment, been glad to.’

Gu continued, 'I told you last week about the start of the fight to control the roads into Spain. Not much happened over that winter. It was cold and wet at times, but we were camped comfortably enough among a cork oak wood. On sunny days it was warm like early summer in Wales. Back in the countryside, I felt at home and drilling didn't seem so bad. After "Oh No", being alive and comfortable was enough.

'Campaigning didn't begin again until after Christmas. There were battles fought by other regiments early in the year, which I heard tell was a difficult time, but we were miles away. We were sent to the fortress city of Badajoz before Easter. We didn't make up a name for that city; none of us would ever forget Badajoz. The British army massed outside its forbidding walls like ants ready to swarm.

'The French had held the fortress for many months; they'd ample time to prepare for an assault. It was frightening to face those blank stone ramparts, Will, they looked to stretch for miles. Each side of the city was protected; either by the river, deep moats with spikes poking through, or else there were high walls, built solid and yards wide years ago by the Spanish. If you go to Kidwelly, look at that castle. Think of facing those walls knowing you'll be ordered to run and attack at any moment. Imagine being shot at with musket fire, cannon blasting, stones and oil set alight pouring down on you, men trying to kill you from the safety of solid stone. We knew the French most likely had reinforced or booby-trapped every point the British could attack.

‘We looked at Badajoz and quivered with fear. Our cannon and mortars pounded the city day and night to make breaches in its thick walls; you couldn’t rest or sleep with the crashes and booms. The French had every chance to partially rebuild any damage each night. Foot soldiers were going to be ordered to run at those breaches, like rats into a tunnel. Each division prayed it wouldn’t be their turn to assault the walls. Like as not, the reason I’m here today is that the 44th wasn’t – we were set a different objective.

‘Orders arrived. The 5th Division and Picton’s 3rd Division were told to sortie out in secret at ten o’clock that night. The 3rd Division’s task was to scale the walls and take the castle. The 5th Division, which was my division, was told to storm San Vincente Bastion – that’s what they called the corner tower of the castle, the one nearest the river. It looked impossible to get over the high wall and wide ditch. Our officers tried to reassure us that once the main battle started at the breaches, defenders would concentrate there. In theory, not many men would be left to guard the bastions and castle; the French would not expect such daring raids.

‘We were about fifty in the Light Company, with no knapsacks, only muskets, carrying thirty-feet long ladders, along with bales of straw and bundles of sticks to help us over the ditch. They were rubbish, those ladders, made of green wood and brittle. One split before we could use it, another was too short, didn’t reach the ramparts, but they were the best to hand.

‘It was a warm night, the ditches were thick with slimy mud, it smelt of rotting food and excrement. When I have my turns, in my mind, I hear again the croaking of frogs and feel squishing, filthy mud beneath my boots. I slither and slip in the ditch-water, with a raw burning fear in my guts, terrified of what will happen when the ladders go up.

'The damned officer leading us that night got us lost. We were supposed to attack at eleven, same time as Picton's men attacked the castle. We were late, lost in the mud and the darkness.

'Finally, we were under the bastion. Somehow or other, we managed to use the ladders and bales of hay to get ourselves across the steep ditch below the walls and break through a palisade of logs. More and more crossed the moat in turn. The French spotted us, but it's not that easy to drop stones or shoot straight down a wall. It's getting to the wall that's risky; many of our number fell to the grape and musket shot. We got two, maybe three, of our ladders up firmly against the walls. Others were shoved away with men clinging on, but the more men you have on a ladder the harder it is to dislodge. We hurried up in turn, stomachs churning, praying that the ladder wouldn't be pushed away while we were on it, petrified of what was to come when we reached the top. Our sergeant stood below with a bayonet, making sure no one dared stop.

'There was hard hand to hand fighting on the parapets. Major-General Walker led us himself and on we went as our young bugler sounded the advance. You keep your wits about you, it's kill or be killed. I can see the eyes of one man as I stuck my bayonet in his belly; he looked so surprised as he collapsed. Haven't thought about him in a while. It is a mistake to look a man in the eyes as he dies.'

Gu mused, 'Could have just as easily been me. He had a mole on his cheek, beside his nose, that man; my own father had one just the same. As he choked in his blood and clutched his belly, all I could think of was how like my father's mole it was. As I pulled out my bayonet, it came out with a sucking feeling, and then I rushed on.

'We 44th got our colours up onto the bastion at last. We were the first regiment to get our colours up that day. The bugle had sounded our success so that the other regiments and command along the walls would know we had overcome the French. That gave heart to the battle. Those breaches I told you about were going badly, men dying like flies under the guns of the French. Wellington had halted the attack.

'A rumour spread that a mortar was aimed at us on the parapet and French reinforcements were advancing. To Walker's disgust, we retreated. He stood there calling us cowards, but once fear gets a hold and men start running, you don't want to be the one left behind at the mercy of the enemy. Back along the ramparts we scuttled, back to the tower. Walker had ordered the 38th to hold it as a reserve; they let us through calmly as anything and then fired at the French who were charging forward as we retreated. The French started to panic, the battle turned and they surrendered.

'We left the walls and went into the town. Picton's damn 3rd Division party had captured the castle, successfully scaled its walls. They started shooting at us. They thought we were enemy troops, you see. It was still dark, no one could see what was happening. We had to run from our own troops, take cover from their fire.

'I couldn't reproach them. The chaos of battle is hard to describe. You have a choice: shoot and kill someone, or risk them killing you. Unless you are certain they are friends, you assume they are foes. I'd like to say we were pleased with the victory, but of the fifty Light Company men that went over the top that night, only eighteen of us were standing at roll call next day, the rest dead or wounded. Through that roll call, our band played *The Downfall of Paris*. I can hear the tune now.' He hummed a few sad notes. 'We survivors hung our heads, shattered and wrathful. We wanted revenge.

'That day was my first experience of the sacking of a city. We blamed the Spanish for supporting the French and were bitter. Our losses the night before in the wall breaches were so terrible – nearly five thousand men dead or wounded. Those that survived looked for retribution and, of course, profit. We'd been under canvas or without shelter for months, had been through hell those preceding weeks. We were far from home and there'd been no women for a long time.

'Our soldiers and Portuguese allies decided that anything in that city was fair game, recompense. For two days, men drank brandy, port and wine from the city's cellars, broke into homes, stole food and whatever else they could find. I won't pretend I didn't steal food, wine and the odd trinket from the houses. What I want you to know is that I didn't join in with some of the terrible crimes committed over those days and nights. I saw silver and gold earrings ripped from women's ears and crucifixes from around their necks. Worse, men were raping women in the streets. Picton's 3rd Division came out of the castle at dawn. Some went into a nearby convent and violated the nuns, evil devils.

'It was horrible to watch. Men, women and children were dragged from their houses and shot or beaten. The Spanish were our allies, despite them only having a government in Cádiz and cowardly armies that wouldn't fight because of their lousy generals.

'I was relieved when Wellington ordered up the gibbets and announced that those found looting or raping from then on would hang. It was necessary to maintain army discipline. More than that, the French were hated, harried and killed by Spanish partisans wherever they went because they committed exactly those crimes so often.

'I can't think why the Duke let it happen. Maybe he was at his wit's end and felt guilty after so many were killed, knew he'd be blamed by Parliament. Hard to judge what Wellington ever thought or felt, really, we soldiers never knew. The only time I ever saw him seem half a normal man was before a battle one time later in the year.

'All of these memories, I don't want or need. The sacking of the city was awful. It's hard to imagine what it would be like if an army came to Carmarthen and did that to us. Think of seeing your mother and little sisters, women and children, bayonetted or worse by filthy ravaging men. It wasn't the ordinary people's fault that the French had forced the city to surrender. War is cruel.'

He stopped abruptly and cleared his throat. 'I'm sorry I told you about Badajoz. It was a bad time for the British, shameful. I try to forget that place. We marched on to

Salamanca after Badajoz. It's a happier story, although truth be known, my poor regiment was dying on its feet.'

Changing the subject quickly, he asked, 'How is your friend John Jones's arm? Is he improving? What is he going to do now that he can't practise his trade?'

Chapter Twelve

Friday 3rd June 1843

All week we woke to news of more gates destroyed across west Wales. Carmarthen town was full of the news but not the detail, everyone waiting to read more in the Friday newspapers. One thing we had heard was that a notice had been pinned to Bwlch Newydd Chapel meeting house door. It said that if anyone paid the toll at the Water Street gate, their goods would be burned and lives taken from them! People coming to market or leaving town were in a quandary: if they paid the toll they were in trouble with Becca and their neighbours, and if they didn't they were in trouble with the law.

Earlier in the morning, John Harris, Talog Mill and Thomas Thomas, Talog shop, along with Samuel Bowen, were called to court in front of Mayor Stacey and Mr Morris as magistrates. Their charge was that they had refused to pay the repaired Water Street toll last Tuesday. John Harris was well known as a radical and agitator. We guessed the three had been deliberately chosen to send a warning across the countryside. They had each been fined forty shillings, with eight shillings and sixpence costs, or else face three months in prison. There was no chance of Miller Harris paying the fine out of principle. Young Sam Bowen worked for his father in The Plough and Harrow; he wouldn't have any savings. I wondered what the authorities would do next.

I set out to walk home on Saturday, but as I rounded the corner of Lammas Street, on to Water Street, I saw Bel walking up the road, struggling with a big basket.

I crossed over to her. 'Can I carry that for you, Bel?'

She started. 'Oh… I want to say no, but my shopping is heavy and it's a long walk home. Yes please, Will. It's not your fault your brother insulted me.'

'He was rude because he was drunk. I'm not going to apologise, he will have to do that himself. I will say he only drank because you'd told him he couldn't marry Ellen. He drinks very little as a rule.'

'I suppose so, but he annoyed me. He acted as if he was doing Ellen a favour by marrying her. My girl is worth her weight in gold. If he wants her, he has to know that. He's the lucky one.'

'I agree, Ellen's a pearl. But why have you refused to let them marry?'

'Two reasons. Firstly, as I told him, she's too young, just seventeen. I'm not having her marry and be worn out before her time or dead from childbirth like some. Nor do I want her to marry in haste when she doesn't have to. That's the main reason: she doesn't have to. I want everyone in the village to know that. I know what everyone thinks of me, they will say the apple doesn't fall far from the tree with Ellen. I had my first child when I was her age, seventeen.'

She looked searchingly at me. I felt my colour rise and had to look away.

'You know, don't you? Does Tom?'

'No, he doesn't. I guessed, then made Mother tell me. She made me swear to keep it a secret.'

'You can promise me the same, I don't want anyone to know. Don't want my boy's memory sullied by how he came into the world. He was with me such a short time. My Dan, born out of wedlock, I loved him so but he ruined me. Who'd marry me after my having an illegitimate child so young? I lied, said I didn't know the father's name. People assumed the worst. I had no choice, there was no point in owning George was the father after he died. Your grandmother, that Susan, was an old witch. She'd have denied it, she made that clear. If I'd tried, she would have told everyone I was blaming a man with no chance of denying it. They would have believed her, not me. I decided it was better not to speak up, to try to forget that awful day.

'Your mother and Ester have always been kind to Ellen and me. They are the exceptions; many of the women are cruel and snide. Men still look at me, appraise me, as if I am one of their heifers, a piece of meat. It's true that in the past, when my children were really hungry, I'd go with one of them for coin or food. What choices do you think I had? You don't know the sorts of things the women say. Elizabeth was told not to allow you and Ellen to play together.

'Now Tom wants to marry Ellen, not some dull farmer's daughter with cows or fields to bring to Cwm Castell. The village gossips will be rubbing their hands, saying she's pregnant, got bad blood. Ellen won't have their respect. She will never be accepted if they rush to wed and a baby follows quickly.

'So I won't agree to it yet, but, if Tom had only listened, I said if they still want to marry in a year's time I'll agree then. It will show the village that Ellen's worth waiting for, it'll give her time to consider. Ellen sees the sense in what I say but doesn't want to admit that to Tom. He tells her it means she doesn't love him as much as he does her. He's a passionate boy but he's young, young and foolish. Won't do him any harm to mature a while either, he needs to learn patience.'

I was shocked but recognised the truth in all Bel said. I had heard tutting and nasty comments about me and Ellen Price. Huw had repeatedly been told by his aunts not to mix with her sort. Father and Mother had told me to ignore them; if Ellen was my friend, that was enough. Many women in the village did treat Bel with suspicion. Was she wrong to make the pair wait? They'd only been courting a few months, after all. I found myself agreeing with her. Persuading Tom she was right was another matter entirely.

We reached the turning to Cwm Castell.

'Shall I carry the basket to the Row for you? It is heavy.'

'No, it was kind of you to take it the last two miles, saved me sweating. I'll manage the last downhill journey.' She patted my arm. 'Thank you, Will. Try to talk some sense to your brother, could you? I don't want Ellen's heart broken, just for them to wait a while.'

After dinner in the Little House, I took Tom aside.

'I spoke to Bel, bumped into her on my way home from work.'

'What did she say? Did you persuade her to give her consent? Can I marry Ellen this summer?'

'No, but I understand Bel's reasoning. I don't entirely disagree with her, in fact.'

'What do you mean? It's not for you to agree or disagree.' He shouldered me aside angrily, then turned. 'Tell me what she said, then.'

'Let's go out to the barn, we can talk without the children hearing.'

We sat on stoops of fresh hay, leaning back. I smelt the sweet-sharp scent of drying grass.

'It's not you that she's against, neither is she against you and Ellen marrying. She thinks Ellen is too young at seventeen and is worried about the local women being unkind to Ellen because she is her daughter and poor.'

'What on Earth do you mean? Why should Ellen and I care what the old wives say? What business is it of theirs?'

'You know how the gossips can be. They will say you are marrying beneath you. You almost said that to Bel yourself at the fair; it's what made her angry. They are likely to say that she is with child and has cleverly trapped you into marriage if you hurry. I have heard one or two of the farmer's daughters being unpleasant to Ellen on occasion when she's been out walking with me. Sarcastic comments about her old dress, with questions and giggles as to why Will Morgan is bothering with her. Implying that she is being free with her favours. They know perfectly well we've been friends since we were small, but that doesn't stop them from being catty. Ellen ignores it but I know it hurts her. In case you haven't noticed, as we've got older different cliques have formed, with the poorer girls sticking together and the farmers' daughters the same.'

Tom snorted but I could see from his expression that he realised it was true.

'Some girls have three babies before they are twenty or worse, die in childbirth because they're barely fully grown. You know it happens, Tom. Remember Ann Jones, Ann Rees that was? It's hard to think of her dying so young.'

It had been the tragedy of the last winter when Ann had died. She was the youngest sister of the Rees brothers, Rhydymarchog, between Tom and me in age. We had known her all our lives from chapel Sunday school and fairs, but everyone in the Hundred knew of her because of her voice. Ann had been born with a most glorious gift: she sang with an astonishingly deep and clear tone.

'A perfect contralto,' Minister Abrahams called it. Ann led the singing in chapel quite unconsciously. Many said she should have gone to London to train for the opera. She didn't, of course, there were no opportunities for that in Newchurch. When Ann was seventeen, she married Michael Jones, Abernant. Nine months later she and her baby were dead, after three long days of labour. Hundreds of people, from every chapel for miles around, came to join the funeral procession for Ann and her little one. In the service, the minister said we had lost "our lovely little songbird".

Tom looked uncomfortable as I continued. 'Bel said if you two still want to marry in a year she will agree. A long engagement will show the farmers' wives you are true loves and Ellen will be respected. If you want to marry, you will have to be patient and prove your affection. If not, then maybe it's better not to wed.'

Tom stomped off, saying, 'A fat lot of help you were.'

I knew he'd come round. Later that night I arrived at the Big House to a great welcome. Ester bustled to get a meal together; they'd eaten much earlier. A fire had been lit in the parlour, it was so cold and wet. Gu was sitting in his old chair staring into it, brooding.

Ester whispered, 'He's had a bad week, Will. Twice he got up in the night with his nightmares, insisting the French were after him. I'm glad you are here but don't trouble him too much tonight.'

She handed me a bowl of thick lamb *cawl* with hunks of bread spread thick with yellow salty butter, telling me to take it in and eat it by the fire with Gu.

Gu looked up and smiled sadly at me, saying, 'I'm glad to see you, boy.'

'How are you?'

'I dare say Ester's told you – not so good. I've had vivid dreams all this week, it was as if I was back there in the army. Ester says I shout out and thrash around. I wake covered in sweat, my heart pounding time and again through the night.'

'Maybe we shouldn't talk about Spain tonight?'

'No, no, I've decided the time has come. I have to talk about it now, I know that. For the first years after I came home, I could no more have told you or anyone else about the war than I could have swum the Towy to Llansteffan.'

Gu couldn't swim at all, so this was a weak joke.

'Then there was no one to tell. People didn't like to ask about it with my wound and everything else. Old soldiers' tales were not welcome anywhere else either. We'd seen terrible things, many were horribly maimed. People no longer viewed war pensioners as heroes who'd beaten Napoleon, but as drains on parish funds. A lot had no choice but to take relief in workhouses. I've heard that in big cities, more died on the streets of hunger. I did all right for myself, but many veterans suffered badly so I kept silent. The memories and the dreams were always there, tormenting me, however much I tried to push them away.

'The first years after I returned from Waterloo were strange ones, quite apart from my unhappiness. Something odd happened to the weather; they were the worst summers in living memory. It hailed in June, then snowed that first September I got back. The year after it was worse. The sunsets were wrong, as if our old sun was bigger and redder than normal, the clouds were blacker, the light weak and thin. Corn didn't ripen anywhere across Europe. The price of bread got higher and higher.

'Although it makes me unpopular, I support the Corn Laws. The laws stop cheap imports of corn from abroad, and farmers' livelihoods being destroyed. Back then in '16 and '17, though, the price of bread was punishing. We managed on the farm – I'd returned with my savings – but folks were starving here in Wales. There were riots across the kingdom. As for the Irish, they had famine. They were terrible times, "the starving years" we called them.'

Gu leaned back in his old chair as I put down the emptied wooden bowl and spoon on the hearth with a clunk.

'Let's move my tale on to Salamanca, shall we? The time I spent there is one of my happier memories, not like the story I told you last week. Maybe that'll cheer me up.

'By the summer of 1812, the main French army had abandoned Salamanca, but they left behind garrisons in three of the city's convents; it took us days to pulverise those convents into submission. That was work for the gunners; we men could rest up. We were camped outside the city walls by the river. After drill each morning we enjoyed ourselves in the city, eating, drinking and yes, whoring for some. Salamanca is a beautiful, golden-stoned city, full of churches, colleges and shops. It had two cathedrals, old and new, with a vast central square where the Spanish ladies dressed in their best embroidered skirts, pinched tight at the waist, flaring out in red and black, silver buttons set off by a silk sash crossed at the front – what a sight. They would walk each evening; it was far too hot in the daytime, they hid away in the day. We were welcomed into the city by the Spanish with singing and dancing. They were delighted to be free of the French. There was no sack, so we soldiers and the locals generally got on. We paid for our food and drink and behaved as well as any army could be expected to. It was a better time and, other than the constant thump of the mortars into the convents, peaceful.'

He looked doubtfully at me then cleared his throat. He lowered his voice. 'Between you and me, I was happy there because I met a little Spanish girl. I was a married man. My excuse – that I hadn't seen Susan in four years and things had been bad between us for years before then – isn't good enough, I know. Maria, the girl was called – they all seemed to be called Maria, those Spanish women. I'd met her after some bad business. To be frank, she'd been violated by a drunken soldier. It wasn't uncommon, I'm ashamed to say, in part because many soldiers didn't respect the Spanish, calling them heathens, and partly because so many of the troops were criminals to start with, joining the army to avoid gaol or the gallows.

'One evening I found Maria in an alley crying, her clothes torn, terrified, too afraid to go home. From what I could work out, her father would have disowned her if he'd found out what had happened. I helped her, cleaned her up, dried her tears, wiped her face and the rest. I had my sewing kit in my knapsack, so together we repaired her dress. I took her home, a respectable enough house above her father's cobbler shop. I returned the next day and she was pleased to see me. She felt I'd saved her, although I'd done little enough. It felt so grand to have a pretty woman waiting to see me, actually liking me after years alone. She had dark, dark eyes, long black hair and a lovely little face. I was very taken, and one thing led to another. What happened next was predictable, she was expecting a child. We couldn't know if it was my child or from the rape really, but to my mind, the assault was once and Maria and I, we were close for some days.

'I was in a predicament. Maria didn't know I was married. She said her father would throw her out into the street when he found out she was pregnant. They were all Catholic in Spain; virginity and virtue was expected of the women. It's not like Wales, where some don't marry when they are expecting a baby. Here, while it's frowned on, it does happen. Maria would have been called a whore, and likely as not had to work as one, if her father had disowned her and thrown her onto the streets.'

His voice lowered. 'Don't you ever tell a soul, but I married her. I knew Susan was alive and it was invalid… bigamy, but I thought, *where's the harm?* You know my views on religion. Catholicism is even more nonsense than the clergy talk here. It would give the babe a name and protect Maria. After all, if it was my child it was only right for it to have my name. Maria knew she couldn't come with the army when we left, she'd seen how the camp followers lived.

'She asked me to promise to come back after the war, but I told her it would be better for her and the baby to say I'd been killed, that she was a widow, and remarry. After all I'd seen in Badajoz, my death in battle seemed a likely thing. I gave her the booty I'd collected. I was better off without them; valuables weigh you down when you march. I gave her French gold coins and a pretty watch, double eagles engraved on the face. I'd taken it from a dead French cavalry officer at "Oh No". Maria gave me a little silver crucifix. I promised her I'd always wear it to keep me safe. I did until Waterloo – it worked – but I tore it off then. I've nothing left of her now but my memories.

'I often wonder if Maria had a baby girl or boy and if the child lived. I wonder too whether Maria is still alive. It was a happy time for me, Salamanca; blue skies, regular pay and a pretty woman doting on me. I was happier for those few weeks than I've ever been since. I don't regret any of it.'

He looked me in the eye defiantly. I was flummoxed. Another family secret shared, another I'd rather not know.

'It's a big secret, that. I realise I can never tell anyone, Gu. Just think, maybe I have a cousin in Spain.'

He replied, 'Aye, but maybe it was never my child either, Will. I'd not have known if I'd stayed. Back to the campaign though… After the three French garrisons were finally defeated we were put to again. Ordered out of the city, we traipsed after the French looking for a place to finally defeat them, but nowhere suited our Duke. It felt as if we might retreat all the way back to Portugal. We were hot, bothered and exhausted. We soldiers wanted to go back to Salamanca or otherwise fight, get on with beating the bastards and go home. It was nightmarish, wandering around a God-forsaken Spanish plain in the hottest July sun in full kit, dragging gun carriages, women, children, horses and baggage. This went on for nearly a month, then when we were between two hills at a place called Arapiles, the French started running across the bare Spanish plain, hoping to recapture Portugal. Wellington was delighted; he'd set up our army to attack, and attack we did.

'The 5th Division was put in the centre of the line near a little wood, which obscured our view. We ended up very close to the French before either side saw each other. The French were trying to manoeuvre so we had the advantage of them. We fired and charged, bayonets fixed. Our dragoons supported us and on their great horses charged them down. Lieutenant Pearce noticed what turned out to be a 62nd French Line officer try to hide their Eagle under his greatcoat. You know what an Eagle is, Will?'

I shook my head; I had no idea.

'Every regiment and battalion has their own coloured flags on poles. They rally to those flags and defend them. It's an honour to hold them and they are given to junior officers to guard in battle. The colours are useful – you can see where your fellows are gathered – but they also represent the regiment's pride. If a regiment should lose its colours, it's lost all its pride, its respect. The French equivalent of that colour is a small golden carved eagle atop the pole above their regimental colours. Napoleon himself gave each regiment their Eagle. I've been told the Romans used the same device; maybe they had an eagle with them up on our Garn Fawr all those years ago. Capturing an Eagle is a triumph for an army and not often achieved, I can tell you – they are guarded to the death.

'There was sharp tussle, Pearce and Finley fighting for the Eagle, my old friend Bill Murray shot a French soldier helping his officer but, helped by some privates and officers of the 30th regiment, Pearce won the eagle. We mounted it on a short spike, called it our golden pigeon we did, and carried it off. What a prize, we were thrilled to a man! The Regiment went down in history for capturing that Eagle. The battle was over in a flash, less than an hour; it was fierce but fast fighting. We kept the Eagle with us overnight, all of us taking it in turns to go up and marvel at it. Lieutenant Pearce was allowed to present it to Wellington the next day, to the Duke's delight. He was generous, was Pearce; he gave the men who helped capture it a share of twenty Spanish dollars. Finley, was even promoted to Sergeant. That was when we got our nickname, on account of us being shorter than many and being the 44th Regiment, we became known as the Little Fighting Fours. We were so pleased with ourselves.

'That was the end for the French. They surrendered and we could march and take Madrid. Napoleon's brother – King Joseph, he called himself – abandoned the city to us. We entered Madrid in high spirits. The 44th were allowed to parade the captured Eagle through the city. It was a nice enough place, but without Maria, it paled for me. We were glad to be safe and rest up, but that didn't last long.

'Soon after Madrid, Wellington attempted but failed to lay siege to the city of Burgos to the north. Before we knew it, after all our triumphs, the army was in retreat. We didn't know why or how. All we knew was that that march back to Portugal was terrible. We revisited Salamanca. There were no celebrations, we were only there a day or so in terrible weather, driving rain and cold. The French army was there too, their numbers much larger than ours. If they'd attacked us, we'd have been defeated. For some reason they didn't; maybe they hated the weather as much as we British. I couldn't get a pass into the city to see Maria. I never saw her or Salamanca again.

'The cold winter rains continued. It poured day after day as we trudged through claggy mud. There were no supplies. Sorties to find food usually failed. The villages around were starving, they had none to spare. The people were thin, bellies swollen, starved. We ate acorns like pigs to stave off the hunger pangs, chewed on our leather straps for sustenance, and all the time the French followed us. No biscuit was issued for eleven days, only a little stringy, tough beef. I've already told you I'd learned my lesson earlier; I knew to hoard food for such times. Saved my life, that lesson, but the food was gone by the second week. After that, I starved with the rest.

'Our last real action as a regiment in Spain was to hold the bridge at a River near Villa Muriel. This was the last straw for the regiment. We had fought all we could but none of us was fit enough to fight. We were broken with marching, the heat, then the cold and rain, and poor provisions on that retreat.

'Had a bit of fun one day before that battle, mind you. A printing press got stuck in a stream; some fool of a Spanish general had decided to bring that heavy machine with him. My Light Company was made to stop to rescue it, pull it out. While we were tugging and straining to shift the press, Lieutenant Grier's greyhounds flushed out a hare. Grier couldn't stop them, they were trained to hunt. Wellington saw them run and he just loved hunting. Then and there, he gave chase after those hounds despite the entire army being lined up and ready for battle. After he caught the hare, he came back to the lines as coolly as anything. He sent an orderly to Grier with the hare and a message, told him they were good dogs but best to send them home, it was not fair for them to be killed in battle. Cared more about dogs and horses than men, it was said of Wellington.

'Grier did as ordered with the hounds, of course, but he kept his little dog, Dash, with him. We all loved that little dog, and Lieutenant Pearce's Welsh Spaniel puppy, Brush, too. Those dogs kept us sane. By stroking and playing with them, they helped some of us survive the terrible hungry times to come. They would flush out birds and game for us, you see; we had the occasional stew if the officers could spare the meat. We mostly starved together on that march, men and officers. You couldn't sleep for the pain of hunger. I felt faint putting one foot in front of another; even marching on the flat felt like climbing a mountain. We got irritable, some couldn't be bothered, not to drink or march or anything. The sergeants had to swear and shout at us to get us to move at all.

'After Villa Muriel, we staggered all the way back to Cuidad Rodrigo in Portugal in November. Only forty or so men from the entire regiment, a handful, were fit enough to fight. I was one of them, no doubt because of my supplies kept hidden in my pack. The proud 44th had started in Cádiz in the spring of 1810, which felt like a lifetime before, with over five hundred men. Less than half that number were alive by the end of October 1812, most so injured or worn they couldn't fight. It was a terrible three years for the regiment, merciless, so many dead. One company, the 7th, was wiped out, only Sergeant Farrell left standing of all those men. They tried to form us into a new battalion in November. It didn't work. Most of us were shipped back to England from Lisbon in spring to recover and recruit more men. I hoped it was all over, that I could sit out my time safely in barracks. That hope turned out to be in vain; there were plenty more battles to be fought.

'Damnation, I'd meant to stop after Salamanca. I didn't mean to tell you of the horrors. That march through the rain, starving, your guts cramping – each step gets harder to take as you weaken. Some lay down in the cold mud and died as we filed past. It doesn't haunt my dreams, but it was a bad time.' Gu fumbled at his waistcoat buttons, anxious and upset.

I felt as dispirited by this tale as Gu sounded. The glories of capturing the 62nd's Eagle were nothing compared with the misery of the retreat. Each week my sympathy and admiration for the old man increased. Would I have survived? How did he return home with no more than a limp and his nightmares? I couldn't imagine. It sounded terrible.

His tale of the girl Maria in Spain astonished me, as much because I couldn't imagine Gu young and in love as because he'd married her knowing he was already wed. It had always been made clear that marriage to Susan was a mistake. I felt sorry for the young grandmother I'd never known, her dreams turned to dust. She had a sad end, dying of a broken heart and melancholy.

Sunday 5th June 1843

Unusually, I'd gone back to the workshop on Sunday afternoon; it was one of the apprentices' birthdays and we'd agreed to meet at The Black Horse for a beer that evening. We missed John Jones; he'd have been at the heart of the fun. I decided to call to see how he was doing and find out whether he might be well enough to join us.

He was recuperating with his mother's aunt on a narrow street of tiny houses close to the quay. I knocked at the door. His aunt, as ancient and small as her house, was delighted to see me. Her home was neat and clean but had barely a stick of furniture, only a small table and two chairs, and there was a little peat fire in the corner on which bubbled a thin *sucan* stew of oatmeal and leek in an ancient pot. A pallet with faded bedding lay in one corner. I asked to see John.

'Come in, come in. John's arm is improving as each day passes, I'm glad to say. You must be the giant, gingery boy from Newchurch. Isn't he a one? John talks about the boys in the carpentry shop all the time.'

Not entirely delighted with the description of my looks, I climbed the narrow stairs to John in the room above. He was in bed but did his best to be cheerful, greeting me heartily as I came through a low doorway into the fusty room.

'I'm getting better, Will, I should be up at this hour, but there is so little to do I went to bed early.'

He'd lost weight; was pale and drawn, with dark rings around his eyes. I tried but failed not to stare at the pinned-up arm of his shirt.

'I can tell by your face – you want to see it, don't you?'

He showed me his stump and I put up my hand over my mouth to cover my shock. Red and raw, pink puckered skin covered the new wound, with black marks all around where stitches had held the skin together across the severed bone. There was no forearm at all – even the elbow was gone. I tried my best to chat about Master David, the boys, the yard and what work we'd got on, but I was shaken.

'How are you really?' I asked.

He shook his head and gazed out of the dusty windowpanes. 'Not so great. What hope is there for me? I lost my right arm and my future when that beam fell. I couldn't be a pot-boy in a tavern with one arm. What woman would look at me now? I could have my pick a couple of months ago. I'm embarrassed to go out. What if one of those girls sees me, disfigured and weak, broken? My aunt has been wonderful but I'm taking the food from her mouth, stopping her sleeping in her own bed. There is not enough money to feed her, let alone me. I'm a burden.' He gulped, half suppressing a sob. 'I've hard choices to make, Will. I can go on the streets and beg, or I can go to the workhouse. I can't let my old aunt starve for me much longer.'

'Hold off doing anything for a few more weeks until your arm is fully healed.' I took out the shilling Gu had given me earlier in the day.

He sighed with relief. 'I'll pay you back as soon as I can. At least we can eat for another week.'

'It's a gift. Think of all the beers you bought me these last years. I'll come back soon with one of the others.'

I started to leave, then turned. 'I wouldn't be a friend if I didn't say this, John. You have to get up and stop hiding away. You may have lost your right arm, but you still have two legs and a left arm. You have to build up their strength. You'd be surprised what a man with one good arm can do. Otherwise, you will end up in the workhouse.'

John glared at me angrily as I retreated down the little staircase.

I thanked John's elderly aunt.

The little woman replied, 'It's no trouble at all, but please call on John again soon. He gets so low alone all the time.'

I'd speak to Master David and maybe Ester, see if they could think of anything to be done for John. We could at least get up a collection to see him through a few more weeks. There had to be work for a bright young man. John's mother was no better off than her aunt; what savings she'd had, she'd spent apprenticing John. His injury was a disaster for his entire family. Somehow we needed to turn around his fate.

As soon as I got back to the workshop, I told David about the visit and John's poverty.

He rubbed his chin thoughtfully. 'I can't employ him. Even if he only swept the yard and did odd jobs, it'd mean putting out old Griff. I could pay back the last year of his apprenticeship indenture money to his mother. Although the doctor cost me a lot, it's only fair. Your aunt and I will have to think about it. It's not easy. Who knows how well he's going to recover? I hadn't heard that he was up from his bed.'

The week went slowly by. Finally, Saturday afternoon arrived and I could go home to catch up with everything happening there. No sooner had I arrived than Da set me to work with Tom, muck-spreading on one of the recently mown fields. With all the rain, it was soft enough to be ploughed next week. Da aimed at getting a crop of Swedish turnips this winter, after all. I wore sacking over my oldest clothes but knew from bitter experience that I'd stink for a couple of nights. I wouldn't be able to go to The Plough tonight.

Sunday 11th June 1843

Sam had stayed in the village with his parents yesterday. He rushed back to the farm with the news. Farmers from Abernant and Talog had attacked Captain Davies's estate in Newchurch in the night. They'd destroyed his house gates and ornamental gardens. It was in revenge for Harris, Thomas and Bowen's arrest and fines.

They'd made a real mess of his gardens. Captain Davies was reported to be furious and Mrs Davies, distraught. When Mother, Ester and I got to the church, the Davies family were not in their grand front pew. We were relieved. No one knew what could be said to them. A few of the congregation might have sympathised, but could not have said anything for fear of reprisals themselves. In any case, many would have sided with the miller and shopkeeper from Talog.

Huw's mother, Mrs Morris, gossiped with Mother outside the church door.

'Thomas Thomas paid the full fine yesterday. His wife is heavy with child, two weeks away at most. Betsy didn't want him to risk prison nor have to run the shop herself with a newborn and two others at her skirts. Miller Harris though is a strong radical, he'd no more pay his fine than fly. I for one wouldn't want to be a constable who tried to take him in. Of course, all the village is with him, he's got the county on his side. That's why all our men are pushed to act. It can't go on.'

Mother looked around as she shushed Mrs Morris. The churchyard was not the place to say such a thing.

It was true that Harris, along with the Rees boys, with their bugles and horns calling everyone to action, were local leaders of the rebellion against the tolls. As a miller, Harris knew how much financial difficulty they made for his customers carting their grain to his mill and back. The tolls were damaging his trade and causing the price of bread to rise. A cartload of wheat cost nearly double to transport than it had a few years before, the same with lime and coal. I wondered at the implication of Mrs Morris's "all our men".

Chapter Thirteen

The church service dragged. The curate won himself no favours with his sermon about rendering unto Caesar what was Caesar's. He was suggesting we should pay the tolls. It was as well Tom didn't ever go to church; he might have walked out.

On the way home I thought again about what Mrs Morris had said. Had Father or Tom joined the destruction? Things had gone too far. There was justification for breaking the tollgates but trampling Mrs Davies's garden and house gates was another matter. I knew Thomas Thomas could ill afford the forty-eight shillings fine, nearly a year's wages for some. However, as Father said, two wrongs didn't make a right. As attitudes hardened, something really bad might happen, someone might get killed. I didn't want my father or brother getting hurt.

I didn't get a chance to ask Da before dinner that day, but he knew I was wondering. After eating, Da went out to the cowshed to give it its weekly clean, despite it being Sunday.

He called Tom and me to help. Da's strong arms swept the besom steadily across the cobbled shed floor as Tom and I drew water from the well and threw it down before him. Father cleared away each morning and evening, but the cowshed and yard was given a thorough clean once a week. He believed it was important the shed was kept clean to stop the milk souring. Many said it was fairies' spells or witches that made new milk turn sour, and kept a hare's foot in their pockets when milking. Da believed it happened more often in dirty yards or when the weather was hot. We had less trouble than many, but still used hawthorn pails for choice, to help keep Satan out of the dairy.

I started to quiz him about the gates and the attack on Captain Davies's home.

'Did you go? Did you see the fences taken down? What about the Water Street Toll?'

'No, it was only Talog men at the Davies's. They didn't ask Newchurch men to go; they knew our loyalties might be split.'

He hadn't answered about the gate. I thought he was avoiding my eye.

'Did you join breaking down the Water Street gate though?'

Tom butted in excitedly. 'Da has been out for nights now with the Rebeccas. He is Charlotte! They look to him for sense and calm, he is one of the leaders of the revolt.' He stopped, took a deep breath, then looked worried as Father paused his sweeping and turned.

'What? You've been out breaking tollgates, Da? You, you are Charlotte?'

'Hush. Of course I have. The right is all with the people, Will, you know that. Your mother and I have been at war over this for months. She is terrified that either I'll be arrested, or Gu will get to hear of it and have one of his tantrums. I'm having none of it. I can barely afford to pay the rent and buy food for the family now. I'm standing up for the rights of the matter. Thomas Lewis's opinion is neither here nor there, I'm going to do what I damn well think is right.'

I was staggered. There had been so much speculation across the county as to who Rebecca and Charlotte really were. Were they even just two men or several? People were always asking who really led the revolt. Da was taking an enormous risk for his beliefs. No wonder Mother was afraid. No one in the village would give him away. I had to hope that, like me, others were ignorant of his identity.

I said slowly, 'In that case, I'm proud of you. I understand and respect what you and the other farmers are doing. I can't help asking why you haven't told me before. Don't you trust me?'

He sighed. 'No Will, I do, but… Don't tell me you never go out drinking in Carmarthen with the other apprentices, I know you do. You are close to your grandfather in a way that none of the rest of us are. I didn't think it was fair or sensible to tell you. When you are in the taverns, who knows what might slip out, who you might be sitting near? You aren't living in Newchurch amongst us anymore. Tom was kept in the dark too and look how he blurted out my involvement. He didn't mean to give away the secret, but it's not always easy to keep silent. As they say, what the eye doesn't see, the heart doesn't grieve after. It felt safer for me and for you to say nothing.'

Tom looked mortified as Father spoke; he had given away their secret in a moment.

Still stung, I said, 'Let's get on with cleaning this shed then.'

Resentful not to have been trusted, I made my excuses once the floor was cleaned and went on down to the Big House. On the walk down the lane, I realised Father's speech explained a lot. Tom was always the talker and had made his views on the unfairness of English Government policies on the lot of farmers clear. Da was a man of few words but known to be radical in outlook. He'd been the one who'd given me his well-thumbed Thomas Paine's *Rights of Man* almost as soon as I could understand, not only read. He always turned first to the political columns of *The Welshman*. It explained why he was so tired some mornings, and why he and mother were always arguing. I remembered Mr Enoch saying how clever I'd been "considering". Now I knew why he'd said that. How stupid of me to have missed the clues. It still hurt, though, that what was happening in my own family hadn't been shared.

I was impatient to know what happened to Gu those years ago, my own problems small beside his back then. It felt impossible that my old grandfather had lived through such terrible times, seen as much, and travelled as far as he had. That he might have fathered a child and married bigamously was astonishing. Gu had never spoken of those times. As his tale unfolded week by week I could see why. No one would want to think about it, anyone would have nightmares and worse.

When I got in, Ester had already told him about the Davies' gardens and he seemed subdued. After supper we went into the parlour where a fire had been lit, although it was warm enough without. I could tell he'd been waiting for me.

He began, 'Let me tell you a little more of my tale, Will. I don't know if it will help, I only know I have to try. You know from last week that we 44th had finally been shipped home from the Peninsular.

'At the end of November 1813, we were sent to the Low Countries, the Netherlands, to fight. We were poorly led. General Graham, he knew nothing of tactics, not like Wellington or Picton. After a poor job capturing Merxem near Antwerp came the siege and battle at Bergen op Zoom. The Little Fighting Fours, with our new recruits to make up regimental numbers, did the army proud. We got into the town, took nine of their bastions, and flew our regimental colours high. Unfortunately, the other regiments weren't of the same mettle; they couldn't fight their way in through the gates. We'd fought our way in, but were stuck inside the town walls, like rats in a trap. The regiment and our army took a terrible pasting. The French had the support of the townsfolk. The Dutch didn't want us there.

'Many died that day, including my comrade of many years, old McCullop. He was a lad; a real chancer, always in trouble, never taking orders as he should. He'd been sentenced to nine hundred lashes in sets over nine weeks before the assault. A terrible sentence – he'd hit an officer you see. McCullop begged to be released from detention to join his comrades in the battle, saying he was "a bad soldier in quarters but a good one in the field". He was allowed the chance to fight and I heard it said he killed at least nine sentries. Poor man, he died that day too. He might have been better taking his punishment, but nine hundred lashes – that could well have killed him.

'The French took hundreds of us prisoner. We'd fought long and hard to get in op Zoom but then there was no way out. The 44th fought so bravely the French recognised it; they gave us back our colours. As prisoners we were well treated, and the army managed our release a few days later, thank heaven. You had to respect the French. They were men of their word. It was rare for them to kill those they defeated if they surrendered. There was a code, you see, that both sides stuck to. Not like those Indians in America that'll scalp a soldier as soon as look at him. Our first battalion was said to have been scalped to a man by those savages in the French-Indian war, years ago. Imagine that. We were pleased they let us go straight away. French prisoners of war were kept rotting on captured ships and in barracks for years at home and we feared that might happen to us.

'It was after that battle, in the winter of 1813, that a letter came telling me of George's death.' He paused. 'He was a strange lad, my George, it's hard to say why. I never understood him. As a baby he was irritable, didn't like to be hugged or fussed. He had routines that he needed us to stick to, clothes he liked and didn't like. We had to do as he wished or there'd be screams and tantrums galore.

He led his mother a real dance. It was another sticking point between us. I said she had spoilt him. She said I didn't understand, George had to have things that way or it'd cause him real distress. He was an odd child, hard to love. I didn't feel his death as the blow I should have. I feel guilty about that too. I failed my sons. I couldn't feel the same for him as I did for Tommy and your mother. It was as if there was a piece of glass between us; we never really touched. I don't know, as I say that, it sounds unfeeling of me.' He looked sad and perplexed. 'Let's carry on with my story, shall we? I don't have any answers for that question of my feelings for George.

'The war seemed to have ended when Napoleon abdicated and went to Elba in April 1814. The 44th weren't sent home; instead, we were stationed in Ostend for all of that year and into the next. It was a comfortable billet, Ostend. We liked the locals and they liked us. The girls were pretty. Loved their lace, those girls. They brewed the best beer you can imagine in Ostend. Monks brewed beer there like everyone else.

'I fell on my feet, posted in Belgium on the coast. Lots of us lads who had trades continued them. So if you were a cobbler, a cordwainer or a smith there was work aplenty if you had time spare, as we did in Ostend. You are wondering what my trade was. I could hardly farm now, could I?' He laughed. 'It was smuggling again, contraband. The channel itself was free enough then, Napoleon imprisoned on Elba. Taxes were still high, so of course, there was always a demand for cheaper wine and brandy, and I was stationed at a port, after all.

'I called on a network of old acquaintances, ships' masters and mates, as interested in making money as me. I bought brandy and gin from the Dutch a few miles away, and other luxuries – such as lace, although lace was not so fashionable then – and shipped it back to south Wales. The wares went in on ships that were bound for home, picking up coal or copper or dropping off timber. You could bribe the Ostend customs men as easily. Who was to notice a few extra barrels or crates going over the water? It made me plenty of money over that year. I was careful; small shipments in flat-sided half ankre tubs, that's a little over four gallons of brandy, but it'd make me three pounds profit each tub. I never over-extended myself; ships sink regularly enough, and too much supply reduces the price of your stock.

'The consignments went to Susan's brothers in Pembrokeshire. If the excise men were around there'd be signals made and the captain would sink the tubs with a sack of coal marked with a little buoy and feathers. It'd be collected when they'd left. Your uncles and I used the Black Ox bank in Llandovery to make sure we kept our profits safe. They sent me gold coin and Bank of England notes through some of the captains we knew from Pembrokeshire. Your uncles put away my share of the profits back into the bank. You need a network you can trust to do right by you and those men and I were kin. I'd like to see those boys, your great-uncles, again, talk about old times. I often wonder how they're doing. I suppose I should have gone with Ester on her summer trips to Tenby. I'd have seen them then.

'Smuggling was and still is a way of life across the English channel between France and Britain, with taxes so high. In Dunkirk, Roscoff, Rye and Deal there was so much smuggling, it was their main trade – it may be still for all I know. That Rye was known as the main route helped me. The English customs men weren't interested in boats full of Norwegian pine bound for Wales or Ireland. A boat stopping off to pick up a few barrels along with a load of coal wasn't noticed or remarked on.

'Smuggling was so common that soon after the war, the Government introduced a coast guard down on the channel to stem the flow. Didn't succeed, of course. The only thing that will stop smuggling is a free trade, cutting the taxes so there is no profit to be made. Parliament is debating free trade now, or so the papers say, but unless and until it happens there will always be smuggling, in my estimation. I doubt they'll agree myself, too stupid to see high taxes means more smuggling and people avoiding taxes. It's what lost us our American colonies; they called it a tea party, taxes so high on tea. A pound of tea would cost a few pennies in France but sold for shillings at home, more in America. The colonists threw tea into the harbour in protest.

'Look at all the problems around Carmarthenshire with the taxes so high. If they don't do something soon, there will be riots. They don't understand us in Wales, that London Government. I could do better, so could many. The problem is our representatives are all from the gentry, they know little of everyday trade and life. All they are interested in is their own pockets. They say there's been reform; it's true I've had a vote these last ten years, but who can I vote for who might understand what's needed? A choice between one wealthy fool or a different fool; neither represent the interests of those who elect them, unless they are rich. That's not a real vote.' He looked at me hard. 'Don't you go telling your father I said that. Don't want to be taken for a radical now, do I?'

'In Spring of 1815, once the news that Napoleon had escaped from Elba reached us, we knew there was trouble coming. Regiment after regiment began to arrive in Belgium from all over England and Ireland. The 44th unloaded the equipment – artillery, cannon, horses, shot and the like – into port. It was hard work; most of that equipment was landed onto the beaches and needed pulling ashore before the tide spoilt it. Dragging heavy equipment across the sand is not easy. Then the 44th was marched on to Brussels to join the rest of army.'

He'd started breathing faster. I could see droplets of sweat forming on his forehead.

'Are you well, Gu? Are you sure you want to carry on? I don't mind if…'

'Damn it, don't fuss me, boy. You, Ester and your mother. You're all the same. I'm not infirm, nor am I stupid.' He stood up, then glared around the room. 'I'm going to bed. I've had enough mollycoddling.'

Chapter Fourteen

Monday 13th June 1843

I set off for work as usual next morning, but as I got to Trevaughn there was a commotion. Carts and animals were stopped, blocking the road. Marching towards me in heavy black woollen uniforms were four of our town constables: Woolcock, Woozley, Evans, and Martin. They were followed by a jeering crowd. A carter hoarsely called an aside to me, loud enough for everyone to hear, especially the constables.

'Word has already gone up the valley. These bastards are off to visit Harris and Bowen, as they have refused to pay their fines. They'll try to confiscate their belongings instead. The people will stand by our champions. They'll fail to get a penny piece, you'll see.'

The constables pushed past, truncheons in their hands, avoiding catching anyone's eye. I smelt sour sweat and realised they were afraid. Like everyone else. I jostled them back, shoving as hard as I could against Woozley, an unpleasant thug who swaggered round town, leering at women and glaring at young men like me. I couldn't resist joining the throng and following, although I knew Gu would have told me not to be seen with the protestors. I'd be in trouble with Master David too, late for work again. The hedgerows were full of people and there was a hum and muttering as we went on for the next miles. At The Plough, the crowd following got larger and the noise increased, as did the excitement. What would happen? Might Rebecca herself appear?

Sam Bowen's father insisted Sam had no money or property of his own, he was simply a lodger, so the constables moved on towards Talog Mill. By then the word was really out. I heard a horn sound. Two or three hundred people had gathered around the mill, many dressed as women with blackened faces to disguise themselves. Most of the men were armed with scythes, picks, axes or crowbars. The constables looked terrified. Woozley's truncheon hand started to shake. They had no choice but leave without attempting to execute their warrants. In the face of the huge crowd, no one with any sense would have attempted it. The entire district was up in arms, more rushing to the call with every moment.

The leaders in their gowns told the constables, 'More tollgates will be broken over the weeks to come. We will be heard. The fines are unfair.' The four left to boos and hisses; one woman threw a clod of earth at them.

The lead Rebecca told her off, saying, 'We are not a rabble or rioters, but protesters simply asking for fair play and our rights.'

I got back to Master David's workshop by around midday. As I'd expected, he was annoyed that I was gallivanting when I should have been working. When I explained what had happened and where I'd been, he grunted and told me my mother would be cross but admitted he would have done the same. I was off the hook.

As the week went on, more and more news circulated around the town about the Rebeccas and their resistance to the tolls. The town and county magistrates were worried and started asking townsmen they trusted if they would agree to be sworn in as special constables. David was asked, like many others.

He had told them, 'No, I don't want to be involved in this dispute. I do business with farmers too, not only in the town. There may be reprisals if I sign up.'

The whole county felt at war, especially my own Hundred, a battle about to begin. The magistrates met to decide what to do next later on Friday afternoon. We heard they'd agreed to try again to take goods in lieu of fines from the two men who had not paid. Anticipating trouble and resistance, they called out all the town constables, along with some twenty or so pensioner militia and special constables.

David told me what happened next from one of his friends who was in the militia and had gone with them.

'Several Welsh constables, including the head of police, John Pugh, claimed they were unwell and couldn't join; the English bully boys, Woodcock and Woozley, went, of course. A force of around forty men, headed by Mr David Evans, road surveyor, set out early at three on

Tuesday morning, hoping to avoid the Rebeccas. Some were tipsy; they'd stayed up drinking the night before to keep up their courage. A number of the town constables drank, the taverns were expected to give them beer free, or suffer the consequences. When the group got close to Talog Mill at around five-thirty, they saw a Becca in a cap keeping watch; a little later they encountered forty "ladies" standing, observing them. The surveyor tried the mill door but it was locked. The group finally found a key and gained entry. They took two boxes of Harris' property and set off back to Carmarthen.

'The constables and veterans went a little way but were quickly surrounded by hundreds of people, dressed in women's clothing, with faces blackened or masked. Around half were said to have guns and the rest sticks, scythes and axes. The leader ordered the constables to give up their guns and the boxes. Mr Evans drew out his pistol and threatened them, trying to force his way through the crowd. At that, Constable Richards was knocked to the ground and kicked. Surveyor Evans was seized, threatened and his pistols taken from him, then they were forced to walk on to Trawsmawr, Magistrate Davies' home.

'The leader of the Rebeccas asked for the warrant to be read, which Constable Richards did, but in English. The crowd started to interrupt and shout as, of course, most could not understand a word he was saying. The constable was made to translate it into Welsh and the crowd demanded the names of the signatories for the warrant. Mr Morris and Mr Stacey had signed the document. The leader of the Rebeccas asked if Captain Davies had signed too. He was told no, but that the Captain had backed the warrant.

'At that, the policemen and veterans were made to take down the recently repaired garden walls of Trawsmawr. The force was finally allowed to leave, with taunting and shoves from all sides, women poking at them, men spitting at their feet. They were quaking in their boots. The Rebeccas told them they'd knock down the workhouse as well as the tollgates one day soon.'

David said, 'Our Beccas believe they've won a battle and the tide is turning in their favour. They want to keep up the pressure on the establishment, but the magistrates think the local population is out of control. It won't end well. The authorities are bound to take action.'

Since the Chartist tragedy in Newport in Monmouthshire, there was little doubt in anyone's mind what that action would be: they'd call in the army.

There were reports that the farmers had asked Mr Lloyd Hall, a radical lawyer and supporter of justice, to act for them some days ago. Representatives from each parish attended a secret meeting with him to ensure he had the information to put across their case fairly to the mayor and magistrates, and to the government.

On Wednesday night the leaders called gatherings of farmers across the Elvet Hundred. They decided to demand from the Newcastle Emlyn Turnpike Trust a debtor and creditor account for the last eighteen months, to check if the tolls had been taken honestly. They agreed if they found their books in order they would leave the Water Street tollgate alone; if not, they would destroy it again. The farmers determined to call on the entire county to demonstrate and hand a petition to the Mayor.

They issued notices on chapel doors across the Hundred. The notice told that, "Every adult man, rich or poor, under sixty-five years of age must join a march for rights, unless they should be ill, when they should send a representative. Those with horses should ride. Those who do not join will have their barns burnt."

In several meetings, people demanded that the workhouse should be destroyed, as well as the tollgates. The march was announced for Saturday, but by the time I finished up work at midday there was no sign of any demonstration, so I set off for home as usual. When I arrived, it seemed unduly quiet. Mother was as terse as I've ever known her.

'It's you, is it, Will? No doubt you'll be wanting to talk to your father and brother. I dare say you'll want to take the same risks with the constabulary as those two.'

I was not sure how to reply. I'd no idea what Da had said or what had happened all week at home. I mumbled something about the magistrates not being able to arrest every man in the county, and that I hadn't done anything she needed to worry about. Mother looked cross and stalked out into the yard.

Da shushed me, gesturing toward the young ones, saying, 'Let's speak in the barn in a while. I'll tell your mother I want a hand repairing one of the wheels of the cart, which in point of fact I do.'

I sighed, guessing he'd want me to hold the cart up if the wheel wasn't turning properly. Fixing it could take a while; my arms would ache tonight. We went out and stood to inspect the wheel. I pointed out that two of the spokes were cracked through, the wheel was bowing without their support and couldn't turn true.

Da looked grim as he turned to me. 'Will, you have to join the march, whatever your mother thinks. The mood is ugly all over the county; our family have to be seen to support this action. I'm worried about Gu and what he will say and do. I can't see him joining in the march on Carmarthen, but he's sixty-three, not sixty-five, so he will be expected. The idea is that every farmer joins so no one can divide us and pick off ringleaders. Everyone, even the gentry, let alone farmers like Gu, is expected to march. This will demonstrate to people that you have to be with us or against us. The leaders will probably accept Gu is ill if he offers a substitute, which we will say is you, Will. He will be vexed at being represented. I'm tempted not to tell him and get on and do it.

'Right then, good boys, we must get on. Lift while I knock this wheel off.'

Tom and I strained to take the weight. To my relief the wheel came off cleanly. After last week I found myself pleased, felt a surge of joy at joining in at last. Hearing about the gate breaking as if I was an outsider had been frustrating me more and more these last days. It was as if I counted for nothing now I was a carpenter, not a farmer. It made my old feelings of being second best at home swirl back. I was glad to do something for the cause.

Tom spoke up. 'Da, once we have finished repairing the wheel, would you mind if Will and I go for a stroll?'

Da glowered. 'Fine, go on then, go.'

'Whew, I'm glad to be out of there,' Tom whispered later. 'Mother and Father have done nothing but argue and bicker all week. She's worried we are going to get arrested and gaoled with the Rebeccas. Nothing Da can say will convince her otherwise. He's not budging in that he will stand up for his rights with the other farmers.'

'What has Gu to say about it?' I asked.

'We've been avoiding him all week. Da doesn't want to argue with him too, Gu's his landlord. If Gu told him not to go, it'd put Da in a tight spot, he wouldn't be able to pretend to listen. I've no idea how much Gu knows. I doubt the farm hands will tell him anything unless asked. He's tucked away down the lane, he may not have heard much. What did you tell him last week?'

'Nothing, he'd had a bad week with his turns and wasn't interested. He wanted to talk about the past.'

'That's just as well. He'd be outraged if he thought he was expected to go on the march next week. Da has told people already that you will go in his place. Imagine if they burnt Gu's barns.'

'So it is going ahead? I'll be in Carmarthen, will that matter?'

'No, it's where we are off anyway. Make yourself visible to the men from the village so everyone knows you came. Be sure you don't tell Mother either, she's angry enough with me and Father. I'm off to see Ellen. I'll see you tomorrow.'

He hesitated, then put out an arm to delay me. 'I've something to show you. It's finished.'

Bashfully, he drew out a love spoon carved from plum wood from his breeches pocket. He'd been working on it for weeks.

'What do you think? Will she like it?' His face was a picture of doubt.

'It's beautiful; she will love it. It's very well worked and has polished up beautifully. That's the thing with plum, takes a lovely lustre with beeswax.'

He looked so relieved I had to laugh out loud.

'Brother of mine, you've got it bad, haven't you? I'm sure she'll like it. Look at how you've worked the hearts and diamonds into the design, and a wheel at the top. Master David couldn't have done better.'

Tom hugged me, something he'd not done in years.

He grinned. 'You're right, I have got it really bad.' He left, whistling cheerfully.

I wondered if I'd ever find a girl I liked enough to carve a spoon for. Would she love me back? Maybe I should practise. I liked the spoons that had small balls that rattled inside the spoon handle, but that looked tricky. They also signified children. I wasn't sure I wanted too many children, or could manage to carve more than three balls.

I wondered what to do next. No one in the Little House seemed happy, staying wasn't an attractive option. I decided to go up the valley, visit Huw to hear about the protests for the people's cause. He'd certainly know everything there was to know. Huw loved to gossip nearly as much as his mother. He was very friendly with the Rees boys from Rhydymarchog since I'd started my apprenticeship. It was the Rees's hunting horn that called the Beccas out when needed around Newchurch.

Huw was in a lively mood, intent on filling me in, delighted to hear I was going to join the big march as Gu's substitute.

'It's going to be on Monday, Will. We've put it about it will be tomorrow to keep the authorities guessing, but agreed we'll draw up the banners and the procession will start from The Plough. The aim is to hand in evidence and petitions on Monday afternoon at the Guildhall. We're at the heart of it in Newchurch, we'll make the government listen. We have to eat, we can't be bled dry by taxes and tolls. If they don't listen then there will be trouble all over Wales, and England too.'

He told me who was marching. I was surprised so many women were joining the procession.

'Why would they miss it? It's the most exciting thing to happen here in years.'

'But what if they send for the troops, Huw? Many were killed in Newport, Peterloo and Bristol by the army. I know we don't have a garrison here in Carmarthen but it's not so far from Brecon or Cardiff.'

He snorted. 'They don't know when we'll be starting though, do they? It's a long way from Brecon if you haven't set out until the news reaches you. It's there and back, you see.'

Huw's mother called out to us from her kitchen. 'Tea's ready. No doubt that big, soft Will Morgan is as hungry as ever, though he is nearly a master carpenter now.'

When we were younger, Huw and I ate as much in each other's homes as our own, often with little Ellen in tow. I felt comfortable sitting with Huw's brothers and sisters around the table. His father used a bone-handled knife to carve thick slices of pink ham to be topped with eggs and cheese. There were mugs of tea for the children and warmed small beer for the men. The talk was of how the crops were growing and the barley was doing nicely, and the price of silks and ribbons. Mrs Morris didn't like political talk at her table. She ruled her kitchen as firmly as any captain his ship.

When it came to gossip, she was queen. She delighted in telling us all about poor Miss Louisa Bowen-Morgan, Knightsford House. Knightsford was one of the best houses in the village. Miss Bowen-Morgan had been called before the court as a bankrupt this month. She was staying with cousins over in Glangwili. *Would the poor woman be sent to debtors' prison?* we wondered. Surely one of her wealthy relatives would help her. How would she cope if she was?

Mr Morris said cynically, 'Maybe if she'd had fewer dresses for church and spent more on labourers for the farm, Miss Bowen-Morgan wouldn't be in the position she is now.'

Mrs Morris jumped to her defence. 'Times are hard and lots of people are going bankrupt. Thomas Griffiths, the butcher, and Robert Richards – who has two jobs, miller and policeman – are in court for bankruptcy next week. Dowman's Tinplate work has gone under too. How can a woman be expected to manage a farm alone? Her father should have sold and given her an allowance, not expected her to run the farm.'

Huw's youngest sister interrupted. 'But Mother, you keep telling us women manage money much better than men. That we should make our husbands let us manage the household's funds if we can, so our men don't waste it.'

Mrs Morris looked embarrassed as her husband, Huw and I laughed at her.

'Caught out, my dear,' boomed Mr Morris, 'but I will own that not every woman has your excellent abilities to manage a farm, money and your men.'

The bankruptcy was no surprise to any of us. Miss Bowen-Morgan was kindly but distractible. She found it impossible to be strict with her servants and farm workers, who took constant advantage. No doubt they regretted it now; well-paid farm work was hard to come by. We knew she'd loaned money to prop up her brother-in-law's failing jewellery shop. We agreed it must have been another sore for Mrs Davies, Trawsmawr. She and Miss Bowen-Morgan, who lived around the corner, had been firm friends. It left Captain and Mrs Davies ever more isolated in the village now she'd moved away.

The conversation moved on to Lion Israel, one of the few Jews living in Carmarthen, who had taken John Anthony to court. Anthony, a notorious troublemaker, had got drunk in The Crown and started pulling Lion's beard, when things had got out of hand. Anthony had been fined one pound ten shillings, with thirteen shillings costs.

'That will stop him drinking for a while. Too much drinking goes on in Carmarthen in all those taverns,' was Mrs Morris' conclusion. She looked sternly at me while saying so. I quivered. Was that what was being said of me?

It was true, I had been drinking more of late. She was also right that there was at least one inn or tavern for every few houses in Carmarthen. There were nearly a hundred in the town alone; the quay had more taverns than houses or warehouses.

After tea, Huw and I slipped away, aiming to get to the tavern early, despite his mother's injunctions. We were intercepted by the Rees brothers. They'd been around the village collecting any old sheets that could be spared to make banners for the march. I was known for a steady writing hand, so they asked me to draw up the Newchurch banners; other villages would be bringing their own. We couldn't agree whether to make them in Welsh or English. The people would understand Welsh, but the message was aimed at the authorities, who mostly spoke English. In the end, we decided to use Welsh, because it was the true voice of the people. I worked out the spacing to fit and wrote:

TOLL RHYDD A RHYDDID
(Free tolls and freedom)
RHYDDID A GWELL LLUNIAETH
(Freedom and better food)
CYFIAWNDER A CHARWYR CYFIAWNDER YDYM NI OLL
(Justice and lovers of justice are we all)

We finally made The Plough and had a grand time. At last, I felt at the heart of things. Wilder and wilder threats were made as to what we'd do to the local police constabulary and to the workhouse Master and Mistress on Monday. Huw and I tumbled out of the tavern and returned to our homes, worse for drink. Ester looked cross and tutted at me.

Gu told her, 'Leave him alone, he's young and foolish, but so were we all. You, upstairs. Go and sleep it off!'

I woke late next morning. My head ached, I couldn't face my bacon.

Ester had no sympathy. 'Get up and put on your breeches at once, William Morgan. You're accompanying me to church and can drive the trap. Let's hope neither God nor the vicar can smell your breath too well.'

I groaned but complied. I was only called my full name by Ester if I was in trouble. Mother and Da were not wearing their Sunday clothes when we picked up my sisters. They weren't going to a service this week and looked worn and unhappy. Tom had already walked on to chapel.

Attendance in St Michael's was low. The Davieses were still absent. I overheard Mrs Charles say Mrs Davies had gone to Tenby to recuperate from her worries and would take the waters. I could see the vicar shaking his head over the collection plate. People were subdued, bustling away straight after church. There was no gossiping outside, although it was pleasantly warm.

I decided an easy afternoon was called for and sat under my favourite tree in the orchard. Gu came to join me.

He called Simon to fetch his chair and then we sat looking down the familiar green valley in the sunshine.

'It's beautiful, isn't it? So calm and peaceful, you'd never think land could be otherwise. I had another turn last Tuesday, you know? I know why they have started again;

it is because I can't get the memories out of my head. But the worst ones I still block out, dare not think of. I wonder every night how to tell you, how to find the words for what really happened. It was my fault, all mine. If I don't own up now, I never will.

'When we arrived in Brussels, we learned we were to join Picton's 5th Division. We were pleased; he was known to be a fair and experienced general, if reserved. We trusted him, that he was a Pembrokeshire man helped me like him. Picton dressed and looked like any Pembrokeshire farmer, a sturdy fellow. He always wore his old greatcoat over a blue jacket with a black neckcloth and an old top hat. It turned out Tommy and his 95th rifles were in the 5th Division too, although they arrived in Brussels sometime after us that month.

'After nearly seven years, I saw my son again. How he'd grown. He looked handsome, smart in his green drummer uniform. I shed quite a tear or two that day. If you want to know what he looked like, he was a spit of your brother – maybe a little shorter, but the same blue eyes and dark brown curls.

'Tommy was embarrassed to spend too much time with his father because I was a corporal and old by his lights, but most days I'd find a way of catching sight of him. We managed a few evenings together after inspections and drills. I was very proud, especially if any of the 44th saw us. It wasn't unusual for fathers and sons to be in the army, sometimes brothers joined up together too.'

He stopped and sighed. 'I can't do it, I can't say the words, to tell you about it. How can I be sitting here in the sunshine on the farm when my boy never came home? How can that be? We will have to leave it for next week, Will. Let's see how I feel then, shall we?'

It felt as if everything in my world was coming to a head at once. I felt sick but excited. I was going to be part of the rebellion at last, join with my family and friends to demand action from the authorities.

Chapter Fifteen

Monday 20th June 1843

Monday dawned fair, the sky palest blue, hazy with the promise of a hot day ahead. There was no point in my going to the workshop if I was expected to join the procession as Gu's substitute. The march aimed to make the Guildhall and town square by noon, so I'd have to leave work as soon as I reached the yard. Word had travelled; people from the surrounding countryside and many from Carmarthen flocked to join us on our way to Bwlch. Travellers from further west who hadn't known of the march either joined on seeing the gathering or hurried into town to spread the news.

Early in the day magistrates Captain Evans Pantycendy along with John Lloyd Davies came to Bwlch to try to argue against the march. They suggested we put in a written petition to the authorities instead. With hundreds gathered, the crowd was in no mood to send in a letter. It wasn't as if there hadn't been years of debate and complaint. The Mayor and magistrates had made no efforts to represent our views to London and Parliament.

It was, as Father said, 'Too little, too late.'

The lead Rebecca spoke. 'Go home. We will give no undertakings whatsoever, nor will we write a letter. We have been complaining and petitioning for years.'

Captain Evans was trusted and better-liked than most magistrates.

He called out, 'If you won't stop, then at least make sure this march is peaceful. I implore you to leave your weapons here. If you do not, the government can claim you have joined an armed insurrection. That is treason.'

In the end, most took his advice to leave their firearms behind. Old muskets, pistols and the odd rifle were given over for safekeeping at Trevaughn. Everyone was relieved, even gun owners; unarmed men couldn't be called a riot or a civil disturbance. Most still carried sticks and cudgels, although Tom, Da and I didn't. They'd given Mother their word that they'd not raise our arms in anger, simply march. A few women carried stout brooms, to sweep away the foundations of the tollhouse and workhouse.

The procession assembled at The Plough and Harrow, falling into ranks four and five men wide as if we were a regiment. We set off into the bright morning sunlight, led by a band of musicians. We were uplifted, a determined throng with a shared purpose. Our banners held high, we sang Welsh hymns to the band's tunes and kept our steps in time, an army of the just. There were nearly a thousand of us by the time we reached the outskirts of town. Father rode with three hundred other men on horseback at the rear. John Harris on his dark bay horse led the march, looking handsome in his ringlet wig, red flannel gown, and white bonnet. He was surrounded by a posse of tough men for protection. It felt more a carnival procession, everyone laughing and joking, enjoying their day free of work. The noise deafened me, people were singing and shouting, banging pots and pans, curved hunting horns sounding clear across the valley. Tom and I were near the front; we'd got there early, being so close and having to carry up the banners. We were grouped by village so I could see Huw and the Rees lads a few rows in front of me. It felt wonderful to be part of this movement for a change. Nothing could stop us.

In Carmarthen we had to slow to get through the narrow streets. There was a constant push at my back. If you tripped, I thought, there'd be little escape from the marching feet pressing on and on. The air was hot and still, I was covered in sweat from marching and the bodies squeezing around me. Shops and businesses were closed, no stalls were open. From every window and street corner people watched, either cheering or looking frightened. Carmarthen troublemakers, those always up for a fight, tucked into the procession. They'd want to cut a purse or start a fight. They'd no interest in the cause.

We passed Fountain Hall; went down Water Street to the monument, where many more marchers from St Clears joined, then along Lammas Street. As we passed the workshop, I waved to David watching from an upstairs window. We marched around to the quay, on to St Peter's Church and back to the Town Hall, where we gave three loud cheers. I'd expected that once the petition was handed in that people would leave for their homes or go to the taverns in town.

After so much enjoyment and excitement, the crowd didn't want to stop. There was muttering about not only tearing down the tollgates, but the workhouse too. The march wheeled round, moving as one body, making for the Union Workhouse. The force at my back was so strong I could barely breathe as we climbed Waterloo Terrace.

At the edge of the crowd I saw the pale, frightened face of John Jones, his stump bandaged and coat pinned. He was being pushed to and fro, having problems balancing as he tried to protect his wound from the jostling throng. If he fell, he'd stand no chance in the melee. I nudged Tom urgently, pointing over to John, saying we had to get him out of the street and to safety. With difficulty, we forced a path through the crowd over to him. I saw the Waterloo Bakery and tried the door – it wasn't locked. We dragged John in and out of harm's way.

It was dark and warm in the shop. The glass front windows were shuttered and it smelt of yeast, fresh crusty bread and spices. In a corner, looking terrified, then relieved as she recognised us, was Mrs Eliza Jones.

She rushed up to us.

As we tried to explain, she exclaimed, 'Thank goodness you are here. I was so afraid all alone, it was so kind of you to think of me.' She smiled directly at John.

We were taken aback. Tom started to correct her and said, 'No…' I kicked him to be quiet. She asked us if we'd like tea and cake.

'Yes please, Mrs Jones, it's been hours since breakfast, but we must be quick. Tom and I need to get back to the procession. I'm sure John will be delighted to stay to look after you.'

'I've been thinking about you, John, ever since I heard about your accident. I am so relieved to see you today, and looking so well. Sit down, make yourself comfortable, please.'

John smiled, gratified, and settled into her husband's old chair in the corner of the shop. He waved his hand at us as if to say *go, I'm fine*, as Eliza handed around sweet buns and tea.

I gobbled down a currant bun, fresh out of the bakery oven, warm and delicious, then gulped down my tea.

'I'm off back to the procession. In case you find Da first, Tom, I'll meet you by the Water Street Toll in, say, half an hour?'

I swung out of the door and hurried up the road towards the workhouse. There were only a few stragglers left on the street. When I neared the workhouse gates it was another matter: a huge mob was there; some trying to get in, others trying to get out through its narrow entrance. People were shouting and swearing, a horse was rearing, tossing its head, terrified. I grabbed the reins to calm it. That helped; leading the horse got me through the mass and to the wooden gate. My mouth dropped open, there were hundreds inside the courtyard. People were breaking anything they could find, bedding and straw mattresses were being thrown from upstairs windows and crashing onto the yard below. A man was hiding a pewter bowl inside his jacket. Desperately I looked around for Da. This was not a place to be found, there were bound to be reprisals for all this destruction. I needed to get him out and home. I couldn't recognise anyone in the crush and I could hardly speak, let alone see him. I heard a familiar voice shouting to the crowd. It was Frances Evans. She'd been home in Newchurch with her new baby for the last couple of weeks. I spotted her at the head of a group of men.

'Follow me, boys, I know where the master and mistress keep their spoils. We'll get back all they've stolen from honest men and women.'

They went into the master's house and disappeared from view. I spotted a movement inside the gate on the left. It was our grey mare, Dainty. If she was there, Da would be with her. Now where was he?

I heard folk calling for silence. People pointed to an upstairs window. Mr Morse from the Stamp Office was standing upright in its outline.

His voice strained as he bellowed as loudly as he could. 'Please listen. The Riot Act has been read by the magistrates. The army is already on its way. You must leave. This is a civil disturbance, a riot. The consequences for anyone arrested will be severe. Leave this place peacefully. For God's sake, return to your homes, I beg you.'

I still couldn't see Father. Those nearest the gates turned, older and wiser people taking up Mr Morse's advice that they'd best leave. I was swept away from the gate and down the road by the throng.

Then we heard it: a drumming of hooves and screams. I looked down the hill. The military had arrived on horseback; not only that, they had drawn their swords. A petrifying sight, huge horses galloped directly towards us, their rider's weapons glinting in the sun. Everybody scattered wildly to avoid the hooves and horses. My heart raced and blood boiled in my ears. Gu's words echoed in my mind: "If you turn and run they'll slice off your arm, neat as a butcher." It was as if I was watching one of Gu's battles, but no – it really was happening, and here in Carmarthen.

What could I do? I had to get out of the way of those soldiers. I ducked into the nearest hedge. I lay flat in the ditch, hands over my head. The ground shook as they pounded on, inches from where I lay clinging to the soil, praying not to be noticed. The troop galloped past, on up to the workhouse gate. They didn't stop, they rode straight inside. I heard shouting and screaming but no one emerged from the yard. Then there was nothing, a silence. To my horror I saw the gates swing closed. Anyone inside was trapped. Where was Father? What about Tom? Maybe Father had already got out and was on his way home, but remembering our mare, I doubted that. Would Tom have reached the workhouse? I hoped not. The street was still. I couldn't stay lying in the ditch. I decided to go back to Eliza's; it was close and safe. I ran the few hundred yards to bang on the shop door. A scared-looking John opened it a crack at my calls. He pulled me through into the hot room and bolted the door.

I was plied with more tea and buns but couldn't eat or drink. I was too worried. After half an hour I left the safety of the bakery.

John winked as I went. 'I am comfortable here. I will stay a while to look after Mrs Jones.'

Nothing stirred in Carmarthen; every house was barred, the streets deserted. I had no idea what to do. To follow the path of the military seemed to court danger, so I made my way back to Master David's yard. When I arrived, there were other Morgan cousins from around the county taking refuge. To my relief, Tom was there too. He hadn't got as far as the workhouse; by the time he'd left the bakery, the cavalry had nearly reached the town. It was quieter away from the protesters so he'd heard their hooves approaching. Guessing what it meant, he had slipped around the side streets to David's. One of my cousins, the Newchurch village blacksmith, had been near the front of the parade.

He told us, 'The procession got livelier as the march got closer to the workhouse. The leaders lost control, we were swept along by the crush. The streets were so full that those on horseback were unable to turn or stop. When the crowd reached the workhouse, people started hammering at the gate with clubs and sticks. When it seemed at the point of breaking down, we were let in. Just as well, those at the front could have been crushed to death if they hadn't opened it. We entered the courtyard with an aim to level the buildings. There were hundreds of men and women in that yard. People were ripping the evil place apart with bare hands, crowbars, brooms – you name it – as if they'd been let off a leash. I looked into their dining hall and there was that trollop Frances Evans, up and dancing on one of the long tables, calling people to join her.'

He continued, 'I decided to leave, then I heard the army galloping towards us, up the road. In moments a whole troop of soldiers, swords drawn, shouting bloodcurdling threats, were at the gates and charging into the yard, meeting our Rebeccas at the gateway.'

'Did you see our Father?' asked Tom.

'Sorry boys, no – too many people.'

Master David said, 'You two had best get home. I hope for all our sakes that John will be there before you. Come back if he is, Will. I want you in work by seven tomorrow, whatever.'

We walked home in a very different mood to the triumphant march to town. Mother stood wringing her hands anxiously at the top of the lane, waiting for us, Shem beside her. We ran the last few yards and hugged her.

'Where's your father?' she asked at once.

With sinking hearts, we admitted we didn't know and took her inside to tell her about the events of the day. I offered to run up to the Pritchards or Joneses to see if they had heard any more than us.

My sister called out that Gu was walking up the lane from the Big House. It was unusual for him to walk here, so we three went out to the yard. He stomped along furiously.

When he saw us he waved his fist and shouted, 'I've heard all about it, how dare you join a riot in the streets of Carmarthen?'

He looked at Tom and then me and began to cry, sobbing bitterly.

Between heart-rending gasps, he said, 'They sent in the cavalry, dragoons, you young fools. You could have been cut to death like my Tommy, surrounded by hooves, drowning in blood.'

He was near collapse. Appalled, we supported him into the house. Mother was in tears and so were Tom and I. We hadn't admitted to Gu that Father was missing yet, and worse that he was likely to be imprisoned inside the workhouse.

We set him down on the settle by the fire as he continued to sob. Tom and I couldn't think of anything to say so we sat either side of him with our arms around his shoulders. Mother made tea, but kept dropping spoons and rattling plates; all she could do was wonder what had happened to Da. As Gu's sobs subsided, he wiped his nose, sat up and took a sip of tea.

He tried to smile at us and said, 'Aye, you boys have always been a comfort to me, you with your mother. I couldn't have had better, although Tom – your eyes are so much like my Tommy's, it hurts to look at you on times.'

He turned to Mother. Something in her face told him she was not only upset for him.

Looking around, he asked, 'Where's John?'

We shook our heads and a shadow passed over his face. 'Young Sam said he heard the dragoons closed the workhouse gate, said that hundreds have been arrested.'

Mother blanched. White-faced, she asked, 'Is anyone hurt?'

'I don't know, the little Sam's told me I've repeated. Will, what are you waiting for? You have business in Carmarthen if asked. Go straight back and find out what's happening. Take my horse and hurry. Your mother needs to know what's become of her husband.' He looked at her. 'Maybe he's delayed, Elizabeth, helping someone.'

We knew it wasn't true. Da would have come straight home like us. Either he had been hurt in the cavalry charge or he was imprisoned in the workhouse.

I ran out and down to the Big House stable, threw a saddle on Gu's pony and trotted off. I needed to look as if I was going about my normal business, so I tried not to rush.

There were crowds all along the road into town and lots of riderless horses roaming the road and fields. No one I met knew what had happened after they had closed the workhouse gates on the marchers. Only those inside knew that, but I'd heard no gunfire. Lurid rumours were being spread, predicting instant transportation to Van Dieman's land, or those caught being hung for treason as the Riot Act demanded.

I saw Huw hobbling towards me. I dismounted and led Gu's pony toward him.

'Are you all right?'

'My foot was crushed when everyone in the procession saw the dragoons, it's nothing much, just bruised. I was lucky. When I saw the trouble in the workhouse yard, people throwing bedding out of the windows, I decided that it'd be safer not to be associated with the mischief and left. On the way, I helped a man from the workhouse who appeared utterly confused. He was crying as he tried to get out of the way of the crowd rushing in through the gates.

'When the cavalry arrived, like everyone else, I ran at the sight of them. I took him with me and we sheltered by the Baptist Chapel, hid behind some gravestones. It seemed wise to rest there a while until things calmed down.'

He looked at me and said hesitantly, 'That man, he was like your Shem, you know – same eyes and face flatter than ours. A little older than Shem, maybe thirty, and slow. It was so sad outside that terrible place, Will. There were lots of people from the workhouse, dressed in rags, milling around, crying. Tiny children with older ones trying to care for them, old women, yes, and a couple more…' he hesitated, '…imbeciles.

'I spoke with the man, he was so gentle, from St Clears he said. He'd lived with his grandmother until she got sick last year. I think she must have died because he said they'd all gone to see her in the churchyard but when he arrived she wasn't there after all. Then the Parish Overseer brought him to the Carmarthen Union with his clothes and toys. He asked me if I could get them back for him. He told me they weren't his clothes and his granny wouldn't like him not to look smart. Said he missed his little wooden animals, so I promised I'd do my best. I walked him back up to the workhouse and on the way I noticed your friend John Jones at the bakery window. I called up and asked if they had any stale buns spare. You know Eliza Jones, she was down in a flash and had a plate piled high, which James, that was his name, demolished.

'I had to take him back then; the workhouse warders had restored order. James got into line when they called his name and went in by the side gate. He waved at me all the way as he marched in.'

Huw was nearly in tears thinking of it.

'It would be so terrible to have no family and end up there. It's an evil place to fetch up, in rags, not your own clothes, no possessions, being worked to death and not enough food. If I was marching against the tolls before, Will, I'm marching against the Poor Law now. I can't get poor gentle James out of my head. I'll get him some of those carved animals at the next fair and tell him to hide them from the warders.'

Huw said he had to get home and reassure his mother. He confirmed that the gates of the workhouse had been shut, with many from the procession inside. Those gates were still closed when they took poor James back in by a side gate.

I went on into town, once again making for the yard. David had news: the town magistrates, headed by Mr Stacy the Mayor, had set up a court in the workhouse. They had already started hearings for the men and women locked inside the gates. No one knew how many were in there, some said a hundred, others said nearly a thousand. We decided to go to the workhouse gates to find out whether anyone had been released. Every few minutes a subdued man or woman came out and hurried away. We tried to stop one man to ask for Father, but he shook his head and scurried off. Then a familiar, tall, slightly stooping figure emerged. Praise the Lord, it was Da. Master David and I rushed to him. I hugged him, whilst David pumped his hand.

Da grimaced and ran his hand through his hair. 'It's not over, I'm afraid. Most of us have been released on a bond to appear in the next assizes. They haven't decided yet whether or not to bring charges. Elizabeth is going to be so angry and upset, she's said all along this might end in me being transported or worse. I'm lucky to be let out and not sent down to Carmarthen prison. They have sent quite a number to gaol. It is mostly those who are already known as leaders; John Harris, Talog Mill, has been imprisoned. Those bastard magistrates have been itching to get their hands on him.'

Father looked tired, it was near enough eight o'clock in the evening. Seeing me holding Gu's horse, he asked, 'Have you seen Dainty?'

I shook my head.

He sighed. If the horse was hurt or stolen it would be a disaster for the farm.

He nodded and glanced at David. 'I'm going to be in more trouble at home than with the magistrates.'

They grinned at that, briefly able to enjoy the humour, then he looked worried again. In the end, after looking sharply at me, David sent me back home with him, this time to search for the mare.

'I've had enough of all this now, you two. I have a business to run. I need my apprentices here and working, not marching around the countryside day and night. I'm expecting you to take the work more seriously now, Will. Enough of Rebecca, if you please.'

Wearily we set off. When we reached Pritchards' farm we finally saw something to cheer us. Who should be at the gate but Pritchard himself with our horse, his hand on her harness ready to lead her home.

'Well, well, John. I saw her trotting up the road all alone and thought she'd thrown you, and you dead in a ditch.'

It was clear he knew why Da might have been rushing away from Carmarthen. We picked up the disapproving tone in Pritchard's voice. As an elder of the Lammas Street chapel he was unlikely to support any radical activities that risked being illegal. His boys and Mary-Jane were kept under a tight rein; no working for Rebecca or excitement for them as far as Mr Pritchard was concerned. We were just relieved to have found the horse and thanked him profusely.

Father said quietly, almost to himself, 'I couldn't have borne to have to tell Elizabeth I'd lost the horse too, it would have been the last straw. Twenty pounds she cost me last year.'

At the sound of the horses in the farmyard, the family all rushed out of the door. Mother flung herself on Father, sobbing, the little ones looked anxious, Shem confused and upset. He approached Father and Mother tearfully, needing reassurance. Father saw and patted Shem's shoulder with his spare arm. Gu and Ester stayed in the background, so I went to join them.

Ester, whispering, asked, 'Is everything all right now, Will?'

I had to shake my head. No, it certainly was not. Eventually, we went inside. Ester poured tea at a table set out with bread and cheese and jam as Father sat. We waited; he didn't want to talk about it but knew there was no choice.

His deep voice began, 'I'm sure you want to know what happened. It was a sorry afternoon, I'm afraid, after a brave morning's march. My only consolation was that

Tom and Will were not taken prisoner too. There must have been nearly a hundred of us when the dragoons rode up and shut those heavy gates. We were terrified, as you can imagine.'

He looked at Mother. 'I'm sorry, Elizabeth, once the procession became a riot I tried to get out of there, truly I did. The pressure behind the horses made it impossible. The power of people's feeling took over; it was frightening and shameful to see the way so many people took such pleasure in breaking the workhouse down and destroying everything in sight. Respectable folk, those you'd least expect to behave like that joined in. It was as if they'd been let off a leash, egging each other on. What a clamour; there were shouts, screaming, the workhouse alarm bell tolling non-stop. Mr Morse from the Stamp Office tried to warn us. He told us this was a disturbance of the peace and the Riot Act had been read and troops were on the way. After that many left, if they were near enough to the gate to get out.

In the end, I got off the horse and tried to lead her out of the yard. I didn't dare lose her, you see. At that point, the troops rode up. They were a terrifying sight: tall black hats, their sabres drawn and waving in the air menacingly, horseshoes sparking on the cobbles. People ran and pushed each other desperately. I was at the gate when they came and believed I'd drawn my last breath. I thought of you, hit the horse hard to make it run out and pulled back out of the way of the charge and into the yard. Like everyone else, I looked for somewhere to hide.'

We listened, breathless and silent.

Gu spoke. 'You did right, John, no one in their right minds should face a cavalry charge when swords are out. If one had decided to start cutting at the crowd, the injuries would have been horrific. I'm impressed that the troop were disciplined enough not to slash at you; they must be well trained.'

'The crowd was unarmed, there were women and children there. I don't really know why they didn't, we were hundreds strong, plenty armed with sticks and pickaxes. It must have been a close thing.

'When the gates shut they lined us up and we waited and waited, fear in our bellies. After some hours, the town magistrates arrived. On seeing the numbers they decided to hold a court session then and there. Too many to send to prison, I suppose. Each of us was called in turn, our names and addresses taken. We'd agreed to tell the same tale, which is true up to a point. We all said that we had no choice in joining the march, as there were notices all around the county that threatened us with having our homes burnt and our lives taken if we didn't.

'For most of us, that excuse seemed to suffice. I suspect the magistrates thought if they sent all of us to gaol they may cause a more serious insurrection across the county. That might have been right too, it would have added fuel to the flames. They decided to make an example of some, choosing those who had been caught and were already known to them. John Harris and John Lewis, Pencelly, have been sent to gaol. We'll have to wait to find out who else. I have been allowed home but,' he hung his head, 'I am on notice that I will be called to the next assizes and may yet be charged.'

Mother's hand went to her mouth and she groaned. 'You may have to go to prison, John, or maybe worse. They had read the Riot Act, you know what that means.'

Father's head and shoulders drooped as Gu tried to say nonsense, that he was sure it wouldn't come to that.

There was no consoling Mother. We left them together and went out, calling the children to come with us.

Gu looked worried as he limped outside. 'Damn, damn. Well, it's late, all you children go to bed now.'

Then he, Ester and I walked back to the Big House. Gu was muttering to himself all the way.

'I will have to talk about Waterloo on Sunday, Will. There's no avoiding it. I need to tell you about those terrible days in Belgium and how it ended. It's been twenty-eight years, near enough to the day. I re-live those hot, deadly hours every June. When the news of the dragoon charge came, in my imagination I saw you and Tom lying on the streets, covered in blood. I couldn't bear it. You are safe, thank God, and not arrested like your father, the damn fool! I need to tell you what happened at Waterloo, get it out, try to get some peace… if peace is ever possible for me.'

Chapter Sixteen

Saturday 25th June 1843

I worked hard all week. There had been little cheer. I worried about Da, of course, and wondered what was happening at home. The only bright spot was one evening when I visited Eliza Jones in her bakery, wanting to thank her for her help on Monday. Who should be serving behind the counter but none other than John Jones? Eliza came out and hugged me, and John thumped my back as I tried to say thank you.

'The thanks are all mine, Will. I was afraid that the wound on my arm might split open in that press of people. You were right to tell me to stop sulking in my bed, but if you and your brother hadn't helped me in the crowd, by being up to see the procession I might have fallen or worse. I have a work here now. I can serve behind the counter while Eliza oversees the bakery.' He winked at us and went on, 'You'd be surprised how much a man with one good arm can do, isn't that so, my dear?'

Eliza blushed, saying, 'You'll never guess, Will, John has proposed. We are to be married. The riot made me realise how much I need a protector. We've always had such a liking for each other, John and I.'

John said, 'My happiness is all down to you, Will. You made me get up and stop wallowing in my sorrows. You and your brother saved me falling in the crowd, and by chance brought me right to where I longed to be, with Eliza. Would you act as Bidder and give out the bidding invitation letters for us? We see no need to wait. The first banns are being read next week. We'll marry at the end of next month. On the twenty-seventh of July, Sunday, so the bakery will be closed.'

It was an honour to be asked; it acknowledged me as his closest friend. I'd be expected to dress up with ribbons on my hat, knock at friends' and families' doors with a stripped willow rod, and give them an invitation to the wedding. The guests would give a donation, money or furniture, large or small, and come to what I guessed would be a feast made by Eliza's bakery kitchens. In the old days, an amusing rhyme would be read out by the Bidder, instead of a letter. I pondered whether I might reinstate the custom. John and Eliza loved jokes; a cheeky, rhyming invitation poem would fit the bill.

'That is wonderful news. You two are a match made in heaven.'

It was true, they both so loved to laugh and gossip. While there was ten-year age difference, Eliza was a pretty thing still, and John still a catch, far more attractive than fat, old baker Jones, her previous husband. They both had a lot to gain from the marriage. John, as ever, had fallen on his feet. I was pleased and relieved for him. The alternative, as he and I well knew, was destitution and the workhouse.

I walked home on Saturday afternoon with *The Welshman* under my arm for Father. I knew he'd want to see what the paper had to say about the march. He'd hope to see an indication as to what might happen to those bound over to attend the assizes. When I got home, they'd already bought a copy the day before, unable to bear to wait. There were a number of columns and articles on the second page. *The Welshman* told how the English press had exaggerated the troubles. It reported the Newcastle Emlyn and Carmarthen Turnpike Trustees had started taking evidence as to money being collected and the number of illegal tollgates.

The newspaper published in full a letter from the farmers' appointed lawyer, Mr Edward Lloyd Hall. In that letter, Mr Hall pointedly stated the penalty for destroying a turnpike gate could be transportation, implying that no more gates should be broken. Mr Hall also argued that no tollgate other than those on the highway were legal; notably, that any gates in the towns were illegal and that would include the Water Street gate. Despite his article and the high risk of punishment, all week long across the west Wales counties, gates were destroyed. The population had had enough; no troop of dragoons from Cardiff were going to stop the people's cause being taken forward. We had to have reform of the tolls, the farmers were not appeased or cowed. They still demanded "nothing more than fair-handed justice".

The newspaper report of the march confirmed nine men had been imprisoned, six in the county gaol and three in the town gaol. Mother kept worrying about Mr Hall's letter and the penalty of taking down a tollgate being transportation. She could not be convinced that Father wouldn't be sent to Van Diemen's land. Tom told me she had been in a terrible state all week with the worry of it. Ellen was scared as well. Father and he had promised on our family bible they'd have no more to do with breaking tollgates or any marches.

'That is no bad thing. Father has been bound over to the assizes, he will be marked as a troublemaker. If he is arrested again, things might go badly for him,' I said.

Tom agreed. He admitted Gu had threatened him with being cut off if there was any more "nonsense with the law." Gu had told him that he and my father were making Mother ill with worry, him too, and he could take no more. Tom said he thought if things progressed with the evidence to the turnpike trust he'd have to give in; it wasn't worth the heartache for the women.

We were glad to get out of the house and volunteered to clean the yard. Shem joined us, doleful and quiet. Tom was gentler towards him than usual. He said Shem was upset because Mother was upset, he had been anxious all week instead of his usual smiling happy self. Tom had found him crying, tucked away alone in the barn yesterday. When asked why, Shem told Tom it was because Father was going to be sent away, Tom was going to live with

Gu and Ellen, and I was in Carmarthen. Mother and he would have to go to the workhouse. Nothing Tom could say would make him believe this wasn't true.

It hit me then hard and cold, what if Shem and Mother were right? What if Father was transported? The government had sentenced many Chartists and protesters to transportation over recent years. Those men and women never returned, supposing they survived the months at sea. The authorities feared revolution and dissent in Britain after the revolution in France and were ruthless in suppressing any insurrection. It dawned on me that my wish – to have a farm of my own – might come true. I'd have to return home to run the farm for Mother, while Tom farmed Cwm Castell Fawr.

I felt sick. In that second I realised I hated the thought of farming for the rest of my life. To have to look after Mother and the children and farm the land until I grew old was a horrible prospect. I wanted to make money and send my children to a school close by. My wife would wear pretty gowns, not the dull, woollen costume of the countryside. Her hands would smell of warm bread, cake and eau de cologne, not of goose grease to stop chapping, like the Newchurch girls. I wanted to build a business, do what I liked, not tend animals, bring cows in for milking twice a day whatever the weather, or fret over crops. I'd spent years of my life wanting to inherit the farm, but when it came to it, it would be a millstone, a burden.

To distract myself from this prospect, I sought out Shem. Singing while he worked would cheer him up. I asked him to sing us *A Life on the Ocean Wave*, his favourite, as he threw buckets of water over the yard. This charmed him. He told us he was making waves like the ones on Tenby beach. He happily pulled water from the well, throwing the pails out hard. Water sloshed everywhere, over our feet and the cobbles. When we were all tired, with the farmyard neat and clean, I took him to one side.

'So Shem, I hear you've been sad this week?' He nodded. 'Why is that then?'

It came tumbling out.

'Mother keeps asking Father over and over again if he's going to prison or to be sent to a land far away. Mother thinks he's going away, Will, and so does Father.'

'Why do you say Father thinks that?'

'Da shouted at Mother. He said, "If you don't stop going on and on at me, I'll be glad to go, get some peace and quiet."'

'Shem, we all hope and pray Da won't be going anywhere. I don't think he will or he'd have been sent to gaol last week. You don't need to worry. If he did have to go away for a while, Gu, Tom and I would be here. We will always look after you, Mother and the children.'

As I said it, I knew it to be true. Neither Tom nor I could turn our backs on Shem. If he outlived my parents, he would live with me or Tom for the rest of his life. The question for me now was where that might be.

Shem was fortunate; many innocents were treated like poor James. Abandoned, sometimes at birth, or else as they grew older when their parents or grandparents died. I'd read of a movement to provide asylums, sanctuaries for people like him. The Quakers wanted peaceful places where the sick could live separately from those in the workhouse. I wondered if one would be built in Carmarthen in years to come. Even if it was, Shem would still be far happier at home than away from his family and our village, where everyone knew him for a kind, gentle soul. More than that, Shem was valued here in Newchurch. He always helped anyone in need, cheered us up with his songs and antics, and worked as hard on the land as any. He belonged in Newchurch as much as any other villager. Shem seemed comforted by my explanation and carried on cheerfully singing *A Life on the Ocean Wave* all evening until we had to shout at him to stop.

Tom and I made for The Plough later that night. Da stayed home with mother. He had joked when we'd asked him to come with us, saying Mother planned to never let him out of her sight again. Spirits were high in the tavern with talk all of Monday's events. Of course, everyone knew John Morgan had been released on bond and was due before the assizes. Da was hailed a hero, drinks were bought for us both on the strength of it. I'd have far preferred if it had been one of them left in the workhouse than Father, hero or not.

Feelings were running strongly against a number of the local magistrates. It was claimed that Mr T C Morris had headed the military when they arrived to lead them to the workhouse. He'd been heard calling to the dragoons to "cut and slash away" at the crowd. Luckily for all concerned, Major Parlby, the officer in charge of the troop, immediately countermanded this and told the soldiers, "No one is to obey any man's orders other than mine."

Mr Morris could have caused a massacre in the town against the unarmed marchers. It stoked our animosity toward him and the other magistrates who had called in the troops.

We were buoyed up by the support in the village, but the wait to hear if Da would have a charge brought against him weighed heavy on us. Tom said if Da did go to gaol he'd have no choice but remain at home to run the farm until he returned. Neither of us dared voice the thought that should he be transported, our lives would be turned upside down forever.

I walked down the lane to the Big House reflective. Ester was waiting up and told me Gu had been dreadful all week. He'd been worrying about Father, but more about what would happen to my mother if he was transported. He'd been so agitated that his old symptoms had returned. One morning she had found him crouching half asleep by his bed, shouting, 'Get into the square, get into the square.'

Gu had gone up to bed but had been asking to see me all day. She thought I'd best go up, despite the lateness of the hour. She'd bring me up a pastry in a while. Ester knew I was always hungry after drinking; her brothers had taught her that as a young spinster living at home.

Gu sat up in his bed when I opened the door, he looked frail and thin in his nightshirt, older than I remembered.

He smiled weakly, 'Will, it's you, how's your week been?' Without waiting for my reply, he rushed out, 'I've been waiting all these days to unburden myself. I know it's late but I need to tell you about Quatre Bras and Waterloo. There were two days fighting, you see. Everyone calls it

Waterloo, but there'd have been no Waterloo if the 5th Division had failed at Quatre Bras.

'A lot's been said and written about that damn war, what happened on those days remembered by officers. All you know as a foot soldier is to fight to stay alive. You only see smoke, the red flash of the musket. You smell powder, blood, death and men's fear. You feel the slam of your rifle into your shoulder, the scorch of gunpowder, taste the lead of your next bullet. You pray not to be hit or stabbed or feel anything worse.' He took a breath at last and continued, puffed out his cheeks and sighed.

'Sorry, I'm rushing. I've been waiting and waiting for you. I need to get it all into the open. I'll go back to the beginning where I left off last week.

'We soldiers were in high spirits billeted in Brussels, didn't think old Boney was anywhere close. The day before Quatre Bras, no one knew where he and the French forces were. Everyone believed at worst his army was setting out from Paris; our officers were dancing at some fancy ball in Brussels when word came through. Glorious evening, it was, after a long sunny day. We were relaxed, drinking in taverns, talking to the girls, taking our leisure.

'To our astonishment, the army was ordered to make ready, a full assembly call with bugles and bagpipes sounding, at eleven that night. We couldn't believe it. No army would fight at night, you can't see to aim a gun. We were issued with three days' rations and told to be ready by midnight. I've told you repeatedly, if you get rations, then you carry them. So although the weather was hot and we were close to Brussels and plenty of supplies, I put as much as I could at the bottom of my pack. The younger lads threw most of theirs away as we waited for the order to move out, too heavy to carry in the heat. Then we tried to catch a few hours' sleep. The regimental wives made tearful farewells to their husbands, praying they'd meet again.

'We waited and waited in column. General Pack on his big horse got angrier and angrier with the delays. Finally the 42nd Regiment arrived to join us and we marched. We doubted there was to be a battle; Boney was far away. Companies stopped in the woods to cook breakfast. We were laughing and in high spirits. It was a beautiful dawn, the sky clear and blue, birdsong filled the air. Trouble was our knapsacks were full – rations, eighty musket balls, greatcoats, a blanket and more – and it was steaming hot by nine. The heat and the weight of our packs spoilt the mood. When we heard gunshots in the distance, our laughter stopped. General Pack ordered us into formation at crossroads called Quatre Bras. We 44th were arranged at the front of the line, between two woods, the 42nd to one side of us and the 1st Regiment the other. I heard later that Tommy's 95th were way out on the left flank.

'We were pleased, if apprehensive, when we saw Wellington himself ride up to take a position to our right. We could see our Dutch allies falling back into the woods with the weight of battle. Things really started to get sticky. As a Light Company man, I was sent skirmishing to the front across a field as the regiment moved forward. The French guessed it was Wellington with us and swooped. Their cavalry chased towards him as he leapt onto his horse and galloped to the rear.'

He coughed and cleared his throat. 'Next thing I knew, we 44th, along with the 42nd, were too far forward and out of line. You couldn't see a thing or have any idea what was happening for the tall rye crop in that field. I stood quivering with terror like a hare at harvest. I heard horses crashing through the tall stalks, coming towards me, but saw nothing apart from waving golden strands. The sound of musket fire was all around me, along with the cries of dying men. I knew I might be found next, tried to keep still. We were fighting blind, couldn't see their cavalry coming forward. Mind you, they couldn't see much of what was happening either, but on horseback, their heads were above the rye.

'Lancers appeared but they were going slowly across the field, not charging. It was chaos. Those lancers' uniforms resembled the Dutch we'd seen retreating. As skirmishers, the Light Company could clearly see they were the enemy. We ran for our lives back to the line, shouting, "French, French!" General Pack didn't believe us until that cavalry started slashing at the 42nd.

'We tried to get into square, as did the 42nd. The poor sods didn't stand a chance. The horsemen had already reached them, and as they formed, they formed around the lancers. It was terrible. Their shouts and screams echoed across the field, we heard them die. We had a terror of our own; we were too spread out in that crop, so didn't have the chance to form square either. Lancers got between the 42nd and us, they were coming at us from the rear.'

Gu was pale and sweating. I put my hand on his.

'We should have died then by rights. Our commander, Hammerton, gave an order we'd never tried before. He told the rear rank of the line to about-face. They did it calmly, while I, with the rest of the front rank, faced forward. I tried not to think about horses bearing down on my back. We kept bayonets fixed and tried desperately to get close enough and gather to form a square.'

'We had the colours behind us, so of course the lancers made for them. Ensign James Christie was carrying them, he was our Sergeant Major, who'd got a well-deserved promotion to officer. A lancer stabbed him and he fell, throwing himself on the colours, so that the lancer could only tear off a scrap of fabric. Seeing our good Christie fall, we turned to attack, our blood was up. That man was bayoneted down, stabbed again and again for killing our Christie, as we thought. Hammerton's quick thinking had saved us for the moment; we'd seen off the charge.

'There were so many dead, and the confusion was so great that we and the 42nd Regiment were mixed together. Then we felt the thunder of hooves once more. This time it was French cuirassiers headed for us, and we knew their fearsome reputation. They had huge horses, each the size of a carthorse, and wore heavy armour. We, with the 42nd, formed square together where we could. Time stopped as they charged. We knew we should aim for the horse, not the man. As we fired, their horses crashed down, screaming and whinnying in pain, heaving up, hooves thrashing, obstructing any rider following behind. The main body of the battalion retired fifty paces, but the Light Company had to stay with Lieutenants Riddock and Grier as skirmishers to face French skirmishers and protect the battalion line. We fired and fired, mouths getting drier than a desert, faces black with soot from the powder until our cartridges ran out. No more supplies came, we'd nothing but bayonets for protection.

'We tried to fall back but cuirassiers on those enormous horses circled around us. Terrified for our lives, we formed a rallying square of as many of us as could still stand, all facing outwards with our bayonets fixed. We were sitting ducks. Realising this, Riddock ordered us to fight our way back to the regiment. We did so but the battle was still so fierce when we got close that the sergeants didn't dare open the squares to let us in. We had to lie down on the earth as close to the regiment as we could so the lads could cover us and shoot over our heads at them. We could only pray no cuirassier saw we were living, nor charge their great horses over our bodies to crush us.

'We were down to four companies by the time we got inside the protection of the square after their cavalry pulled back. Hammerton had been badly wounded. We'd lost all order. It was mayhem. General Pack ordered us to work as one with the 42nd. They were in as bad a state as us, if not worse. Pack stayed with us, Picton himself was to the left of us. Finally, reinforcements for our artillery arrived with more ammunition; until then we'd had only a few nine-pound guns supporting us against all the French cannon.

'Yet another wave of cavalry started charging down on us. It was terrifying Will, dreadful. O'Malley had taken over from Hammerton. He told us, "You are as brave as lions, men, we will yet repulse them". We started firing faster, cheered by his words. Soon after he said that, I felt a red-hot bolt in my calf – I'd been hit with a musket ball. The pain was grievous but I had to keep standing. If I fell there'd be another space in the square and there were too few left to fill it. Besides, we knew being left on the battlefield with the fallen was often a death sentence, one way or another. If the enemy didn't kill you, looters would without a qualm. I was lucky that the worst of the battle was over by the time I was injured. The muskets and artillery kept firing on into the evening, but at least the cavalry charges stopped. The regiment was in a sorry state. We helped each other stagger to the rear as reinforcements arrived.

'I said to the 30th Regiment as they marched forward past the streams of wounded going back, "Push on old three tens, pay 'em off for the 44th". There were hundreds of us walking wounded; the worst injured were helped or dragged away by comrades.

'The pain in my leg was sharp, but I could see many others far worse off. Faces shot half away, arms hanging as if senseless, horrible wounds to men's bellies. I found a stout tree branch to take some of the weight off my leg, then joined the flood of wounded waiting to see the surgeons in the casualty yard. There were so many men there, the yard was awash with blood. I heard screams as men had amputations or musket balls pulled from their bodies. It looked a shambles; an abattoir would have been tidier and less bloody. I made for John Collins, our regimental surgeon. I knew him from the Peninsular and trusted him. Recognising me, he called me forward in the long line and examined my leg. We spoke of Ensign Christie saving the colours.

'"A lance through the eye and into his tongue," Collins said. "Poor bugger, I doubt he'll survive." It turned out he did, though. I saw Christie a few months later, face a horrible sight, red and scarred, with an eyepatch, but he lived. Collins also told me our Light Company's mascot, Lieutenant Robert Grier's dog Dash, had been injured. We loved that little hound. He'd been found as a puppy in Spain and stayed, begging scraps and spoilt by us ever since. The Lieutenant was sore injured too. I was sad to hear that but more worried about that dog. I knew the lads would be terribly upset when the news reached them.

'I was fortunate with my leg – the bullet went straight on through the calf, so there was no bullet or cloth left in the wound. It was agony, it felt like a burning poker inside my muscle. Collins told me that as long as it didn't get infected I should recover. He wrapped clean linen from sheets found in the village and waved me on wearily; there were dozens more behind me for him to treat. I've limped ever since, but Will, it was my only bullet in all of my time serving.

'The battle ended at ten that night. To my relief and delight, as we wounded walked back, Tommy came and found me. He'd heard from the Lights I'd been wounded and afraid for me, he had decided to search me out, tired as he was. A good thing too; like so many of the newer recruits he'd thrown away his rations and had nothing to eat. I'd picked up a dead cuirassier's breastplate as a souvenir; we liked to cook from them. I heated water from my canteen in it, brewed tea and we shared my biscuit and beef.' Gu started to sob. 'It was the last I saw of him living,

Will. I thank the Lord I saw him, but it hurts to think of him, so handsome, strong and brave drinking that tea.'

Gu was overcome. I sat holding his hand a while as tears rolled down his lined face. He leaned back on his pillow, exhausted.

'I'll stop now. It's late. I'll try to tell you more tomorrow.'

It took me a long time to fall asleep, Gu's tale haunted me. I wanted to know more about Waterloo and felt proud Gu had chosen me to confide in. As if that wasn't enough, I worried about Mother and Father. Like Shem, I wondered how we would manage if Da was sent to prison or transported. I'd slept no more than an hour in the long wait until dawn. I had no heart to face the village stares and questions about Father, so claimed I had a touch of backache and wanted to rest it before work next week.

Ester wasn't pleased, 'We should go to church, hold our heads high for standing up for justice.'

Gu said, 'Leave the boy be, why should he care what Newchurch thinks of us?'

Off Ester went wearing her best dress, with its fine Brussels lace, to collect Mother. She glared at us as she went through the door.

I sat in the kitchen wondering what to do. I didn't feel like doing anything really. There were carpentry chores around the farm I'd been asked to help with but I couldn't face them. In the end, I got out my old knife and started to carve a little pig from a piece of applewood. I was trying to make it look like Buttercup. It looked more like a dog by the time I'd finished. I determined to try again and use a picture and draw the shape first, absorbed, enjoying the task I'd set myself. I'd give the toy to Huw for that poor man James in the workhouse.

Gu clomped down the stairs. 'Not like you to mope, Will. When things get hard, all you can do is carry on. Put one step in front of the other and carry on. Let's take a walk out to the four acre field and see how the corn is swelling.'

I swished a stick from the hedge as we walked, taking the tops off any brambles we passed. Gu said, almost to himself, 'Let's get this over, shall we? Maybe in the daylight, telling will be easier.'

He began unexpectedly, words tumbling out. 'I went to the curate and made him get out the church books of births, deaths, and marriages last week. I didn't know if there'd be any entry, with Bel being so poor. I needed to know whether Bel had had Tommy's child, if that was why she asked me for money. I wondered whether Tommy had left something behind, not gone from the world with nothing remaining. There was a record, but Bel's boy was born early in 1814, a year after Tommy left, so he couldn't have been his child. I was relieved, didn't want to think I'd allowed any grandchild of mine to suffer the way that little family did, so poor and, yes, despised. Bel not being married and babies with different fathers. Bel is a flibbertigibbet with a kind heart, but I was relieved she hadn't given birth to my grandchild, with only a half a crown a month to manage on. The dates are all wrong. Who knows who the child's father was? It's no concern of mine. He died along with your brother and sisters from the spotted fever, so it was of no consequence in the end.'

I was dumbstruck, my mouth dry, in a quandary. I'd promised Mother and Bel not to tell the truth. I didn't know if Gu would be comforted or dismayed to hear that he was right, there was another grandchild, but not Tommy's son. While my mind whirred, Gu carried on talking. The moment passed, I had no chance to tell him. I'd kept my promise to my mother, but not telling those with the right to know felt wrong. I was annoyed with myself, never brave enough, always too much thinking and not enough action. Tom's accusations from last month still stung. Was I being cowardly or was I protecting them?

Gu and I sat together against a tree stump, looking over the tall corn.

'I have to finish, Will. I hope it's not the burden for you that it has been to me for nearly thirty years. It's like having a rotten, black hole in your heart, that however hard you try you can't fill or clean. You try not to think of it, then the memories rush back, sometimes they are so strong that you feel you're there. As if you're in the midst of it. Someone may shoot you at any second with a musket or stick you with a bayonet, or a cannonball roar by. You duck instinctively to hide from the cavalry's swords and sweat with fear. Your stomach churns with horror and your ears ring. I need to try to let light into that black hole, see if it will help.

'The night after Quatre Bras, we walking wounded tramped slowly back towards Brussels. The heat had been terrible all day, so when I passed the 44th at camp I decided my wounded leg would be better rested, rather than trying to make it any further that night. To add to the misery, there was thunder with a heavy rain shower.

'Next morning, no one knew what to do. I was unsure whether to join the next column of wounded or not. I was still a corporal, so I made the lads in my company clean their rifles and collect a full supply of powder and shot. Word came that the Prussian Army had been defeated the day before; Wellington had ordered a retreat. I decided to stay with the regiment as we retreated.

'We halted every half mile or so, still exhausted from Quatre Bras. At one stop, Picton ordered some soldiers flogged, they had deliberately fired away their ammunition. We felt sympathy for new recruits fighting their first battle; we understood it was terrifying, but we accepted discipline had to be kept or else we'd all die. Quite a number of the newer men from our brave 44th had feigned dead or hidden in the woods the day before. They crept back to us as soon as they could that day. We knew better than to tell on them; we would need them fighting with us. A flogged man can barely hold his musket.

'It got hotter and closer with every hour, sapping our energy. It was so humid, you could cut the air. My shirt and breeches clung to my skin, even the backs of my knees were wet, dripping with sweat. As black clouds massed we knew another rainstorm was coming. We prayed that storm would be thunder and lightning and not the crash of cannon. Napoleon's columns were closing in on us.

'It was a deluge, the heaviest rain any of us had ever known, as bad as anything we'd seen on the Peninsular and my God, we saw rain there. One or two of the oldest veterans said it was like the rain in India, monsoon they called it. Inches of rain came down in minutes, it didn't stop. With the feet and guns tramping and dragging, the ground turned to mud that got deeper and deeper. We were already exhausted but the extra weight of sodden clothes and knapsack made it worse, as torrential rain kept falling. Thank the Lord the French didn't reach us before nightfall.

'We were ordered to a spot chosen by Wellington and arranged according to the officer's plans. We 44th were to the left in the 5th Division, with our backs to a wood. We trusted Wellington to choose his battlegrounds well. He was wily, an experienced old fox. He'd have picked those sites where he'd be prepared to fight before any retreat. He dictated the ground if he could, that was why he had so much success on the Peninsular. Napoleon was following on and couldn't dictate the site, but his army had been victorious at Quatre Bras. They believed that they had the upper hand, and that counts for a lot.

'I had no idea what welcome would await the wounded in Brussels. I felt more comfortable with men I knew. Strange as it must seem after all I've said about battles, I decided to stay and fight rather than abandon my pals. It's a strong bond you build when your life depends on your fellows, very close, hard to understand unless you've lived through such times.

'The heavens kept pouring rain. As veterans, we showed the youngsters how to make Portuguese tents to shelter us. We stuck muskets in the ground, smeared one side of blankets with mud, which was in plentiful supply, and got under cover. It kept the worst of the rain off as we sat on our knapsacks trying to sleep through a miserable night. I worried the mud might get into my wound and the pain of my leg kept me awake. General Pack made us stand to, muskets ready because there was a rumour of attack. It was just that, a rumour. The French would have been no better prepared for the weather than us. No one could fight in six inches of mud, so after a tiring hour of standing ready in mud and rain, we were told to try to rest again. Scant provisions came through, although Brussels was close enough, a few miles away, and carters had been paid to deliver to the army. We shared what little food we had left.

'To our relief, it had finally stopped raining. We lit fires to dry our clothes, made tea if we could. All around came the familiar sounds of men preparing for battle, shouts as artillery was hauled into place, the ringing of cavalry swords being sharpened on whetstones. I made my company clean and dry their rifles yet again. Their lives and the battle would depend on them firing; damp muskets, rifles or powder are useless.

'We expected an early attack but Boney delayed, nothing happened until late morning. The ground had dried a little in the sun, still sticky but at least no puddles. We cheered as Wellington rode past in his blue cloak, shouting encouragement to us. Believe it or not, we welcomed civilian visitors from Brussels. Lieutenant Campbell who commanded us Lights, his father, an old general rode up – much to our Lieutenant's embarrassment.

'Then it began: the roar of cannon, howitzers crashing, canister spitting shot. We were outgunned. The French delivering far more cannon fire than our army. At first, you flinch with every roar; it's as if a terrifying thunderstorm of death envelops you. After a while, the pounding becomes background noise. Unless you hear a missile whistle close by, when you might throw yourself down instinctively, although you know it won't help, the noise disappears. The smoke from the musket fire quickly obscures your view; you are fighting in a thick fog; only aware of those few yards around you, your company, and the colours that it's your job to protect.

'We Lights were in the rear, on a knoll beside the Hanoverian brigade, the 42nd too. Initially we didn't do much but watch. The French infantry started to advance, they pushed our Belgian allies, who were wavering under the terrible assault, as were our British lines. Picton ordered our Brigade to support them.

'We saw their vast columns advance through the smoke. Their drums beat out a marching rhythm, Old Trousers, Old Trousers. Dum, dum, dum; dum, dum dum. They shouted "Vive L'Emperor, Vive L'Emperor". They were coming straight for Pack's brigade, for my 44th.

'We were trained to stay silent as the grave until we charged with our bayonets fixed. At the order we gave a roar to scare the dead. Our muskets pored out shot, a murderous blast of fire and their columns fell back. We heard hooves behind us, felt the earth tremble and opened ranks to let our Heavy Cavalry charge through. That destroyed the columns Boney had sent for us. Word came through mid-afternoon, General Picton was dead, shot through the head, top hat and all. We bowed our heads. The old farmer, Wellington's "foul mouthed devil", was gone.

'That was a bad moment, as it was when the French Imperial Guard appeared, Napoleon's Immortals. The Duke rode past us again to cheer us. Yet again our boys fought off them off, our squares repulsing them, but once the horsemen had gone their artillery battered us, our ranks thinned with every passing minute.

'In the lulls, I couldn't help but fear for my Tommy at the front of the action. We 44th had been held back at first, so few fit to fight after Quatre Bras, but the rifles of the 95th were long forward. It was hard to see how anyone could survive, the battle had gone on so long. As a drummer, unless called to drum out an advance, he would have to stay to give out ammunition and water and maybe take the wounded back. It was dangerous, although both sides spared drummers if they could; drummers held no weapons and were so young.

'It was late afternoon when we heard cheers. The Prussian Army had finally arrived. England and the 44th were saved. The French began to retreat at last and the Prussians gave pursuit, at first we tried to follow but the British army were too exhausted to give chase. We were told to desist, go back to our positions. We sat and rested, tried to find water or brandy in the canteens of the dead and took stock. I waited, hoping Tommy would come to look for me – my leg was so sore from its wound – but there was no sign of him.

'I began to ask after the 95th and was waved towards a farmhouse where the fighting was the thickest. Sick with fear, I hobbled on, two of my comrades came with me. Seeing a wounded green jacket being carried to the surgeon on a stretcher by two of his fellows, I asked for their drummer boy, young Lewis. They just shook their heads and walked on. We came to a sandy pit near the farm, strewn with bodies of green-jacketed men. Many were alive, groaning, begging for water, their wounds terrible to see. The 95th had taken the brunt of the cavalry charges, had been slashed at by sabres, crushed by hooves. Some had mortal wounds, you could see and smell men's guts hanging out.

'I needed to see my son. I found him, lying next to his drum.' Gu faltered, continuing slowly with tears running down his cheeks again.

'He looked if he'd closed his eyes to sleep, except his skin was white as Swansea china, a pool of blood staining the sand and his uniform. Flies were already feasting on it. He'd taken a sabre's blow across the neck and bled to death. Sliced through the neck and arm, crushed, a hoof through his belly, my Tommy. Dead meat, already rummaged for valuables, boots stolen, red stockings, one toe showing through a hole. My poor, poor lad, eighteen and gone like so many men around him. I cursed God that day. Why had he let me live through all those battles and taken my son from me in his first? Why was I living and he dead before he'd fully grown? I was the guilty one for leaving home and not facing up to my responsibilities. I can never forgive myself, nor God for taking him and not me, never.'

He shuddered, 'The boys let me go to him. I held him one last time, then had to let him down. Looters would be circling to strip him and his comrades. We began to dig into the soft sand, as deep as possible and laid him into the grave. I put Maria's cross in his hands, then covered him with sandy soil, dragging bodies over the spot to ensure no one would find him. It's terrible what looters do to bodies, they'll steal teeth for dentures for the wealthy from the corpses, not only valuables, the bastards.

'My heart was torn into pieces. How could I be standing alive, when my son, who I'd held in my arms as a baby a few short years before, was gone? How could I have survived seven long years in the army and he be dead so soon after joining? I should have died that day, not Tommy. It was my fault for abandoning my wife and children, running away from my responsibilities to join the army. If I hadn't, he wouldn't have thought of it as a career, would he? I'm to blame.

'We made our weary way back to Brussels and the 44th. There's little more to tell. Days later we were sent back to Colchester, the 2nd Battalion was disbanded shortly after. You know the rest.'

He stopped, unable to speak. Walking back to the house we were both in tears, shoulders low, my arm around him.

Gu told me again what he'd said to me earlier. 'You put one step in front of the other and carry on. You can't get over it, so you have to carry on.'

Ester was walking down the lane as we arrived at the farm. I felt relief hearing her chat quietly about what was happening in the village. Any mention of Rebecca and the arrests had been avoided by her friends. I tried again to carve a pig, whittling with my knife. I needed time alone to think about all Gu had told me, so sat with an old children's picture book as a guide. I roughed out the shape and carved the detail. I was much happier with the look of the creature as I sanded it and wondered about finding pink paint. The work and concentration distracted me from Gu's painful account of Waterloo. I went back into the parlour to check on Gu, who had stayed in there, gazing into the fire.

'Don't worry about me, Will. Thank you for listening to my ramblings. Let's see what happens with my turns now. I'm going to try to do more on the farm these next weeks; there's a lot of jobs left undone by those farm boys. I need to get this place to rights if Tom may be bringing a wife here, by and by.'

It took me hours to fall asleep again that night. I slept badly, dreaming of smoke, shot and floggings, running scared into woods time and again. I woke hoping Gu hadn't passed the nightmares on to me, chiding myself as I thought it for nonsense. I dragged myself up and into the workshop in Carmarthen next day. We all had to wait to see what would happen to Da at the assizes.

Chapter Seventeen

July 1843

The month passed slowly for me. It must have dragged cruelly for my parents waiting to hear if a charge would be made at the quarterly assizes. It had not helped that the weather stayed damp and cold. Farmers worried the harvest would fail unless the August weather improved. Mother got thinner and thinner with anxiety. Ester was worried about her. I'd overheard her telling Gu that when Susan had got so ill after the boys died, that was the way her melancholy had started. Susan had been unable, or unwilling, to eat or sleep for worry.

Rebecca and her daughters' attacks on tollgates didn't stop. In the first week after the storming of the workhouse, seven gates were taken down. Then gates around Kidwelly and Pontardulais were targeted by the Rebeccas. In response the Government sent nearly one thousand troops to west Wales. They were stationed in Newcastle Emlyn and St Clears and the dragoons stayed in Carmarthen. Not a single man had been caught, despite the army and yeomanry chasing across the county time after time. They were embarrassed by their failure to capture a single Rebecca in the act of breaking a gate.

Colonel Trevor, Lord Dynevor's son, returned to Wales and held meetings, hoping to quell the disturbances. Mr Foster, a reporter from the London Times arrived, at the end of June, he wrote a sympathetic article on our predicament.

On the 6th of July, John Pugh, Chief Constable of the Carmarthen police force, was dismissed for cowardice. We knew it was because he hadn't gone to Talog Mill. He'd been there in the workhouse doing his work, all right. In fact, Pugh had been energetically beaten over the head with a bassoon by a band member that day. It had caused hilarity in town, people trumpeting loudly whenever they saw him. The townsfolk in Carmarthen drew up a petition to try to get him his job back. Everyone was outraged that his replacement was that thug of an Irish police constable, Martin, a drinker and illiterate. He'd been chosen because he had no links to the town and did whatever the magistrates told him without question. Our petition on behalf of Pugh failed.

Then came more encouraging news: lawyer Edward Lloyd Hall, in a private prosecution representing David Howell, proved the Water Street Toll was charging exorbitant sums. At last our complaints were being listened to and proven right. The people would not stop until the gates were taken down and the promised public inquiry complete.

Tom and I could laugh and confide in each other again, as we hadn't for months, not since Gu told him he'd wished I was the elder. Tom would always look out for me, and for Shem. He was my brother and I loved him, for all his intensity and his short fuse. He felt the same about me. I had to admit that sometimes these last months I had deliberately set out to annoy and upset him.

In Carmarthen, Master David made us work hard throughout that month. The bad weather had put us behind getting the roof and rafters on a house he'd agreed to complete by the middle of July. He was worried he'd lose money and asked us to volunteer to work Saturday and Sunday afternoons to get the house finished. No extra wages, but an agreement that we could take the time back later in the summer or autumn. There'd be disapproving looks from church and chapel-goers for working on the Sabbath. David insisted that as long as we were seen to go to chapel on a Sunday morning before working it would be fine.

As one of the older, experienced apprentices and family, I had no choice but to help. Taking time back later suited me; as usual, Ester had made plans to go to Tenby regatta and races in August. The three days of the regatta were Tenby's biggest annual fair. All of our Pembrokeshire aunts, uncles and cousins would be there. Ester loved that holiday weekend. It gave her a chance to catch up with everything happening with her family. Her sister relied on her to help out as her boarding house was full to the brim and the servants took most of the days off as holiday. Mother usually went with her, but this year she was adamant she couldn't. She didn't say it out loud, but she was afraid my father might be in prison or being transported to the other side of the world soon. He tried to persuade her, saying a break would be good for her, but she was insistent.

It was agreed I'd go instead. Ester would pay for the steam packet fares to take us there from the quay, using her butter and cheese profits. I was pleased – Tenby was a lovely town on the coast and I hadn't seen my aunt and uncle since starting my apprenticeship.

I had loved visiting the little town when I was younger, playing with my cousins on the sand all day. There are three beaches in Tenby: one faces north, another south and the town beach to the east, so one beach is always sheltered from the wind. Bathing in the sea and making mud pies on sunny days was such fun. If we children were in luck, one of my uncles would have sailed over from Manorbier and we'd be taken out into the bay to fish for mackerel for supper. The horse races along the sand were something fine to be seen, but as a child, I'd less interest in those than I had in my cousins and play.

Ester had looked at me one Saturday afternoon and sighed. 'We need to get new shirts and breeches for you, Will. I noticed last month you've outgrown your Sunday best, again.'

My mother added, 'Your father hasn't got any old clothes spare, I don't know what to do for a jacket. You'll have to make do with second-hand, although I doubt if we'll find breeches long enough to fit.'

Listening, Gu cleared his throat.

'I'm getting Will and myself a new suit each for Tenby, from Ben Phillips on Lammas Street. Will's only ever worn his father's hand-me-downs. I'm going to buy him new, and before you say it, yes, I'll make sure they leave cloth at the cuffs to let down as he grows. We'll lodge in that boarding house on St Julian's Street with views out over the beach to Caldey you talked so much about last year, Ester. I want the family to know we are prospering.'

Ester looked delighted. Gu'd never once in all the years of their marriage agreed to go with her to Tenby.

Gu said, 'I could do with a change. I'd like to see your brothers, Ester, meet their grandchildren. I wonder if any of their boys are as wild as we were in our youth? Tom can manage the farm while I'm away. It'll be practice for him, it's only a week. I'll pay him a wage. Maybe we'll take a trip out to the farm in Manorbier after Tenby, Ester. I'll give you five guineas from the coffer for two new outfits; something showy, purple suits you well. Let the family see all that we are made of, eh, what a handsome woman I married.'

He looked down at his boots. 'Elizabeth, I don't like seeing you so downcast. I want to help, cheer you up. Take two guineas, go with them, get yourself a new dress. You're not to save any, I want it all spent on yourself. Tell John it's for your birthday next month if he asks.'

I watched Ester's face glow with happiness and Mother's with surprise. What was the world coming to? Her father offering money for fripperies! Mother's expression changed, her shoulders went down and her smile died. She'd remembered Father was in court next week. Nothing could stop her worrying over that, certainly not a new dress.

Chapter Eighteen

Saturday 15th July 1843

At last the first day of the assizes arrived. We had warned Mother there was next to no chance the workhouse captives' case would be heard that day. Father walked to the courthouse as demanded by the bond. He, along with sixty other men and women, was told his case would be held over until Tuesday or, more likely, Wednesday. They returned home despondent; yet more days to wait and worry. The judge had to remain in Cardiff that day instead of beginning the assizes. All we were told were the names of prosecuting Queens Counsels, and that the government was paying all the prosecuting expenses.

I'd waited for Father outside the court and he was terribly downcast.

'Your mother is in a dreadful state, and I'm not much better, to tell the truth. When I'm thinking clearly,

I doubt it will be more than prison or a fine, given we are only bonded to appear and no charges seem to have been brought yet. Trouble is, I cannot convince your mother that transportation or hanging isn't a possibility. At night, lying in bed, I wonder to myself if she's right. Your mother keeps saying the Riot Act had been read and the penalty is death. I don't think the Government will want to hang sixty Welsh men and women, it could provoke an insurrection, but they might well transport us to deter others.'

'No, Father, I'm sure it will be prison or a fine. They couldn't send sixty people away to Van Diemen's land.'

We had no choice but carry on with our waiting; nothing would happen on Sunday, the day for church and rest. A travelling circus chanced to be in town: 'The British and American Equestrian Company.' A stud of thirty horses touring south Wales from Haverford West, through Pembroke and Tenby and on to us in Carmarthen. Shem had been talking about the circus for weeks. He loved horses and music; he'd heard there was to be a band playing along. I'd promised to take him to see the show, not realising it was in the same week as the trials. I didn't know if Da would mind.

When I asked, he said, 'No point in everyone being miserable. It'll give your Mother a break if you take the girls too. How much is it?'

He pursed his lips when I told him.

'It's a shilling each, sixpence for children, but I've already agreed to pay for Shem and myself, so it would be only the three girls to pay for.'

With a sigh, he took out the coins from deep in his pocket and dropped them in my hand. We set out in high spirits for the show. I couldn't help notice a number of those damned dragoons in dashing uniforms were there, with – I ground my teeth – the prettiest girls from town on their arms.

We watched as a grand procession wound its way through the streets, led by a man in a top hat calling out for people to come to the circus. An excited crowd gathered to watch and wonder. First, eight matching grey horses pranced by, a woman standing upright astride the front pair, wearing pink knitted stockings with a blue silk skirt that barely covered her bottom. She balanced on one leg briefly as we gasped in admiration. Shem watched the horses, but I was more interested in admiring her. You didn't see a woman's legs bared for all to see in Carmarthen very often.

The band followed playing popular airs, then came more fine horses led by men dressed as if hussars. What a spectacle, it felt like a carnival. Shem was entranced and I was impressed. The crowd followed the parade on to the Priory Field to watch the show. The youngsters' mouths were open wide with wonder as we walked into the ring and took our seats. The band marched in and started to play. One by one, acrobats and performers in colourful costumes danced and somersaulted into the great ring in front of us. The horses pulled chariots, walked on their hind legs and galloped around the ring to a fanfare of trumpets, then more popular tunes were played. A wonderful sight. For a little while, we forgot our troubles and enjoyed that show. We walked home happy, Shem most of all.

On Monday the judge, Sir Rolfe, arrived in Carmarthen at around eleven. I saw his carriage draw up and a lean man with a strong nose and large eyes slanted down emerged, along with piles of boxes and valises. He and the county magistrates attended a church service in St Peters, then took "luncheon". The hearings finally started around three in the afternoon. A wasted day, so the gentry could socialise, whilst being paid their fees. We felt bitter against these men, called our betters.

David and I went to the court session, where Judge Rolfe presided in a scarlet silk robe and hood. That afternoon, to everyone's surprise, he gave a rousing and encouraging opening speech. He criticised the town magistrates for not using the powers they already had to keep law and order in Carmarthen. He suggested they had not made clear enough the penalties of such behaviour to their local populace. Judge Rolfe talked eloquently of the Staffordshire Plug Riots last year when miners went on strike and some were shot.

He said, 'After those riots, many men were sent to spend their days wretched and in exile away from their families. This must not be allowed to happen elsewhere in our great country.'

To the courtroom's delight, he continued that there needed to be, "An inquiry into the real foundations of the complaint that the Trustees have violated laws, and that tolls have been demanded more than the Act allows." He continued, "Either there is just cause for grievance, or there is not. Until that is resolved and set right if necessary, it is difficult to administer the law firmly and impartially."

We were much cheered by this speech. Maybe London and Cardiff had heard that there was a real cause for complaint by the farmers and carters of Wales after all.

There were two local cases heard before the end of that day's session. John Williams was found guilty of stealing a watch and sentenced to hard labour for six months and a private whipping. This was followed by a lengthy case as to whether or not Mr Thomas had been badly beaten by Henry Griffiths and his sons at Dryslwyn Fair last year. In the end, a verdict of guilty was reached, with twenty shillings damages awarded.

David and I went back to the workshop encouraged by Judge Rolfe's attitude. On Tuesday more minor cases were heard. Da had to attend each morning in case he was called, but the court officials told him the case was unlikely to be reached, so he left as soon as they allowed, to get back to the farm and bury himself in working his land.

All week long the court had been packed full, with family, friends and the curious attending. We hoped the case would be heard on Wednesday, but there were yet more cases of theft and assault. Finally, on Thursday, after nearly a week of agonising delay, the Rebeccas cases were announced in court. I was there with Tom and Gu, who insisted he wanted to go to show support for his son-in-law. Mother had not been able to bear to come to court and waited nervously at home each day.

The men in gaol were called to the bar first. Each was told that they were to go on fresh bail to appear at the Queen's Bench on 30th October, at any place determined. Most of our Rebecca leaders were bailed for £50; David Thomas was bailed for £100; but John Harris, Talog mill, was given an enormous bail of £200. John Lewis, who we all knew as John Pencelly, caused a stir after he told the court he'd only gone to the workhouse to hear Mr Morse, Stamp Office, speak! John, one of the ringleaders, claiming that made everyone smile.

Mr Morse was there and said, in that case, he should contribute to John's bail and gave £25, with Mr Thomas, the stationer, kindly offering the same. John Lewis himself paid the rest as his bail was set at £100. Job Evans had not appeared, so a warrant was made out for his arrest. It was sad to see these proud men dishevelled and dispirited after their month in gaol. It seemed they were to be made scapegoats by the authorities, for what we believed were reasonable actions of the people. We wondered what would become of them.

Next up were those men and women, including my father, who'd been ordered to attend in person in case a Bill of Indictment was preferred. To everyone's relief, no indictments were offered by the magistrates for any person that day. His Lordship Rolfe observed that in attending they had "fulfilled their obligation of recognizance", as he put it. As no bill had been preferred, the bond and the charges would drop as a matter of course. They were all discharged!

The room gave a mighty cheer. What a reprieve for so many families. There was huge sympathy for the twelve men who still would have to wait on bail, but at least they were not to be held in prison any longer. Tom and I hugged each other as we waited for Father to break away from the group. We climbed into Gu's trap and set off as fast as the roads would allow. Gu chuntered and criticised all along the road.

'Keeping all those people waiting all week, instead of telling them there was no charge. Outrageous! How would that Lord Rolfe like it? Wouldn't have happened to the gentry.'

On and on he went until Da told him, 'Thomas, enough. I'm a free man, praise the Lord. I thought I was going to be transported. Let me enjoy the moment.'

Shem was waiting at the entrance to the lane. When he saw us he ran for Mother, who emerged wiping her hands on her apron anxiously as we drove into the farmyard. Father was with us, not detained in gaol to be sent away, as she'd feared. She could see from our smiles the news. Father told her the case was dropped. She screamed, throwing herself into his arms, crying with relief. Shem looked worried when Mother started to cry, so I explained to him it was good news and her tears were happy ones. He looked bewildered but started smiling too. Then he began to sing; it was his favourite. We heard *A Life on the Ocean Wave* ring out across the yard and fields. I glanced sideways at Tom with a grin. We each put an arm around his shoulders and joined Shem in his song.

If you enjoyed this novel, and want to hear what happens to Will and his family next, watch out for the sequel. I hope to publish it by late 2020. It covers the "Treachery of the Blue Books" perpetrated by the English Government, and much more.

If you are interested please visit my website:

semorganhistoricalfiction.wordpress.com

The website has a free short story, "Ester's Tale", and there are photographs of Cwm Castell Fawr farmhouse and other places mentioned in the novel.

Epilogue

This novel started from verbal family history, which, as I researched the detail, proved to be somewhat inaccurate. I decided to keep faith with the family narrative as this is, after all, a novel. Will Morgan and his family's personal tale is partly fictional. However, I dramatised actual events and timelines, rather than fabricate the actions of the Napoleonic War and the Rebecca uprising, using first- and second-hand accounts wherever practical. Cwm Castell Fach and Fawr, the Big and Little Houses, still stand in Newchurch, above Carmarthen, near the golf course.

Thomas Lewis was one of a number of men with the same name that fought on the Peninsular and at Waterloo. Once this novel was complete, I discovered that 'my' Thomas probably served in the 95th then 96th Regiments. The 95th Regiment's service in the Peninsular and at Waterloo has already been extensively documented; several officers wrote memoirs. Consequently, it seemed reasonable to leave Thomas fighting with the 44th, those

Little Fighting Fours who served so bravely. It was another Thomas Lewis of the same age who fought in and survived those battles with the 44th, according to Chelsea Hospital records. Instead, Gu's fictional son Tommy fought in the 95th. I found Thomas Carter's 1887 historical record of the 44th Regiment when searching for details about Lieutenant Grier's dog. This provided excellent source material, including the tale of Wellington diving off to hunt a hare before a battle, and confirmed the greyhounds were linked to the 44th. They were Lieutenant Grier's dogs, and the hunt occurred before the battle at Villa Muriel.

Will became a carpenter in Carmarthen and is likely to have worked building St David's Asylum, as did his son John William. The farms were left to other family members, but family stories recall visiting and children being given a sovereign each from an oak coffer bach. While John, Will, Elizabeth and the other children lived there, Tom and Ellen's tale is fictional. There is no real evidence that John was Charlotte, one of the ring leaders of the revolt.

I have aligned the novel to the historical accounts of the Rebecca Riots in and around Carmarthen that spring and summer of 1843. *The Welshman* newspaper was my primary source in researching the novel. Editorially, it was possibly more balanced than the conservative local papers of the time such as the *Carmarthen Journal*, which were also harder to access. Pat Malloy in his account used the *Journal* extensively, so there is background from both contemporary records. *The Welshman* newspaper is freely available online. The Commission into the people's complaints of that year also provided first-hand witness accounts of the events.

The 'Rebeccas' were active until the end of 1843 across Wales and into England, and sporadically even later. While it was mostly gates that were attacked, gradually the people started addressing inequities and grudges such as the failure to acknowledge illegitimate babies. There were cases when people were being blackmailed as well, then perhaps inevitably, violence escalated. One elderly lady was killed and an old man robbed of a gold sovereign, with a policeman attacked and injured. The increased military presence failed to catch even one Rebeccaite, but when large rewards were offered, Beccas were taken into custody.

In March 1844, the bailed men from Talog, along with those who stormed the workhouse, were finally tried. They must have expected transportation but were given relatively short sentences for the times, of eight months' imprisonment apiece, with John Harris receiving a twelve-month penalty. Thirteen ringleaders were transported, but only those who had committed additional crimes that would have always merited such sentences. Many more were fined or discharged on the promise of good behaviour.

The Attorney General sensibly decided it was better not to provoke resentments and political unrest any further in west Wales. Huge social inequity at that time inevitably led to bitter resentment, and consequently political, social and financial unrest. The Rebecca riots' genesis was severe rural poverty, although for many, social justice was also a driver. Historians now place the Rebecca Riots in the context of the wider movements of social discontent across the UK. There was a "log jam of inequity": high rents, poor harvests, low market prices, evictions, the Poor Law and the tithes biting hard in rural communities, as Britain moved to become an industrially focused nation. This discontent was superimposed on the earlier Corn Law protests, Chartism, famine in Ireland and high taxation.

In rural Wales, there was a deepening divide between Welsh-speaking communities and English-speaking landowners, with laws being passed by a British Government who had little understanding or interest in the different nationalities within the Union.

Women were very much part of the march on the workhouse and the protests. This demonstrates that women, until the law's introduction, arguably suffered less inequality in Wales than England. Not only were customs of inheritance different, but the position of women in Wales was also dissimilar to that in England, based on ancient and more progressive laws dating back to Hywel Dda in the 10th century, and often even before that to the Celtic Brehon Laws of Ireland and Wales. Women customarily managed the family money, notably more recently in the valleys' mining communities where "Mam" would take the pay packet for all the family and dole out pocket money each week.

Women had more rights in divorce and could reclaim any dowry. They were owed compensation if their husbands were found with another woman, and if it happened three times could ask for a divorce. There were also strict grounds as to when a man was allowed to strike his wife, otherwise again she was entitled to a compensation payment. In Wales, unmarried mothers had more rights for financial support of their children. Unsurprisingly there was opposition to the bastardy clauses in the new Poor Law, which reduced women's rights. In some towns, the Rebeccas would threaten fathers of illegitimate children with violence if they did not support their offspring, or the community would shame them using the *Cefl Pren*, a wooden horse.

Gradually, the agrarian revolt died down, although political dissent and complaint had become more acceptable. The British Government remained afraid of revolution in Wales. The scandal of the Blue Books and suppression of the Welsh language lay ahead.

The Royal Commission Report, 1844, into the Turnpikes concluded that the people's complaint was a fair one and a new Turnpike Road Act was passed only five months after its publication in August. In south Wales, the Trusts were abolished and given to Road Boards in each county. The sidebars were largely removed, and tolls on lime halved. By 1888 across England and Wales no new Trusts were agreed, the task of maintaining roads given to county councils. The railway revolution had made most turnpike trusts unprofitable long before then.

Most of the anecdotes and people in the book are drawn from the newspapers from those months, or contemporaneous accounts, to give some flavour of life in Wales and the British army at that time: Lieutenants Grier and Pearce's dogs in the Peninsular, McCullop's lashing, the atrocities at Badajoz, poor Mr Tucker's suicide, Miss Bowen-Morgan's bankruptcy, bidding wedding custpms and the Royal British Whale curiosity show are factual. The terrible harvests after the war were, we now know, caused by Krakatoa's eruption in 1815, although it was the 1816 and 1817 harvests that were worst. If you'd like to imagine what Maria looked like, take a peep at Sorolla's *Types from Salamanca*, which shows them in their charra costumes.

Researching this period has been fascinating. I have drawn from Joseph Jenkins, a Cardiganshire's farmer's contemporary diaries; *Pity the Swagman*, analysed by Bethan Jenkins. His diaries are on the syllabus for children in the State of Victoria in Australia, although little known even in Wales. They bring vividly to life the challenges of living through these times in rural west Wales.

Smuggling was widespread until Free Trade was introduced in 1845. It was particularly prevalent across the channel and Napoleon encouraged it despite his blockade, hoping to leach gold away from the British Government. Gravelines and Dunkirk became cities of smugglers with a specially constructed compound. Brandy, gin and French prisoners of war were sent back to the continent by up to 300 English smugglers.

William Cobbett in his Cottage Economy has a diatribe on the evils of drinking tea and the health benefits of beer and is worth reading for that section alone. Cobbett was a radical thinker, journalist and hero of this time. His books are free from Gutenberg online. Cobbett was imprisoned for treason after writing about the evils of flogging in the British army. At that time an officer was allowed to give as many lashes as they wished as punishment, often for minor crimes or misdemeanours. Poor McCullop's experience shows that many men were sentenced to hundreds of lashes. McCullop was relatively fortunate to be given the lashes staggered over weeks to allow intervening recovery. Some were given hundreds at a time – effectively a death sentence.

I greatly enjoyed Bernard Cornwall's Sharpe series and Adrian Goldsworthy's novels. Writing about war was a new experience, so their well-researched insights into the day-to-day lives of those fighting was a great help. Individual ordinary soldiers' accounts transcribed in their lifetime were wonderful sources. Joseph Sinclair's *A Soldier of the 71st* was, for me, the most engaging. Of note was the only real reference in the texts to what must have been commonplace – men finding comfort, intimacy and partnership with other men. Sinclair's description of hearing of the death of his bedfellow, then seeing his body thrown on a barrow with others ready for mass burial after an outbreak of fever was heartbreaking.

In addition to the newspaper accounts, William Tobit Evans's book *Rebecca and her Daughters*, written in 1910, along with Pat Molloy's account, *And they blessed Rebecca*, were essential in giving me the detail and the wider picture of those agrarian riots across south Wales and beyond. This period is taught in many Welsh schools and widely known in Wales, but less so beyond our borders. The Welsh adopted Nonconformism with enthusiasm, with services mostly in Welsh, their native language. Chapels and the Sunday schools movement meant that Wales was to become one of the most literate societies in the world at that time.

What we now call post-traumatic stress disorder, as well as survivor guilt, was not recognised until the First World War. For those who fought and survived prior to that, there will have been little understanding of their symptoms; many will have simply been considered mad. Will, unknowingly, is trying to help using a technique we might now call guided reminiscence. Depressive disorders, such as Susan's melancholy, were recognised as they were common, but as there were no treatments, illnesses had to run their natural course, with families caring for individuals as best they could. Intellectual disability, as experienced by Shem, was integral to society then as now, but many people suffered terrible discrimination and treatment. All were, and are, part of the human condition and of everyday life in any century.

REFERENCES

The Welshman, weekly newspapers, spring/summer editions, 1843

Report from the Commissioners of Inquiry for South Wales. Vol. XV1, 1844

Rebecca and her Daughters, Henry Tobit Evans, 1910

And they Blessed Rebecca, an account of the Welsh Toll-gate riots 1839–44, Pat Molloy, 1983

Petticoat Heroes; Gender, Culture and Popular Protest in the Rebecca Riots, Rhian E Jones 2016

Pity the Swagman; A Diary of a Welsh Swagman; The Australian Odyssey of a Victorian Diarist, Bethan Phillips 2002

Historical Record of the Forty-Fourth the East Essex Regiment, Thomas Carter, 1887

A Soldier of the 71st from De la Plata to Waterloo, 1806–1815, Joseph Sinclair, Frontline books 2010

Picton's Division at Waterloo, Philip Haythornthwaite 2016

"Incorrigible Rogues", the Brutalisation of British Soldiers in the Peninsular War 1808–1814, Alice Walker. bjmh.org.uk

Napoleonic Lives, Carole Divall 2012

Matador

Lightning Source UK Ltd.
Milton Keynes UK
UKHW020641241221
396187UK00010B/649